MERRY & BRETT

TITLES BY MEGAN BYRD

Take a Chance on Me

One Sweet Love

Merry & Brett

MEGAN BYRD

ARDENVILLE PRESS

For questions or inquiries: megan@meganbyrd.net

To my fellow seasonal readers who love reading
Christmas-themed books in December

and to Hadley James and her momma, the real Ali

1

OCTOBER

Brett

THE CAR DOOR slams shut behind me as I start up the sidewalk toward the house I called home my entire childhood. I still have mixed feelings whenever I visit. So many wonderful memories were made inside those walls for the first sixteen years of my life. Followed by two years where the absence of a brown leather recliner in the living room reminded me every day of what went wrong one fateful Christmas. The sting of fingernails digging into my palm forces me out of my negative headspace and I uncurl my fists.

I study the exterior of the house, my brain trying to tell me something's not right. The house is still painted brown, though more paint is peeling off the white shutters since I was here last. How much of a pain it would be to sand them down and repaint them? I'll add that to my to-do list. The bushes in the flower beds look the same, though overgrown and wild. Better take care of that while I'm here. The sagging basketball hoop still has its shredded net. What am I missing?

That's when it hits me. My truck is the only vehicle in the driveway. Mom said she'd be home when I arrived, but maybe she had an errand to run. I prop open the glass door while fishing in my pocket for my keys. The faded black door swings open and my mom pulls me into a bear hug. "Brett, you're here!"

I wrap my arms around her. "I didn't think you were home."

"Why's that?"

"Your car's not in the driveway."

She releases me and turns toward the kitchen, waving a hand over her shoulder. "Oh, that. It's in the shop."

I close the front door behind me and follow her toward the kitchen, catching a whiff of tomatoes and chili powder. My stomach rumbles. "It smells incredible in here."

Mom stirs something on the stove, then opens the fridge and rummages around before pulling out a bag of shredded cheddar cheese. "Thanks. I made my famous chili just for you."

"Yum." I can't wait to dig in. I have yet to find a chili that tastes better than hers. I grab a bag of corn chips from the pantry and two bowls from the cabinet. "What's wrong with your car?"

"Oh, the fuel pump or something."

That sounds expensive. "When will it be ready?"

"Whenever. Will you see if I have any sour cream?"

I stick my head in the fridge, moving glass dishes of leftovers around. Is that tamale pie? It'll be my lunch tomorrow. I find a small container of sour cream in the back corner. The expiration date is today. I open the lid. It smells fine, so I set it on the counter next to the cheese. "How are you getting to work?"

"I'm taking the bus."

I frown. There's nothing wrong with public transportation, but I'd feel better knowing Mom can get around on her own schedule. If I lived up here, I'd take her wherever she needed to go, but my apartment in Asheville is nearly two hours from the house here in Boone. "Can't you get a rental from the shop until your car's fixed?"

Mom pulls a tray of cornbread muffins from the oven. "We're all set. Fix a plate and take a seat. What can I get you to drink?"

Reaching into the cabinet nearest me, I remove two glasses and fill them with ice and water. "I've got the drinks. You make your food and sit down. I'm sure you've been on the go all day. I can take care of myself."

She pats my cheek. "I know you can, dear, but it's nice to be able to mother you. I don't get to do it that much anymore."

A knot of guilt twists my stomach. I know she isn't trying to make me feel bad, but I already feel like a terrible son having moved so far away. We both know I needed to, but it doesn't ease my conscience any. I haven't been able to convince Mom to join me in Asheville, and I can't blame her. She's been here longer than I've been alive. Her friends are here. Her job is here. But the past is here, too. I suppose she's learned to live with it better than I have. I do my best to visit when I can, but time slips away from me and lately I've only made it up about every other month. *Do better, Brett.*

After setting the glasses on the table, I fill my bowl with chili and all the fixings, then join my mother at the table. "So...why no rental car?"

Mom is unusually focused on stirring her sour cream and melting cheese into the chili. "I'm saving my money for the repairs."

The fact that she still hasn't met my gaze makes my heart flutter with concern. "How much did they say it's going to cost?"

She finally looks up at me, sighing. "Don't worry about it, Brett. I'm a grownup. I can take care of myself. How's work going?"

I frown, not liking her answer but knowing she's closed the door on that conversation. I'll just have to do a little investigating later and find out for myself. I know she can take care of herself, but she's my mom. She took care of me, loved me, sacrificed for me. If there's anything I can do to make her life easier, I'm going to do it. Even if I have to be sneaky about it. "Work's great. I think I've about got Sarah convinced to let me host a weekly story time."

Mom finally meets my eye and smiles. "Oh, Brett, you'd be great at that. You've always been so good with kids. I hope your boss agrees to it."

"Thanks. If we start in the next few weeks, I bet it'd help our holiday sales numbers. The parents could browse the shelves while their kids are occupied. And I get to share my favorite children's books with a new generation. Sounds like a win-win to me."

Mom squeezes my hand and smiles. "Speaking of work," I say. "Is there anything new with yours?"

She sets down her spoon and turns to me, her eyes dancing. "Actually, my boss approached me earlier this week about a position opening up in January. Walt is taking a new job in Denver to be closer to his wife's family, so they'll need a new salesperson."

My mom is great with people. She's a perfect fit for meeting with customers one-on-one. "Mom, that's fantastic!"

Her smile dims a bit. "It is. The only issue is the job requires visiting local businesses, but, because I wouldn't leave the city, it doesn't come with a company car. I will be reimbursed for mileage, though."

She's already shut me down on the car topic, so I know better than to bring it up again. Still, it makes me more determined to figure out how I can help. In the meantime, I opt for encouragement. "Things will work out. I'm excited about the opportunity for you. You will be a spectacular salesperson for Griggs Hauser."

❄❄❄

After breakfast the next morning, I grab the hedge trimmer from the garage and hack away at the bushes in the flower bed. I dig up the dead impatiens and plant a few crocus bulbs I found next to the gardening tools. I hope it's not too late in the season for them to root and bloom in the spring. Time will tell.

I researched everything I'd need to sand and repaint the

shutters and it's too big of a job for this short weekend. Maybe I can get it done when I'm here for Christmas. I should be able to set everything up in the garage to stay warm and knock it out in a few days. Especially if the car's not parked in there. It reminds me of something else on my to-do list.

When the yard work's finished, I head inside to the office. Mom took my car to run some errands this morning. Hopefully, I can find what I need before she returns. If she discovers my snooping, she'll hide everything away where I can't find it. I never discovered where she hid my Christmas presents and, believe me, I was one of those kids who tried as hard as I could to find them. I don't care about being surprised on special days. It's better to know what's coming so I can look excited even when I'm not. Besides, not all surprises are pleasant.

In the file drawer of her desk, I spy a folder marked Car Stuff and pull it out. Inside are receipts from oil changes and tire rotations. In the back is a work order dated a couple of weeks ago for a transmission replacement. The dollar amount at the bottom makes me groan. She might as well just save up for a new car. Her Camry is at least fifteen years old and has well over two hundred thousand miles. It's probably not even worth as much as the cost of the transmission.

I hear the front door shut and quickly stuff the folder back into the drawer. I glide out of the office on stealthy feet and into the bathroom across the hall, silently shutting the door. For good measure, I flush the toilet, then wash my hands before exiting. Mom's in the kitchen unloading a bag of groceries. "Are there more I can carry in?"

"Yes, thank you."

I slide my feet into flip-flops by the front door, then retrieve a few bags from the trunk of my car. It takes three trips to get everything inside. "Are you cooking for a crowd tonight?"

She shakes her head. "No, just figured I'd stock up."

Because she doesn't have access to a car. And hasn't for several weeks. I don't like it. But she won't accept my help outright, even though I can see how excited she is at the prospect of the sales position. I'm going to have to find a way to help her without her suspecting anything. Maybe I can pick up more hours at the store, especially as we get into the holiday season, but I probably need something that pays better. I love my job, but it isn't the most lucrative. However, I'd give up working at Page Turner Books if it meant making sure my mom was taken care of. My brain works through a myriad of possibilities for how I can come up with more cash fast, but I still don't have a solution when I return to Asheville.

2

Meredith

IT'S A BEAUTIFUL, crisp autumn morning. My breath comes out in white puffs, underlining the cooling weather. We're only weeks away from the best time of the year—Christmas! I already can't wait for the stores to put up their displays and the radio to play holiday classics. I should start making a list of gift ideas for my family.

"Earth to Meredith. Can you hang this web from the gutter?"

I blink out of my thoughts, grab the white spider web made of shimmery garland from my sister and clip it to the house. The ladder wobbles a bit, and Ali steadies it. "Are you sure you're okay up there?" she says. "I can hang it up if needed."

I wave away her offer. "No way. Rich would kill me if I let you up here when you're nearly eight months pregnant."

Ali sighs and rubs her protruding belly absently. "He has been a little overprotective lately, hasn't he?"

"There's nothing wrong with protecting the people you love."

This makes my sister smile, and she stares off into space, probably thinking about how awesome her life is with her marvelous husband and future amazing child. I may be a little jealous of her family. Not that I wish she was single like me. Rather, I wish I had someone who looked at me the way Rich looks at Ali when she's not paying attention. Like she's the best gift in the world and he can't believe Santa made all his wishes come true. Longing for a love like theirs thrums in my chest.

Ali grabs the bottom sections of the web, wrapping the strings around the porch railing. When she's satisfied with its positioning, she retrieves the big black spider with twisty legs from the bin and hands it up to me. I arrange it on the web, trying not to get irked when Ali micromanages the process. The shiny orange eyes stare at me like they can peer into my soul. *Yes, I know, Spidey. It's not even Halloween and I'm already thinking about Christmas.*

I climb down from the ladder and dig around in the bin for more decorations. I retrieve half a dozen ghosts and tie them to branches of the tree in the front yard. Paige, my other sister, is working on the graveyard on the other side of the driveway. All the headstones are in place, and she's artfully arranging skeleton hands and feet so it looks like people are trying to dig out of their graves.

It's no surprise where I get my love for holidays from, though Halloween has never been my favorite. I don't like scary things, though I enjoy dressing up as mythical creatures and getting candy. Past costumes include fairy, unicorn, mermaid, and Aphrodite. I like the lighter, happier side of Halloween. My sisters, on the other hand, go all in on the horror and gore. They preferred witches, dragons, ghosts, and goblins. Thankfully, they weren't allowed to scare me too much since I'm the baby of the family.

Ali tests out the fog machine, adding an extra layer of creepiness to the graveyard. When the kids come by to trick-or-treat next week, they'll be in for a fright. Paige has taken to dressing up like a zombie and hiding among the headstones, waiting for unsuspecting victims. To her credit, she usually only jumps out at the teenagers, which, I must admit, is hilarious to watch. It's quite entertaining how loud the screams are and how fast they hightail it out of our yard.

With my job done, I head into the house to see if Mom needs help with dinner. The aroma emanating from the kitchen smells delicious. I give Mom a side hug where she's standing at the stove. "What are we having tonight?"

She kisses my cheek and lifts the lid of a giant pot. "Chicken tortilla soup."

"Looks and smells delectable. How can I help?"

"Can you get out bowls and spoons? Then tell everyone it's time. Your dad and Rich are in the living room watching football."

"Sure thing."

After assembling the dishes and cutlery by the stove, filling glasses with ice water, and setting them on the table, I peek my head into the living room. My sisters must have finished decorating outside because Ali's now laying sideways on the couch, her arms resting protectively over her baby bump, while her husband rubs her feet, his eyes on the TV screen. Dad's reclined in one of the La-Z-Boys, his eyes closed. Paige is sprawled sideways on the other one, her eyes glued to her phone. She's probably texting with her boyfriend Elliot. I walk over to Dad and gently nudge his shoulder. He startles awake. "Dinner's ready."

Dad pushes down on the side handle and rockets up out of the chair, marching into the kitchen. He wraps his arms around Mom from behind and kisses her neck. It's both endearing and a little cringe-inducing. I'm happy my parents are still in love after all these years, but it's another stab in my gut reminding me how solidly single I am. Everyone in our family is happily coupled up except me. Not that I've had time to date. I just finished my MBA this summer and am now on the hunt for a full-time job. I can't guarantee I'll be staying in Asheville for work, so it makes little sense to get involved with anyone.

Not that anyone's been asking. Nor am I keen on getting away from here. I love being near my family. Mountains, hiking, and a cute downtown area are also things I love about Asheville. If I could find a job I'm passionate about, I'd gladly stay here for the rest of my life. I love working at the Arboretum helping with their events, but it's a temporary gig that ends after the new year. I also love selling Christmas-themed handmade items on Crafty, an online marketplace, but that's a fun passion project more than a moneymaker.

Rich helps Ali off of the couch and places his hand on her lower back, guiding her into the kitchen. Paige is still glued to her phone, her face flushed with happiness. I tap her on the shoulder. "It's time for dinner."

She smiles, but her eyes don't leave the screen. "Okay, I'll be there in a sec."

I leave her to it. When we're all seated around the table, minus one, Ali rolls her eyes. "Paige Archer Larson!" Dad yells.

I hear one of the recliners rocking back and forth and Paige dashes into the kitchen, an embarrassed stain on her cheeks. "Sorry, sorry."

She quickly fixes her soup and plops down into the empty chair next to me. Dad says grace and we dig in. The conversation revolves around Ali's baby shower next week and what other preparations need to be made for my niece or nephew's arrival after the holidays. By the look in Mom's eye, I know all of Ali's Christmas gifts will actually be for the baby. I'll make sure to get her something she actually wants. Well, and something for the baby. I'm just as excited as everyone else for a new family member.

Paige nudges me in the side. "So, Meredith, have you figured out what you're going to do with your fancy new degree?"

All eyes are now on me. I shove a spoonful of soup into my mouth for time, having to immediately open my mouth and huff out breaths as the piping hot liquid scalds my tongue. Gulping some water helps cool things down. "I'm not sure yet. Ideally, I'd like to find something local, but, at this point, I'm willing to explore all possibilities."

It's quiet for a minute before Rich speaks up. "Have you thought about seeing if the Biltmore is hiring? They're one of the biggest companies in the area."

I can't believe I hadn't thought of that. Biltmore Estate is a huge tourist attraction and has a variety of enterprises on the estate. Plus, it has an outstanding Christmas program. I bet my experience at the Arboretum would be a plus. It hits all of my criteria and then some. "That's not a bad idea, Rich. I'll check it out, thanks."

Ali points her spoon at me. "I have a contact in New York City that could help you find a job up there. You'd get tons of exposure and experience that would help you climb the ladder. I'll send him an email this week."

I wrinkle my nose at the thought of moving so far away. However, New York City is like the mecca of Christmas celebrations, so I can definitely see the draw. I don't have any prospects right now, so I might as well explore every avenue. I'm glad to have such a supportive family. "Thanks, sis."

When dinner's over, Paige and I clean up while everyone else moves to the living room. When she hands me a dish to dry, she touches my shoulder. I look over at her and she gives me a warm smile. "I don't think I've said this yet, but I'm really proud of you for completing your MBA. I know it wasn't easy, but I think Mom and Dad appreciate it."

"Thanks." My smile wobbles and my insides squeeze in discomfort. The whole family knows Oliver's the reason I chose the path I did. I want to make them all proud and honor my brother's memory. If that means altering my work goals some, so be it. I'm sure I can find a way to make everyone happy.

3

Brett

IT'S BEEN HARDER to find additional part-time employment than I thought. Most places want daytime help, but I'm looking to pick up evening hours so I can work after my shifts at Page Turner Books. I've already told my co-workers I'll cover any shift as long as I'm not already on the schedule. This probably means I'll be working most weekends for the foreseeable future, possibly both morning and afternoon shifts. Which is fine. My personal life can take a backseat until my mom has a car again. I saw how much she hoped for the promotion, but it can't happen if she has nothing to drive.

In between ringing up books, I've been looking through the newspaper and searching online help-wanted sites. There are loads of ads seeking Santa impersonators for the upcoming holidays, but that isn't happening. Evening shifts at restaurants are the most coveted, so that's a nonstarter. There are a few retail stores advertising, so I'll submit applications to them. If I can't find something, I really will have to consider finding a full-time job that pays more than the bookstore. Maybe actually look for something that requires my communications and marketing degrees. Let's hope it doesn't come to that. I sigh, discouraged at the lack of opportunities I've found.

"What's wrong, Brett?"

My co-worker, Rachel, is standing across from me, her forehead creased in concern. Time to deploy some gentle ribbing, my usual form of deflection. "I'm trying to figure out how to let you know you've got lipstick on your teeth."

Rachel runs a finger across her teeth, but stops mid-swipe, shakes her head and rolls her eyes. "I didn't put any on today. What's really going on?"

Shoot. Should have said her sweater's on backward instead. "I'm fine."

"It's not the holiday doldrums, is it? I didn't think that started until closer to Thanksgiving."

I both love and hate that Rachel knows so much about me. She should, seeing as how we've worked together for five years, but I don't even want to get into a discussion of my yearly funk with her. She thinks I just don't like Christmas, but it's deeper than that. I probably should tell her the complete story sometime, but it won't be today. "My mom's car needs some serious repairs and I'm trying to make extra money to help her, only it's been harder to find something I can work around this job than I thought."

Rachel's face softens, and she places a hand on my arm. "Oh, Brett, I'm sorry. I'd offer to lend you the money, but I already know you'd decline. So, instead, I'll keep my eyes and ears open and let you know if I hear of any opportunities."

What did I say? She knows me well. I don't like being a charity case. It was tough being pitied by others after everything that happened with my father during my junior year of high school. Those sympathetic frowns, patronizing pats on my shoulder, and whispered condolences. And all the whispers about my mom. I glower just thinking about how awkward and terrible that time was. I'm never going to allow myself or my mom to be in that situation again, even if it means I have to sacrifice things I love, like my job, to keep us afloat. "Thanks, Rach."

She squeezes my forearm before pulling away. "And if you need a reference, I'm your gal. I'll gladly tell all potential employers that you enjoy teasing and torturing your fellow employees for entertainment." My face must show my shock because she laughs. "I'm just kidding, Brett. I'll only tell them about your stellar work ethic and your willingness to help your co-workers whenever you can."

I give her a half-hearted scowl. "Now I sound like a big softie."

Rachel shrugs. "If the shoe fits." She leans in and lowers her voice. "But don't worry, I won't tell anyone."

4

NOVEMBER

Meredith

MY BOSS, JOANNE, pokes her head through the doorway. "How are the job position posts going?"

"I've got radio adds scheduled, a social media post all set to run in local users' feeds, and billboards on Hendersonville Road and I-26. I've also made some fliers that I'll take to local businesses to keep in their stores."

She gives me a quizzical look. "You think stores will let you poach employees?"

I hadn't really thought of it that way. "We're not really poaching. This is seasonal work, and it's mostly in the evenings. But maybe I should look more at places where people gather outside of work. Maybe the local libraries? They have public bulletin boards."

Joanne nods. "Yeah, that'll work. Perhaps post offices as well.

Otherwise, it sounds like you've got everything covered."

Her praise warms me. I've been working hard trying to get us prepared for Winter Lights, our biggest event of the year. It doesn't bring in as much money as the wedding events held on property (which has its own budget and coordinator), but it's the largest concentration of people through our gates all year and we get a lot of annual memberships from it, so it's worth doing to the best of our ability.

The North Carolina Arboretum is open year-round for people to wander through the 434-acre public garden which overlaps with Pisgah National Forest and Bent Creek Experimental Forest. There are gravel roads for jogging or biking and multiple trails to explore. It's also home to some black bears, though I've never seen one here in person.

In addition to the Winter Lights program, the Arboretum has an immersive floral installation in May called "Bloom with a View." It also holds classes for children and adults, hosts school field trips, and runs children's day camps during the summer.

This year, I'm in charge of everything related to our open-air walk-through light show. I've worked at Winter Lights in some capacity since high school, but have been interning here since I finished my master's degree, which focused on hospitality management. Our previous events director retired in September, so I'm the temporary replacement until they find someone to fill the position permanently. It's a lot of responsibility, but I feel like I've been handling it well.

It's only two weeks until opening night, but most of the lights and displays are already in place. I'm confident we'll be ready on time. The biggest obstacle for me right now is finding staff for all the different activities and locations. We still need a Santa and some elves, a few people to work drink stands and the s'mores station. That's why I'm using every avenue to advertise in the area for help.

"Do you need me to do anything else around here this morning? If not, I'm going to go hang fliers. I'll probably head home when I'm finished."

Joanne waves her hand. "Sounds great. And thanks again for filling in while we look for a replacement. You've been a lifesaver."

"No problem. I love Winter Lights and the Arboretum."

I gather the papers and my coat and head out to my car. I'll start in south Asheville close to the Arboretum and work my way up to downtown. Then I'll hit the upper part of the county before going home to my parents' house in Montford, the historic district just north of downtown. It contains cool old houses and a funky vibe. The cemetery where Thomas Wolfe and O. Henry are buried is there and we often see bright purple buses with mustaches cruising through with tourists. I took one of those Vroom tours once, just for fun. The guide was hilariously punny and the brewery we stopped at was cool, though I don't drink. We didn't pass by where I live, but I saw a few friends' homes.

My sisters like to tease me about still living with our parents, especially Paige, who has a place in west Asheville. She offered me the second bedroom after her last roommate moved out, but I'm afraid we'd get on each other's nerves like we did when we all lived at home. Sure, we're grown up now, but she's very particular about things, like keeping main areas picked up and clean all the time, and I'm, well, not. I'd rather keep our relationship on good terms, especially since I'm perfectly content with the current living situation. I'll move out once I have an official full-time job. Until then, it's just easier to stay where I am and save money.

After hitting the libraries and post offices in the south and west, I drive into downtown and park in the deck attached to the downtown library. I pin a flier to the bulletin board inside, then step out onto Haywood. While I'm here, I might as well pick up some delicious chocolate from Little Shop of Sugar. It's too early for their Christmas selection, unfortunately. I love the Content-mint, a mint-infused truffle with candy cane pieces sprinkled on top. It's to die for.

An inspection of the case shows pumpkin and pecan pie

truffles. There's a leaf-shaped caramel with maple and walnut flavoring. Chocolates in a variety of shapes—turkeys, leaves, pumpkins. I select some sea salt caramels for my parents and get a Peanut Butter Bomb and a Chef's Kiss for myself. The tiny chocolate lips on top always make me smile.

Remembering my original reason for being downtown, I ask the clerk behind the counter if I can put the flier anywhere. She takes it and hangs it in the window, facing out to the street. Brilliant! I thank her, compliment her hair, which is bright orange like the leaves in fall. Very bold, but she pulls it off quite well.

Back out on the sidewalk, I ponder where else to go. The book display in the window across the street catches my eye. I use the crosswalk to get a closer look. It's a table with books on plates. *The food we eat feeds our body, but the novels we read feed our mind* is painted on the glass above it. So fun. I notice a flier advertising a new children's story time in the window. Maybe they'll stick mine up there as well. Only one way to find out.

I pull open the door; the chime signaling my entrance. Not sure who to talk to, I head toward the checkout counter. There's a man with a few days of stubble on his face and a serious, almost scowly expression. The brooding look suits him and I'm curious to find out if he has a deep, gruff voice to match. I'm intercepted by a woman with brown hair, pretty blue-green eyes, and a bright smile.

"Welcome to Page Turner Books! I'm Rachel. Can I help you?"

I look over at the counter, but it's now empty, so I turn back to the woman. "Hi, Rachel. I'm Meredith Larson. I work at the Arboretum."

Her eyes light up and she clasps her hands together. "I love that place!"

I grin widely, delighted by her enthusiasm. "Me too. Um, this may be an odd request, but I was wondering if it's possible to stick a flier up in the store? Perhaps you have a bulletin board or something? We're looking for seasonal workers to help with Winter Lights."

Rachel's eyes widen, but then she quickly nods and starts looking around. "Yes, of course. We can stick it in the front window."

"That's great, thanks." I rummage in my tote bag for the folder of fliers. I pull one out and hold it up. "Here we are—"

She looks down an aisle off to her left and holds up a finger. "Stay right here. I'll be right back."

I'm suddenly on alert. Did she see something concerning? Should I leave it on the counter and come back later? I'm just about to drop the flier and dash when Rachel comes back up the aisle, pulling someone by the wrist. She stops in front of me and swings her arm to her side, bringing the man with the stubble to a stop next to her. His eyes take a cursory glance at my face, then swoop down my body before looking away, a frown causing his forehead to crease.

"Brett, this is Meredith. She says the Arboretum is looking for seasonal help." When he stays silent, Rachel continues. "What are the days and hours you need workers?"

I'm not sure what's going on here, but it's an opportunity to solicit help, so I can't turn it down. "It's evenings from five until around eleven, beginning the third Friday of this month through the first weekend in January. We also need help right now in the evenings to finish setting everything up, but if someone can't start until the event opens, that's okay. We'd just need them to come in some time before the event starts for training and instruction."

Rachel nods and looks at Brett, but he's now studying the fingers of one of his hands. "Just evenings, that's good. What positions are you seeking to fill?"

This is weird, but I try to ignore the awkward tension coming from the sullen man. "We have openings for people to work the beverage stands, but workers must be twenty-one because we offer wine and beer in addition to hot cocoa and water. People are also needed to hand out maps and provide information to patrons. And we need a Santa and a couple more elves. And there are also some manual labor positions."

Rachel nudges Brett in the ribs. "Did you hear that Brett? They need a Santa."

He straightens up and glares at Rachel, but she just smiles back at him, clearly enjoying whatever's happening. I hold out the flier to Rachel. She takes it from me and offers it to Brett, who holds up his hand in refusal. That looks like my cue.

"I'd better go. I have more fliers to hand out. Thanks for posting it."

Rachel beams at me. "No problem. Good luck!"

"Thanks." I give her a nod, then realize the guy's no longer with us. I turn and find him back behind the counter. Wow, he moves fast. I give him a little wave, but his frown only deepens. Okay, whatever. I push through the door, the chime wishing me a fond farewell, and head down the sidewalk, trying to decide where to go next. *Coffee shops are great places to advertise!* There's one a few blocks away, so I take two left turns until I'm standing in front of Hill of Beans. I sure hope these fliers work. I'd hate for Winter Lights to flounder the year I'm in charge.

5

Brett

IT'S A WONDER there isn't steam coming out of my ears as annoyed as I am. I cannot believe Rachel ambushed me like that. Technically, she's trying to help, but the teasing about Santa was uncalled for. Though, I can't be that mad at her because she doesn't know the truth. How can she know that ribbing me about playing Santa is as uncomfortable as being stabbed by hundreds of tiny needles? I should tell her. But then she'll feel sorry for me and I'd rather not have to deal with that. Better to just let it go.

Normally I wouldn't be so affected, but that woman looked so much like a ghost from my past that I felt sixteen all over again. The long, black hair and short, curvy body resembled Vicky so much I wondered if I'd time traveled for a second. Of course, Vicky, my father's second wife, doesn't have bewitching brown eyes that can pierce your soul or plump, pink, heart-shaped lips. Nor does she have multiple studs in her ears like this Meredith woman wore. I counted two earrings in each lobe and one in the cartilage at the top of her ear. Does she have any other body piercings? I'd say it's possible because I noticed some ink on her wrist peeking out of her coat sleeve. Surprising details for someone who looks like she rescues kittens and gives her spare change to anyone who asks.

I bet her life's just been easy sailing. No trials or tribulations, so she had to create her own drama. Her extra piercings and tattoos are probably leftovers from her teenage rebellion phase. I'd almost bet money that the tattoo is something cheesy about growth or transformation, like a butterfly or ladybug. Maybe one of those Chinese symbols for love or prosperity. I chuckle at my own thoughts.

"What's so funny?"

Rachel's standing to my left, hand on her hip, her head cocked to the side. It's her attempt at a mom posture and it makes me chuckle again. "You are."

Rachel straightens up, now with both hands on her hips. "What is up with you today? First, you're a stone when I share a potential job opportunity with you, and now you're giggling like a maniacal clown. Spill, Brett."

Did my chuckle sound evil? It's definitely a possibility. I've got my scowl down pat. Might as well add a devilish laugh to the package. I motion to her posture. "You have a long way to go to capture the stern mom look you're shooting for. Your kids are going to run all over you."

She drops her hands, relaxing her body. "I'll just have to keep practicing on you, then."

I grin, anticipating all the enjoyment I'll get from seeing sweet, caring Rachel try to devastate me with glares and power poses. "I look forward to it."

"The Arboretum job sounds perfect for you."

My smile turns down into a frown. Not this again. Rachel is undeterred.

"I'm serious. Maybe not the Santa thing, but the hours would work with your job here. You should at least apply and find out what they're paying." She snaps her fingers. "Shoot, I should have asked about money. Sorry, Brett."

I shake my head, amused that she's remorseful over something she shouldn't be. Her heart's in the right place. "You're a good friend, Rachel. I'll think about it, but I have an interview today after work for High Fashion down the street. If I get that job, I'll be set."

Rachel pulls me into a hug. "Oh, yay! Good luck, Brett. I'm sure you'll get it."

"I appreciate the enthusiasm."

She pulls back, a mischievous smile on her lips. "Just remember to smile."

❄❄❄

"Brett, it says here you have over ten years of experience working retail?"

I nod at Blaire, the interviewer who asked the question. "That's correct. I worked at multiple clothing stores in high school and college before relocating here and starting at Page Turner Books, where I've been for over five years."

He looks down at his notes before nodding. "Very good. It sounds like you'd be a good fit for our company. I have no more questions. What about you, Cherize?"

My gaze moves between the two interviewers. Cherize taps her pen against her chin, looking off to the side. Her eyes return to my face and she scrunches her nose. "We pride ourselves on maintaining a certain look here at High Fashion. One of our preferences is for the staff to have a preppy look. How willing are you to style your hair and maintain a clean-shaven face?"

The question catches me off guard. Are employers allowed to ask that of employees? They can dictate what we wear, and we represent them, so probably. I doubt they'd say anything that could open the company up to a lawsuit. "I'll do whatever you want with my hair, but I can't shave my face."

The interviewers exchange a concerned look. "Do you have it for religious or medical reasons?"

So there are exceptions to their policy. I could lie, but then I'd have to keep it for as long as I work for them and I'm already dreading the itchiness that's sure to start soon. I'll endure the discomfort, but prefer not to keep it longer than I have to. "No."

There's a beat of silence as another look passes between the two of them and my stomach sinks. It looks like I won't be getting the job.

The interview wraps up with generic pleasantries and I head home, feeling defeated. It had seemed like such a good fit. They were willing to work around the hours of my other job, but for some reason, beards are a sticking point.

Working at the Arboretum is not ideal, but the hours fit, and it ends in January. Most other places I inquired at weren't too keen on me working for only a couple of months. As long as I can serve drinks or work behind the scenes, it should be fine. I won't love the atmosphere, but I can grit my way through since it'll help my mom. Of course, I have to actually apply and get an offer first. There's no guarantee that they'll hire me. Especially if they want people who are psyched about Christmas.

My friends goaded me into attending Winter Lights a couple years ago and I can see the appeal for most people. They probably haven't had life-changing events turn them off of the Christmas season. Since it's an outdoor event, I bet they'd have no issue with my facial hair. It'll certainly keep me warm as the nights get colder. My only deal breaker is playing Santa. That will never happen. I'd rather take money from Rachel.

6

Meredith

WE'RE LESS THAN one week away from the start of Winter Lights, and I still have half a dozen spots to fill. Hopefully, today's round of interviews will produce the help we need. We've got ten applicants, so if everyone seems like a hard worker and good fit, I may have to make a few tough decisions.

The first couple of interviews are with college students. They're still too young for the beverage stands, but their peppy spirit would make them excellent elves for Santa. One even has some photography experience so she could fill in for our regular photographer when they need a break. Of course, we still need a Santa for people to take pictures with. Normally, we have that position filled in September, but the guy we've used in the past retired and moved to Florida, so we're starting from scratch. It's too late to hope for a Santa with a real beard, but I've acquired a bright red suit complete with white, curly hair and beard, so whoever wears the suit is set.

The door opens and a well-dressed man with styled blond hair and piercing blue eyes enters, filling the room with his presence. He marches over to me, thrusting out his hand and hitting me with a bright smile. "Hey, there. I'm Connor."

I shake his hand, leaning back in my chair so I can look into his face. "Hi Connor. Have a seat, please."

He plops down in the chair, draping one arm across the back of the chair, and propping a leg up on one of the arms. His smile doesn't waver. The confidence oozes off of him. He's definitely a guy used to getting his way. I need to maintain control of this interview, so I clear my throat and start with the questions. "Mr. Phillips, why are you interested in working at Winter Lights?"

He waves one of his hands while he speaks. "Oh, you know, I love the festive atmosphere and it seems like it'd be fun."

Not a terrible answer, but it doesn't tell me much. Like how dependable he'll be. His casual resting position and the designer black dress pants and button-down shirt he's wearing make him look like a rich boy just doing it to have a story to tell to his country club buddies. I bet his shoes cost more than my entire outfit. And no socks in November? *Don't judge, Meredith. Stay professional. Continue the interview.*

"It *is* a fun experience. Have you considered which position you're most interested in filling?"

He grins wide, his straight teeth an unnatural shade of white. "Why, Santa, of course. This face needs an audience." He circles his face with his hand for emphasis.

He is attractive, I'll give him that, but he's a little much for my taste. "Do you have any previous experience as Santa?"

"No, but I played the Easter Bunny at Asheville Racquet Club for a couple of years and the kids loved me."

That seems like a good omen. Still, I need to be sure he's not just saying what he thinks I want to hear. "Do you have a reference I can talk to about that experience?"

Connor pulls out his phone and starts thumbing through it. "Sure. What's your number? I'll send it to you."

Nice try. He's not the first guy to try to get my contact information this way. "Read me the name and number and I'll write it here on your application."

After a few more questions, I wrap up the interview, then stand and offer my hand. "Thanks for coming, Connor. I'll let you know by the end of the week."

He takes my hand, turns it so the back of my hand is facing up, then brings it up to his face and kisses it. I blink in disbelief. "Thank *you*, Meredith. I look forward to working with you." He finishes his statement with a wink, then turns and strides out of the room.

I'm stunned. Did that just happen? I don't have time to process my interview with Connor, because there's a knock on the door frame and my next interviewee comes into the room with a scowl on his face. Oh boy, it's the guy from the bookstore.

I shuffle my papers to find his application form. Joshua Jacobs. For some reason, that doesn't seem right, but the paper can't lie. I smile and offer my hand. "Hello, Joshua, thanks for coming."

He takes my hand, glancing back at the door he just came through. "I prefer to be called Brett." He drops my hand and sticks his thumb toward the door. "Was that Connor Phillips?"

I motion for him to have a seat, and we both sit. "Yes. Do you know him?"

The lines in his forehead deepen. "I do."

There's obviously a story there, but Brett seems to be a perpetually gloomy person, so I doubt he'd offer an unbiased opinion of Mr. Phillips. Though, I'd definitely be interested in hearing his thoughts. I got a weird feeling about Connor in the interview, but it could be my own prejudices against preppy guys. In high school, they didn't give me the time of day and I'm still carrying a bit of a grudge against their snobbery. But I can't let my past get in the way of doing my job.

"So, Brett, why are you interested in working at Winter Lights?"

His forehead smooths out and, while he's not exactly smiling, he no longer looks angry either. "I'm looking to make some extra money and the hours would fit nicely with my other job."

I've definitely had plenty of responses include wanting to make money, but usually they also talk about the fun, cheery atmosphere. "Have you attended Winter Lights before?"

"Yes."

I was expecting his answer to include his thoughts on the event, but I shouldn't expect him to be a mind reader. "What did you think about it?"

"There were a lot of people."

I wait for him to continue, but when he offers nothing else, I move on to my next question. "Have you considered which position you're interested in filling?"

He scratches his beard. It's in that slightly patchy in-between stage where men either commit to growing it out or give up and shave. I wonder which one he'll choose. I've never really been into beards, but Brett's face would look good with one. He'd also probably be attractive without one as well. Actually, the stubble he has right now is kind of sexy. I bet it'd feel scratchy against my hand. I realize I've been gazing at the lower half of his face too long, and blink, hoping he didn't notice my blatant stare. *Be professional, Meredith.*

"I'd prefer to do behind-the-scenes stuff or possibly the beverage stations. I've been in charge of multiple events at the bookstore and am comfortable talking to a crowd and multitasking."

So he *can* speak more than one sentence at a time. The brief responses he's giving me aren't unprofessional, just unexpected. I guess I'm used to more talkative job candidates, like Connor. It's what you expect for customer-service positions. Though, Brett's other job is very customer-service oriented, so he must have some hidden people skills I just haven't seen yet. Time for my whimsical question, just to learn a little more about his personality. "What's your favorite thing about the Christmas season?"

His eyes, which were aimed at the ground, now raise to meet mine. I see surprise mixed with something else. Panic, maybe? The forehead creases are back. He sighs. "I have to be honest with you. I don't really like Christmas." The surprise must be evident on my face because his next words come out in a rush. "But I'm a hard worker, dependable, and will make every guest's experience a pleasant one. I'm willing to do anything you ask. Well, except play Santa. I absolutely can't do that."

We sit in silence for a moment as I digest everything he just said. *He doesn't like Christmas? How can someone not love such a magical and hope-filled holiday? And why in the world would he want to work at Winter Lights if he doesn't like Christmas?* I realize too late that I spoke my last thought out loud.

Brett swallows. "The truth is, I need the money to help my mom and have been turned down at every other job I applied for. I promise you won't regret hiring me. Check my references. They'll confirm I'm responsible and give everything I have to my jobs."

He gives me an earnest look, the creases in his forehead now from concern rather than displeasure. The vulnerability he's displaying tugs at my heartstrings, and I want to offer him the job on the spot just to put him at ease, but I still have to go through the process. "Thank you for your honesty. I'll let you know whether we're going to offer you a position by the end of the week."

He nods, appearing resigned, and it's all I can do not to reach out and give him some reassurance. As long as his references are good, he's got a position. He stands, shakes my hand, then exits the office.

I slump down in my chair and release a deep breath. Who knew interviews could be so emotional? I didn't know this job was so multi-faceted. I have to get the event up and running, make sure everything goes smoothly, and, apparently, manage the employees and their various personalities. Am I cut out for this much responsibility? Joanne seems to think so, at least temporarily. A knock at the door lets me know my next candidate has arrived. I shuffle Brett's application to the back, plaster a smile on my face, and shift into boss mode. Next time I'm planning breaks between interviews. Back-to-back times five is grueling.

7

Brett

ON THE DRIVE home, I replay the interview in my head. Did I shoot myself in the foot by being honest about needing the money? The interviewer really seemed to want staff who are enthusiastic about Christmas. That's just not me and I can't fake it, even though it feels like my last shot at making extra money unless I go after a new full-time job that pays more.

It was a struggle to maintain eye contact with her, since she looks so much like Vicky. That's not her fault, of course. She seems to have enough Christmas spirit to cover both me and herself. I noticed the little Christmas trees dangling from her earlobes and the string of colored lights winding up the outside of her ear. It was a cool, funky look, but way too festive for my tastes. I looked for her tattoo, but the pink sweater she was wearing had sleeves that nearly swallowed her hands.

Of course, none of this matters because I probably won't get the job. Especially if I'm competing against Connor Phillips. Though he prefers the spotlight, so I bet he's angling to be Santa. Which is fine by me. He's perfect for that job. The guy seems to have the magic touch, getting whatever and whomever he wants. Even if they're already in a relationship.

I'm tempted to call the Arboretum and rescind my application so I don't have to deal with Connor and reminders of the past, but then my mom pops into my head. She's worked so hard, especially after my father left us. Mom deserves the promotion, and a broken-down car shouldn't keep her from it. She's worth a little discomfort on my part, working with people I don't particularly care for. And now I'm back to worrying that I flubbed the interview and all this is moot.

❄❄❄

The next morning, I'm arranging one of our display tables when someone hugs me from behind. Only one person is bold enough to surprise me with personal contact. "Good morning, Rachel."

She lets go and moves into my line of vision. "Hello, Brett. Congratulations!"

I frown, giving her a skeptical look. "For what?"

Rachel's smile falters. "Um, for acing your interview yesterday?"

"Yeah, I don't think that happened."

"Are you sure? Because I got a call from Meredith Larson, checking your references. I told her you're a wonderful team player who will take on any job. That you're good with details and a pleasure to work with."

I huff out a disbelieving laugh. "A pleasure to work with, huh? I'm sure she saw right through that."

Rachel softly smacks my shoulder. "Come on, Brett. You know we have fun together, even if it is mostly you teasing me. You always have my back and you *are* a hard worker."

One side of my mouth quirks up as I think about how much I enjoy messing with her. We've been friends long enough that I can be more myself around her. I trust her. This new job would be with people I don't know or definitely can't trust. "I appreciate your positive words, at least. Though I'm not as optimistic about my odds of getting the job. She asked me what I love about Christmas and I was honest."

Rachel purses her lips and nods. "She did ask me about your Christmas aversion. I said I didn't know the details, but that it doesn't affect your ability to be kind and respectful toward customers and co-workers."

I'm relieved Rachel doesn't use this opportunity to pry into the details. She respects my privacy, which makes me feel like I can trust her with the truth. "Okay, I'm going to share something with you, but promise it stays between you and me. I don't even want your husband to know."

Rachel mimes zipping her lips and tossing a key over her shoulder. All I can do is shake my head, but her loyalty warms my heart and bolsters my confidence that this is the right thing. "The reason I don't like Christmas is that my father left me and my mom on Christmas Eve my junior year of high school. Every year, all the lights and decorations remind me of how awful that time was."

The way Rachel's face crumples in sadness on my behalf makes me feel a little uncomfortable. I don't like people feeling sorry for me, but I know she's sensitive toward others' feelings and it does kind of make me feel justified in this hate I've harbored for nearly fourteen years. "Oh, Brett, that sucks. I'm so sorry."

"Yeah. Sometimes I feel like I should be over it because it happened so long ago, but I just can't move on. I think it's because he never seemed remorseful about it. I mean, he started a new family and everything. It's like we didn't matter to him, like he made a mistake with us and then moved on without a backward glance."

Rachel grabs my hand and squeezes in support. "Wow, that's rough. How old were you?"

"Sixteen."

A wrinkle appears between her eyebrows and she frowns. "It's got to be hard to lose a parent at any age, but I'm sure it's even tougher when they leave on purpose."

It actually feels nice sharing this with someone, even though it feels like my skin is being flayed with the vulnerability the admission requires. "I hadn't really thought about it like that."

Rachel shakes her head. "If I were in your shoes, I'd probably be grumpy at Christmastime, too." She lets go of my hand and wraps her arms around my neck. I hug her back, appreciating her concern. She really is a good friend. The staff here is one reason I love working at Page Turner Books so much. "If you need to vent at all this holiday season, let me know. I don't care if it's two in the morning. You need all the support you can get, and I'm here for you."

I loosen my arms, and Rachel does the same, stepping back. "Thanks, Rach."

I'm considering telling her about the people issues I'd be sure to encounter if I got the job, but then the opening chords of "All My Rage" by Metalhead, my favorite band, play from my pocket. "Oops, guess I forgot to stick my phone in my locker. I'll be right back."

I pull the phone out and silence it, but the local number on the screen piques my curiosity. I'm already in the staff-only hallway leading to the break room, so I answer it. "Hello?"

"Hi, this is Meredith Larson from the Arboretum. Is this Brett Jacobs?"

My shoulders drop, my improved mood from confessing to Rachel evaporating. Here we go. The phone call to say I didn't get the job. "Yes."

"Great. Mr. Jacobs, I'm calling to say that we'd love to have you as part of our Winter Lights staff for the season."

What? They want to hire me? Even with my Christmas aversion? Rachel must have really talked me up. I don't know whether to buy her some chocolate or curse her. I could turn down the job and continue the search, but, unfortunately, I know this opportunity is my best bet for helping my mom. "That's great. What will I be doing?" My tone is less than enthusiastic, but I just can't conjure peppiness at the moment. Or most moments, as a matter of fact.

"I've got you listed as the cocoa shack operator. And also, maybe help with some last-minute light hanging and setup if you're interested in starting work before opening night."

I won't turn down the opportunity to make more money. Especially when it sounds like I'll be doing the least-festive job available. "Yeah, that sounds great."

"Excellent!" Her already chipper voice raises an octave. I bet she's one of those people who wakes up full of energy, bounces out of bed, and greets the day with an enthusiastic 'Good morning.' I can't even imagine. "You'll need to come in for a training session, and you'll be paid for your time. We have one this evening at six, and then a morning and afternoon option this coming Saturday. The training will last about three hours. Do any of those work for you?"

Wow, we're just jumping right in. I suppose it makes sense since the event opens next weekend. "I can come tonight."

"Great! When you get to the gate, give the attendant your name. Drive back to the main garden parking lot and come into the Baker Exhibit Center where you interviewed. I look forward to working with you."

Really? I seriously doubt someone so happy-go-lucky will enjoy my presence at Christmastime. If I don't break her spirit, it'll be a miracle. Not that I'm going to try. I'm not that kind of guy. I just know that my dour mood has the tendency to rub off on those around me. I guess we'll see.

8

Meredith

I'VE GOT EVERYTHING ready for tonight's training. Half of the new hires can attend, the others I'll see on Saturday. I'm glad we've got all our spots filled. A few of the applicants didn't seem to realize they'd be working nearly every evening for the next six weeks. I know it's an enormous commitment, but we pay better than most part-time jobs and we give them one night off each week, staggering which night so everyone can have at least one free Friday and Saturday night during the event.

I have a few people lined up to fill in for the regular staff for the inevitability that someone gets sick or quits. It's a challenging schedule, but it's a lot of fun, so it doesn't really feel like work. At least, that's how I feel about it. I've worked Winter Lights nearly every year since I was in high school. It's one reason I was chosen for this temporary role—I'm practically an expert on how the event runs.

A glance at the clock on the back wall of the room tells me the trainees should be here soon, if they're not already. I head out to the lobby and see three of them huddled around the fireplace. The mantel is festooned with real branches cut from trees on the property. Pillar candles in hurricane glasses are spaced across the top. Pine cones and red berry clusters are artfully arranged in between the candles. With the roaring fire, all that's missing are little stockings hung along the front. But that would be a fire hazard.

A large Fraser fir is to the left of the fireplace, wrapped in white lights and beaded natural wood garland. Birds of every color are clipped to the branches along with ornaments made from round, unfinished wood slices depicting various flora and fauna native to North Carolina.

Several smaller potted fir trees wrapped in colored lights are situated around the room. They'll be planted on the property after the holiday season. Garland and other decor grace the walls. The information desk and stair banisters mirror the mantel minus the candles. It feels like a winter wonderland. Especially with the instrumental version of that song playing over the speakers. My body fills with warmth at all the memories of Christmases past that float through my mind. I breathe in, capturing a hint of fir tree as I do.

I must make an audible sound when I exhale, because all three heads turn in my direction. Smiling, I wave. "Welcome, everyone. It looks like we're waiting for one more person." I check my watch, seeing it is two minutes after six. The building door whooshes open and a fourth person rushes in.

"I'm here, don't worry." He gives the room a confident smile and walks directly to me. "Let's get started."

I have to work to keep my smile from turning down. I don't like how Mr. Phillips is trying to take over my training already. Or that he was late. If this is going to be a regular thing, I may need to look for another person to play Santa. "Now that everyone's here," I say, giving Connor side-eye, "follow me back to the training room."

When everyone's seated, I take a minute to orient myself with who's here. Connor, of course. Ava and Genesis, elves and backup photographers, and Brett, beverage purveyor and miscellany work. "Thank you for coming. Connor, Genesis, and Ava, you all will work together at Santa's Workshop in the Education Center, so, in a little while, I'll send you up there where Joanne will walk you through the routine and have you practice some." Connor runs a hand through his hair and winks at the two girls, who blush. He's got to be at least ten years their senior, so his action feels a little creepy to me. I'm going to have to keep an eye on him. "Brett, you'll stay with me and we'll talk about your responsibilities. For right now—"

"What's he doing?"

My gaze swings over to Connor, perturbed at the interruption. Is he going to be hard to work with? "Please raise your hand if you have a question. Brett will work in the cocoa shack."

Connor smirks in Brett's direction. "Aren't you worried about him scaring the kids away with his angry face?"

As if in confirmation, Brett glowers at Connor. Better move things along. "You just worry about yourself. Like I was saying, we're going to start with an intro video that talks about our expectations for you as staff of Winter Lights, along with a history of the Arboretum." Connor groans, but when I pin him with a warning look, faces the front and says nothing. "When it's through, you'll take a short quiz and then we'll discuss the answers to make sure everyone is clear on things."

I hit a button on my computer and the video plays through the projector onto the screen in front. I watch the people, making sure they pay attention. At one point, Connor pulls his phone out of his pocket, but when he sees me watching him, he gives me a sheepish grin and puts it away. He then winks at me before turning back to the video.

❄❄❄

While Santa and the elves are in the Education Center with Joanne to go through the photo and visiting experience, I take Brett to the cocoa shack. The obvious friction between him and Connor is still weighing on my mind. Brett tensed up when Connor came through the door making me wonder if he's preparing for a fight. Surely they're mature enough to just keep their distance from one another, but if it's going to be a problem, I'd rather deal with it now. "What's the history between you and Connor?"

Brett doesn't seem surprised by the question. He obviously knows things were weird in the classroom. "We went to college together, but were never really friends, obviously. He's not my favorite person, but I can ignore him."

"I don't want this to be an antagonistic workplace. Is this going to be a recurring issue?"

He shrugs. "I won't respond to his provocations. Nor am I going to blame you for his harassment, if that's what you're worried about. I'll even sign something if it makes you feel better."

Does Brett think I'm worried about being sued? I hadn't even thought of that, though I probably should have. I'll have to talk to Joanne about it. "That shouldn't be necessary. You won't be working together, so you'll only really see each other at staff meetings. I assume you both can handle being in the same room, along with four dozen other people, for ten minutes."

We reach the shack, and I unlock the door. Inside there are boxes of insulated cups for hot cocoa. There are also plastic cups of two different sizes for beer and wine. "When you're in here, you'll be serving hot cocoa, beer, and wine. We'll also have bottles of water. There will be bottles of three different local beers that you'll pour into the large plastic cups. Do not give them the bottles. We don't want to risk having broken glass where someone might step on it. You'll put red and white wine in the shorter plastic cups. Insulated cups are for the hot chocolate, obviously. Any questions so far?"

Brett shakes his head, so I continue.

"You'll pour four ounces of wine, which is about halfway up the cup. Eight ounces of hot cocoa and we'll have mini marshmallows and whipped cream for those who want them. On weekend nights, there will be two of you working in here to keep up with the crowds. Monday through Thursday, you'll be in here alone. If you run low on anything, you can radio whoever's lead for the night and they'll bring more."

He nods, looking thoughtful. "What are our payment options?"

Excellent question. He really pays attention to details. "We take cash and cards. At the end of the evening, you'll inventory the beverages and restock. Re-cork any partially used wine bottles and use them first the following evening."

I can't tell if all this information overwhelms Brett. He seems to be following along just fine. "Did that all make sense?"

"I think so, but could I get some practice with the device we'll be using for electronic payments? Maybe go through some fake transactions?"

Ooh, a man after my own heart. I love people who take their job seriously. "Did you read my training notes ahead of time?" When he gives me an odd look, I wave my hands in front of me. "Sorry, that was supposed to be funny. To answer your question, yes, that's actually next on the schedule. Follow me to the kitchen where I'll walk you through the device and we'll make some drinks."

After twenty minutes, I'm thoroughly impressed. He's pouring drinks like a pro and handles the transactions like he's been doing it for years. He hands me a steaming cup of cocoa topped with marshmallows. "Is there a designated number of marshmallows I'm supposed to use?"

I take a sip of the beverage, using the cup to hide my smile. He's one of the best people I've trained this season. Even if he doesn't love Christmas, I know he's going to be an excellent employee. "Nope. Follow your heart on that one."

He looks at me quizzically but says nothing. Connor could take some lessons from him. Though, maybe his boisterousness will make him the perfect Santa. I sure hope so. Speaking of which, I should probably go check on their progress. Brett seems set, so I feel good about letting him leave early. "You seem to have everything down. We've covered everything I wanted to, so you're free to go."

"What about helping with any remaining set up?"

That had completely slipped my mind. "Oh right. Tomorrow, there's going to be a crew working on the lights and decor around the mini railroad. If you want to help with that, be back here around six-thirty."

Brett nods. "Great. I'll be here. Do I just give my name to the attendant?"

I snap my fingers. "Thanks for the reminder. Come with me."

We return to the classroom and I hand him a lanyard with his name on it. "There's a barcode on the back that you can scan at the Member's Line to get in. It also means you can come visit the Arboretum during the day anytime you want. And free admission to Winter Lights on your evenings off."

He frowns. "I don't need days off. I'll work every night."

I shrug. "Sorry, it's not optional. We don't want you to exhaust yourself. Oh! Another thing I haven't mentioned yet. Santa and the elves have costumes, but there's a dress code for everyone else. Jeans and tennis shoes are fine, but we require a festive shirt. It can be as simple as a red or green sweater or sweatshirt, or as fun as an ugly Christmas sweater. Nothing lewd or profane, though. This is a family-friendly event. Hats are optional, though we'd love it if you donned our official Arboretum Christmas hat."

I hold up a green Santa hat with white trim and puff ball. Our logo is embroidered on the trim. I extend it to him, but he shakes his head. "No, thanks."

"I'm required to give them to each employee. Whether you wear it is up to you."

He sighs and takes it from me, turning toward the door. "Do you have antlers and a red nose for me as well?" he mumbles.

I chuckle, not sure if he meant that as a joke. "Not unless Santa decides he needs a reindeer."

Brett gives me a concerned look. "You're joking, right?"

I rein in my smile, not wanting to risk offending him. "Yes, that was my lame attempt at a joke. Which obviously fell flat."

His posture relaxes. "No, sorry. It's just…" He pauses, then shakes his head. "Never mind."

I can't let him leave like that. "It's just what? Please tell me."

"I don't want to speak ill of others."

It's not too hard to put the pieces together based on tonight's experience. "You think Connor would make you dress like a reindeer?"

He doesn't confirm my assertion, just shrugs. My mouth forms a straight line. I don't like this weird undercurrent between two of my new employees, but I need them both for our event to be fully staffed. To be on the safe side, I'll supervise Connor closely, especially when Brett's around. Guess that means I'm signing myself up to be one of Santa's helpers this year. It's not a bad gig. I'll get to witness all the smiles and joy on kids' faces when they see Santa. The anticipation lightens my mood. I can handle this. Everything will be just fine.

9

Brett

AFTER SCANNING MY new badge in the Member's Line, the bar raises and I drive down the long, winding road until I reach the main parking lot. When I get out, I grab the green sweater I bought last night to meet wardrobe standards. It's better than having to shave my beard and, while the color evokes thoughts of a Christmas tree, it's not too festive. The hat, however, is never touching my head.

When I enter the lobby of the main building, there's a small group of people in old work clothes—faded, paint-splattered jeans and holey long-sleeved shirts that have seen better days. Not one of them is wearing red or green. Oh. Guess the uniform is only for when Winter Lights is open. I'm tempted to return the sweater to my car, but know I'll regret it once the sun sets. At least it's not bright red, so I can still pull it off as regular clothes. That are brand new and still have the tag on them. The white price tag dances on my sleeve like it's mocking me. I yank it off and stuff it in my pocket, then join the crowd.

An older gentleman wearing a tool belt and a bright yellow toboggan hat counts us with his eyes, then claps his hands once. "Looks like everyone's here. Let's head out to the railroad shed and get started. If you didn't bring work gloves, there are extras in the shed. Just grab a pair."

He turns and heads down a hall without another word. After glancing at one another for a second, we scramble to catch up with him. I don't know his name, but I like that he's no nonsense. Maybe I'll like this job after all. Especially since it doesn't look like Connor signed up to be early help. I suppose his "talents" would be wasted on behind-the-scenes work.

The man pulls out an orange Home Depot bucket, and it hits the ground with a thud. Several of us retrieve a pair of brown leather gloves from the bucket and put them on. The man in charge hands us stuff from inside the shed. There are oversized candy canes, light up toy soldiers, teddy bears, and gingerbread men. "Hey Roy," a guy wearing a plaid hat with earflaps says. "Where's the design map so we know where all this stuff goes?"

Without a word, Roy reaches into back pocket, extracting a folded up piece of paper. Plaid guy takes the paper and smooths it out before orienting it to the surrounding landmarks. "Okay, the candy canes line the path nearest the railroad. Space them four feet apart. The toy soldiers flank the stairs that go up to the main gardens. Bears and men are to be scattered around the yard, except for the biggest bear which will be hung on this shed. When we get that set up, I'll tell you the rest. If your decoration needs spikes, you can find them and hammers in the blue bucket."

Roy unceremoniously heaves a big blue bucket out of the shed and drops it next to the other one. Alright. Guess it's time to get started.

After several hours of instruction, mostly from the guy in charge of the map whose name I learn is Jonah, we're finished, and it actually looks pretty good. We drop our gloves back into the bucket, which Roy returns to the shed and locks the doors. "Thanks all," Jonah says. "We need lots of hands tomorrow for finishing Santa's Workshop. We'll meet up at the Education Center at six. If you can come, raise your hand."

My hand goes into the air. I look around and see most of the others have also volunteered. I suppose everyone here is looking to make money for Christmas. Mom is the only person I've bought anything for in a long time. Some of us at the bookstore do a White Elephant exchange, but it's a twenty-dollar limit, so not a financial hardship. But this year, I'm hoping to pull off the best Christmas surprise ever.

The next evening, I arrive at the Arboretum in regular work clothes. I'm not sure what we're doing for Santa's Workshop, but I wouldn't be surprised if there was some construction work and possibly painting. Traffic was heavier than normal, so I'm a few minutes late and people have already been assigned tasks. I look for Roy among the workers, but my eyes snag on a pair of red and green Christmas leggings. I can make out candy canes and reindeer in the print. Whoever's wearing them is bent at the waist, so all I see is a very nice rear end. The woman straightens back up, and the hem of her baggy red sweatshirt falls down over the aforementioned backside. I feel a tug of disappointment at the loss of the view. Her dark hair is up in a springy ponytail that's bouncing back and forth while she talks animatedly with another person. She turns in my direction and points at something, and my gut twists when I realize I'm ogling my boss. I quickly try to scrub the image from my mind, but closing my eyes only seems to burn it deeper into my memory.

When I open my eyes again, Meredith is standing right in front of me and I jump from the surprise. She reaches out and touches my upper arm. "Did I startle you?"

Lie or lean into it? "It's my fault for meditating in public."

"You were meditating?"

I shake my head. "No, lame joke."

She blinks at me and embarrassment wells up inside. *Way to be normal, Brett.* "Anyway, I'm here to help, but traffic made me late, so I don't know what there is to do."

Meredith pulls me over to an area with sheets of plywood stacked on the ground near a saw and a few cans of paint. "I'm making reindeer. I thought we'd mix things up a little this year, so Santa's throne is going to be his sleigh. Kids can pretend like they're joining Santa to deliver presents all over the world."

Okay. Seems unnecessary, but I don't feel like squashing the excitement radiating off of Meredith. "I'm not very good at drawing."

She waves away my words. "No problem. I'm hand drawing them. I just need you to cut them out and then we'll paint them together."

Oh. So we're working together tonight. That's cool. Maybe being around her Christmas cheer will help get rid of this tiny bit of attraction that's lingering from when I first spotted her. I mean, look at her cheesy reindeer earrings that she must have worn because she knew what she was working on tonight. Are those carrots in her second holes? Because that's what reindeer eat? Oh boy. This woman is too much. I shake my head, then pick up the saw on the floor and start cutting out the first reindeer.

We draw and cut in silence for a few minutes until Meredith announces that she's going to paint the first deer, so we have a reference for the rest of them. I notice there are only two more cut outs to do, making the total reindeer only four. "I thought Santa had eight reindeer."

Meredith looks surprised, whether from my comment or the fact that I'm starting a conversation, I'm not sure. "We don't have that much floor space, plus they'd get cut out of the photo, anyway. The focus is on Santa and the kids."

That makes sense. When I finish the last reindeer, I turn to see that Meredith's already completely painted one reindeer. I'm taken aback by how realistic the deer looks. I can just picture it grazing in a meadow. "Wow, that's realistic. There's no way I can paint a deer to look like that."

She smiles. "No problem. You can paint the brown bodies and I'll focus on the faces and extra details."

An excellent proposition. I can do brown paint. I nod and get to work. An hour later, I sit back and study our work. "These look very realistic. Where did you learn to paint like that?"

She shrugs. "I've always been artsy. I've been creating things since I could hold a pencil."

"Have you considered doing this for a living?"

Meredith shakes her head. "I just finished my MBA and probably should use it to make the time and expense worthwhile."

Wow. Beautiful *and* smart, in addition to being hardworking and kind? Meredith's quite a catch. Not that I'm interested. She's my boss, so that wouldn't be professional. And besides, I'm not looking for a relationship right now. Especially not with someone who looks so much like Vicky. Maybe if I keep her talking, I'll find out something that will squash the annoying hint of attraction I feel. "What are you looking to do?"

"My focus was on hospitality management, so maybe something with hotels or large entertainment property."

"Like the Biltmore?"

My question earns me a wide grin. "Exactly like the Biltmore. It seems like it could be the perfect opportunity to do something I might enjoy and keep me at home."

That last bit snags in my brain. "You like living here?"

She nods. "I love Asheville. My family's here and I enjoy being close to them."

Someone comes up to where we are and whistles. "Whoa, Merry, these look great! In fact, they look just like the little wooden Santa and his sleigh set I ordered off your website."

Mary? Is that a nickname or something? She introduced herself to me as Meredith, so that's what I'm going to call her until she instructs me otherwise. She beams at them and, for a second, I wish it was me she was looking at like that. "Thanks, Zach." She gives him a side hug and my jealousy flares. What's up with that?

When he leaves, I can't help myself. "You have a website?"

She waves her hand from side to side. "Kinda. I'm on the Crafty platform."

I've heard of it. It's like a small business site for people who create kitschy items and want to sell them. I wonder what she makes. "What's your name?"

"MerryDesigns. No space between the words."

The name of her store raises new questions for me. "How do you spell it?"

"M-E-R-R-Y, like Merry Christmas."

"Is Merry a nickname or something?"

"Yes, but only people at the Arboretum call me that. It's what's on my name tag."

I look down at her lanyard. *Meredith Larson.* She must see my confusion because she grabs the tag, chuckling. "Not *this* name tag. The one I wear during the event."

"Why do you go by Merry at Winter Lights?"

"It's kind of a funny story. When I first started working here in high school, another Meredith was also on staff. She suggested we use our middle names to distinguish ourselves, and I agreed. I became Mer E, for Meredith Elaine, and she was Mer C, Meredith Christine. The other staff thought it was funny to call us Merry and Mercy, and it stuck. When I was assigned to work in Santa's Workshop, I thought it would be fun to lean into the name and become Merry the Elf. Now, I don't think I could go back to being called Meredith even if I wanted to."

Maybe I can start the trend of returning her to Meredith. Assuming that's something she wants. She might really like her nickname. I definitely understand about names defining us. It's why I changed mine. "Is that where your store name came from then?"

"Yes. And the fact that everything I make for the store is holiday themed."

That doesn't surprise me. It's obvious she loves Christmas. "I bet you do your best business right about now."

"You're right, but I make steady sales throughout the year, believe it or not."

Are there really that many Christmas-obsessed people in the world? I guess you have to be one to know one. Which I'm obviously not. But to each their own. I look around and realize we're the only people left in the building. Where did everyone else go?

"I guess we're finished for the night," Meredith says. "We'll let these dry and tomorrow we can attach them to stands so they'll stay upright. Then we'll add their collars and ropes and be all set. Thanks for your help tonight, Brett. I wouldn't have finished all this without you."

Her words stroke my pride, even though I really didn't do much. "Anyone could have filled my shoes. It was just a little sawing and painting."

She touches my sleeve, giving my forearm a light squeeze, before pulling back. "You were the perfect person for the job."

Meredith's just being kind, I try to reason with myself. That's who she is. But a part of my brain, the part that seems to have forgotten all the reasons I shouldn't be interested in Meredith, hopes her words and touch were specifically for me.

10

Meredith

"ALRIGHT, EVERYONE, THE first night of Winter Lights is here!" My body is buzzing with energy and the tiny bells on my green and red elf costume jingle with the slightest movement. A glance through the crowd of employees confirms I'm not the only one excited for tonight to begin. "Everyone has their assignments. You all look great, by the way. I love the unique flair you've put on your outfits."

I really do like that everyone seems to have gotten into the Christmas spirit. I've had my green and red elf costume for years, but my body hasn't changed much since high school, so it still fits nicely. Ava's elf costume is green and yellow, reminding me of Buddy the Elf. Genesis has red tights, a pink tunic with white trim around the bottom and sleeves, and a matching pink hat with red trim. We're all different, but go well together. Connor, of course, is a much too in-shape Santa. I brought some stuffing to round out his belly. He hasn't put on the beard yet, but I'm sure the heavy costume heats quickly. As long as he puts it on before he leaves the building, I'm okay with it. I'd hate to ruin the magic of Santa for a child.

The rest of the crew has cute Christmas sweaters depicting things like reindeer, snowflakes, and candy canes. One has a festive Darth Vader sweater which, I suppose, is technically okay since it's red and white. Sure, the white balls are little death stars, and those are TIE fighters instead of snowflakes, but from far away no one would know. My gaze pauses on a plain green sweater. I'm not surprised to see it belongs to Brett. It fits the dress code, but I almost think I prefer Darth Vader.

"Joanne is everyone's main contact person tonight. If there's an issue, use your walkie-talkie. I'll come by at some point to check in with everyone and make sure you have what you need. Are there any questions?"

I swing my gaze over the group. No hands go up. "Okay, then. Everyone head to your stations."

The staff disperses, and I rush over to Connor. "Hey, please make sure you're wearing all parts of your costume before you exit this building. We don't want to traumatize any of our younger patrons."

Connor pulls the beard and hair over his head. "How's this look?"

I reach up and adjust it until it looks almost real. The only giveaway that Connor's not an old man is the smooth skin of his cheeks. I take the hat from his hand and place it on top. "You're almost perfect. I've got some stuffing up at the Education Center I want to put in your jacket to complete the look."

Connor rolls his eyes, but stays silent against my critique. He hooks an arm around my shoulders and gives me a warm smile. "Let's go entertain some kids!"

I let him lead me up the stairs and outside to the Baker Garden. We walk along the pathway, around the giant metal Christmas tree that rests over the fountain, up four more sets of stairs, and to the

Education Center.

Inside, I grab the stuffing that I'd set in the sleigh and push it up under Connor's coat, manipulating it with my hands until it looks somewhat like a round belly. I step back and survey my work. "You look good, Connor."

He gives me a wolfish grin. "I always look good. You look great yourself. That costume fits you like a glove." His eyes make a slow down and up perusal, which makes me squirm a little with discomfort.

The other two elves arrive, saving me from having to respond, and I give them instructions, even though it's the same stuff they heard at training. I tend to over-explain when I'm nervous. And opening night is giving me the jitters. I know everything will be fine, but it still doesn't stop me from worrying. "I'll be here for a while, but once everything is running smoothly, I'll head out to check on everyone else."

Connor takes his place in the sleigh and, I must admit, it's an idyllic scene. The kids are going to love it. Speaking of which, here's our first family. Two girls dressed in matching green smocked dresses who look to be early elementary age run straight to Santa and climb onto his lap. A harried looking woman with three scarves around her neck and two small coats in her hand races after them. "Girls, you're supposed to get in line. The elves will let you know when it's your turn with Santa."

The girls climb back down and meet their mother at the front of our red velvet-roped line looking chastened. "Mom, there's no one else here," the older one says.

"I know, sweetie, but it's not polite to jump on Santa. You want him to put you on the nice list, right?"

The girls nod solemnly. Connor looks at me, and I give him a slight nod. He beams at the family. "Ho ho ho. Who do we have here? Come, come!"

He motions to the girls, who light up, but walk rather than run to the sleigh this time. He pats his thighs and the girls sit up on his lap. "Sorry, Santa," one says and her sister echoes the apology.

"Don't be sorry," Connor says, his smile wide.

Are his eyes twinkling? All he needs are rosy red cheeks and I'd believe he was Santa. Maybe I'll put some rouge on him tomorrow.

"I love an enthusiastic greeting," he continues. "It's not every day I get to spend time with two beautiful girls like you. I've spent the last few months supervising my elves in the workshop. Now tell me, what is it you two would like for Christmas?"

I realize my mouth is hanging open, and I shut it quickly. Connor has transformed into Santa right before my eyes. Who would have thought he'd be so good at it? He chats with the girls for a few minutes about school and how he appreciates that they listen to their mother. He suggests the girls make their mom a Christmas card of all the things they love about her and the woman lights up. He's managed to charm everyone, me included, in just a couple of minutes.

When another family enters the queue, he wraps things up and takes a picture with the girls and their mom. The girls take a candy cane from the big red sack next to the sleigh, while the mom leans in and whispers something to Connor. He nods in response and gives her a warm smile. When she turns, I can tell there are tears in her eyes. Wow! Connor sure knows how to schmooze. I mentally pat myself on the back for looking past his arrogance and hiring him.

An hour later, the Santa line is ten families deep, but everyone seems to have things covered, so I whisper to Genesis that I'm going to check on everyone else and head over to coffee and snack stands on the other side of the room. No one there has any issues, so I visit the s'mores station just outside the building. Several families are roasting marshmallows around the firepit. "How's it going?" I ask Zach.

"Everything's great."

"Good." I wind through the gardens down to the railroad. The younger crowd is enjoying watching Thomas the Train's eyes move back and forth as he chugs around the track. He passes a red train on a second track. The staff member is talking to an older gentleman. I step closer and hear the patron discussing the maintenance of trains. It's obvious he worked in a train yard in his younger years. I wave to my employee and give him a thumbs up. He nods, letting me know all is well here.

I retrace my way back up the stairs and head over to the cocoa shack in the Baker Garden. There isn't a line at the moment, but I see people milling around with plastic cups in their hands, so it seems to be doing well. I approach the window, which Brett somehow senses because he doesn't look up when he says, "How can I help you?"

"Hey, there. I'm just making my rounds. How's it going here?" He meets my eyes and I smile, noticing that his sweater mirrors the green in his eyes. His beard has filled in more. It makes him look quite handsome. I realize I've been staring too long and look down at my fingers, which are drumming against my thighs. *Get it together, Meredith.*

"Fine."

Ah, right. Don't know why I expected him to expand on that. "Great!" Someone steps up behind me. "Well, I'll get out of your way. If you need anything, let me know."

Brett's brow furrows. "I thought Joanne was the contact person tonight."

I twist a strand of hair around my finger. "Oh, yeah, you're right." He just looks at me. "Okay, bye."

I give him a little wave, then turn and hurry into the Baker building. *Smooth, Meredith. Were you trying to flirt with him or something? Because that wasn't flirting.* My body's warm with embarrassment. Brett probably thinks I'm super strange now. Oh well.

I check on the staff inside the building. Everything's fine, so I make my way back up to the Education Center, taking a roundabout way to avoid the cocoa shack. Back inside, the line to see Santa is even longer than before. Ava gives me a wide-eyed look of panic, so I rush over to her. "Sorry," she whispers, "but I need to use the restroom."

"Go." I wave her away, taking her place at the head of the Santa line. I have a front-row seat to watch Connor charm not only the kids, but the parents as well. Charisma definitely seems like the key ingredient for a quality Santa impersonation.

At the end of the evening, we reset the scene, repositioning a reindeer that somehow ended up facing backward and refilling the candy cane stash for the following day. While replacing the candy canes in the supply closet, I hear the other two elves whispering about how cute they think Connor is. I peek my head out and see Genesis with a swoony look on her face. I follow her gaze and see Connor bent over, sweeping something into the dust broom. That reminds me of something I forgot to mention at our opening meeting. Well, I'll add it into the wrap-up meeting.

When everyone is reassembled after cleaning up, I clap my hands together to get everyone's attention. "Great first night, everyone. I heard several wonderful comments about tonight from patrons. If you heard anything positive about tonight, write it on a slip of paper in the break room and put it up on the bulletin board so it can encourage us. On the flip side, if you heard anything negative, please tell me or Joanne so we can address it. One last thing I wanted to mention. The Arboretum has no issues with staff dating one another as long as it doesn't affect work performance. Please keep physical affection reserved for outside of work hours and preferably off of the property. Just like other work infractions, you'll be issued a warning for the first incident. The second warning will result in a dismissal. If we feel it is something egregious, then there will be no warning, just immediate termination."

I pause, realizing I don't want to end on such a somber note. "Like I said, everyone did fantastic tonight. Kudos to our new Santa, Connor. You were fantastic with the families. Keep it up! You all are dismissed."

Connor winks at me, then turns to Genesis, who touches his arm, then rocks up on tiptoe to whisper something in his ear. He grins at her and nods. The elf works fast. Well, good for her. I look around in search of Brett, but he's apparently already left. The tug of disappointment in my gut surprises me. I mean, we're not even friends, so what does it matter that he didn't stick around to say goodbye? Still, I can't help wishing he had.

11

Brett

MY WEEKDAY NIGHT shifts at the Arboretum feel pretty much the same, but I don't mind routine. I've got things in the cocoa shack down to a science. My muscles know the exact amount to pour for wine and cocoa. My scoops of marshmallows are nearly uniform as well. There was only one hiccup when a kid knocked over a cup of cocoa while reaching for it, causing the contents to spill off my side of the counter and into the cash box. A few paper towels and things were good to go, minus a few damp dollar bills.

Maneuvering in the aptly named shack with a second person on the weekend took an adjustment. Thankfully, we're so busy that there's no time to chat and get to know one another, which suits me just fine. I'm here to make money, not friends.

My new boss, Meredith, has stopped by at least once a night to check up on me, though I never need anything. I probably should feel perturbed that she keeps stopping by like I can't handle it on my own, but I'm sure it is standard procedure. She seems to be a stickler for the rules and thorough in her job duties. The more time I spend with her, the less perturbed I am by her friendly personality and that she gets excited about small things like a staff member's Christmas sweater or photos of babies and cute animals. She knows how to make everyone feel seen and appreciated. Definitely excellent traits to have when one is a manager of people. I bet she'll be fantastic in hospitality management.

Tonight, I plan to go home after my shift at the bookstore and sit on my couch wearing all black to celebrate my first night off from the Arboretum. Why black? Because it seems like the antithesis of Christmas cheer. Only a week and a half of working Winter Lights, and I've had more festive holiday goodness thrust in my face than in the last ten years combined. Plus, I'm exhausted from working two jobs every day.

Actually, the Arboretum really hasn't been that bad. I don't feel pressured to go crazy with Christmas spirit and, as long as I stay far away from Connor, the rest of the staff is cool. It certainly doesn't bother me that our work stations are on opposite sides of the garden. He's definitely been playing up the Santa gig. One day he brought mistletoe and pinned it to his hat so women would 'give Santa a kiss.' Even thinking about it makes me wince with disgust. He's definitely taking advantage of being able to date other staff. I just hope no one gets hurt with as casual as he is with others' feelings. I mean, that's how I remember him. He could have changed, I suppose. And maybe no one's looking for anything serious, in which case, more power to them.

I, however, am not going to risk the messiness of engaging with a co-worker. Not that there's anyone here I'm interested in. *Liar*, my brain retorts. Okay, so I definitely don't hate Meredith's presence, but she's my boss. Even if staff can date, I doubt that implies to the people in charge. Besides, there's no realistic scenario in which she'd ever be interested in me. A bubbly personality like her probably prefers someone equally outgoing, not someone who likes books, is quiet, and bah humbug about Christmas. *Someone like Connor?* my traitorous mind asks. No, not him. Though, there doesn't seem to be any danger of that happening. She's too smart to fall for his fickle charm. But she was pretty effusive that first night about Connor's stellar performance as Santa, so perhaps even she can be swayed.

Not that it's my problem. She's a grown woman and can date whomever she likes. Still, as someone who's well aware of Connor's craftiness, I feel like it's my duty to warn her. *Why? Because you like her?* Curse this rogue brain of mine. I finish filling a book cart and push it out onto the floor, hoping the routine of work will squelch these unwanted thoughts.

❄❄❄

I've just plopped down on my couch, ready for an evening of mindless television, when my phone rings. I don't recognize the number, but it's a local area code, so I answer.

"Hey, Brett. It's Meredith. From the Arboretum."

She really didn't need to add that last part. Her voice is permanently etched in my echoic memory. Obviously, not just hers. My mom's is in there. And Rachel's. And, as much as I wish I could erase it, my father's as well. Not that I've heard his voice since my high school graduation.

I didn't want him there, but couldn't exactly ban him from a public event. Though he gave up trying to connect with me once I became an adult. He still sent me birthday cards for a while, but I was pretty clear about not wanting to have anything to do with him and he finally got the message. He chose someone else over me and my mom. Why would I choose to put myself through the pain of seeing him happy with another family?

Despite everything, Mom still keeps in touch with him. Initially, it was just to keep him updated about me, since I refused to talk to or meet with him. But I guess enough time has passed that they're now kind of cordial. I wouldn't call them friends per se, but they have some sort of understanding. I don't really know the details because I haven't asked. Regardless, it doesn't make sense to me.

"Are you there?"

I blink, realizing my thoughts have gotten away from me. "I'm here."

"I know this is your night off, so feel free to say 'no,' but several of us are going over to Nothing But Wings for trivia night and I wanted to see if you're interested in joining us."

She's got to be an extrovert, opting for a crowded restaurant with people on a free night over a quiet night at home. My stomach growls, reminding me I haven't eaten dinner yet. And I do like trivia challenges. I watch Jeopardy most nights. It'd be an opportunity to get to know her outside of work, which intrigues me for some reason. I wonder if she's always been super excited about Christmas. Not that I'm interested in getting to know her as more than a friend, of course. "Yeah, sure."

"Great! What flavor wings do you like? I'll put in an order for you."

"Garlic ranch as long as someone else will eat some. Otherwise, I'll just have whatever the group wants."

"Yay! Those are my favorite, but no one else will touch them. They're worried about their breath. I say you only live once, so you might as well enjoy it."

Her enthusiasm brings a smile to my face. "Okay, well, see you soon."

We hang up. I look down at my faded black sweatpants with a bleach spot on the leg and T-shirt with a huge gash in the side. I should probably put on something less ratty to go out in public. After changing into a black sweater and dark jeans, I grab my keys and head over to the restaurant.

When I arrive, the parking lot is packed. I snag a spot when someone pulls out. It's loud inside, every booth and table taken by groups of four or five people. A waving hand catches my attention, and I squeeze through the crowd to a U-shaped booth back against the wall. Meredith pats the space next to her and I slide into the booth. She lightly squeezes my forearm, a warm smile on her face.

"So glad you could make it, Brett. I don't know if you've met everyone. This is Ava. She's one of our elves." She gives a small wave and I nod. "This is Jonah. He keeps our railroad up and running, and that's Zach, our s'mores expert."

"Nice to meet you all," I say. "Has it started yet?"

Meredith shakes her head. "We've got about five minutes."

A server appears at our table, setting down two trays of wings, mozzarella sticks, and nachos. She passes out small plates and then turns to me. "What can I get you to drink?"

I glance around the table. The guys have beers and the women have cocktails. "Can I get a Cold Mountain?"

She nods and disappears.

"Dig in," Meredith says to the table, then turns to me. "What are your trivia strengths?"

Her question catches me off guard. Is this a serious team? Not what I expected with as casual as she made it sound. That's fine with me. I was part of a few prize-winning trivia teams in college. "I'm pretty good with music that isn't pop or country."

She nods. "What else?"

"World news, geography, movies."

Meredith grins like I gave a winning answer. I remind myself this is just a low-key night with co-workers while ignoring the warmth blooming in my chest from her smile.

"Great," she says. "Ava has pop culture and celebrities covered. Jonah knows cars, TV, and slogans. Zach is our guy for toys and games, and I'm our general knowledge guru."

"It sounds like we've got everything covered."

❄❄❄

An hour and a half later, my words almost seem prophetic. We whipped up on all the other teams and the gift card, which was our prize, covered all of our food. I didn't love the team name, though. *Merry Quizmas*. It's obvious who came up with that one, but I really can't blame her. Meredith was the star of our team. She knows a lot more than pop culture and general knowledge. She probably could have won the night single-handedly, except she deferred to whomever we had declared the expert on the subject at hand. I noticed halfway through the evening; she has a tell when she knows the answer. She plays with the earring in the top of her right ear. I probably noticed because I was sitting on that side of her.

I also learned that the women weren't drinking cocktails like I thought. Ava had a Shirley Temple and Meredith's clear drink was ginger ale with a slice of lime. Is it to stay sharp for trivia or do they not drink at all? Maybe Meredith doesn't allow herself to cut loose when she's with employees, even if she's off the clock. That's probably it. She seems very serious and professional when it comes to her job.

The rest of our group was fun to talk to and get to know as well. I wonder if we'll always have the same nights off. I guess I'll find out at my next break. I definitely enjoyed seeing a new side of Meredith. I didn't know she was so competitive. She has a serious game face, but I found it endearing. There's so much more to her than what I thought.

Ava mentioned Meredith's Crafty shop again. I'd forgotten all about that. I'm extra curious now to see what she's selling on there.

Driving back to my apartment, I feel strangely energized. Guess I needed a fun night out more than an evening of brooding solitude. I'm definitely looking forward to seeing everyone tomorrow. Maybe this job isn't so bad.

12

Meredith

I'VE SPENT MY morning at home searching for full-time employment. There are a few hospitality management positions listed on the job site board I'm scrolling on the computer. My breath catches when I see a listing for Biltmore Estate. They're looking for a manager for their hotel properties. While the mansion is now a museum, the property has three different lodging accommodations—the Village Hotel, the Inn, and private cottages. I haven't stayed at Biltmore overnight, just toured the house and wandered through Antler Hill Village and the walking trails. I've always wondered what the views are like up at the Inn on top of one of the hills. Spectacular, no doubt. I fill out the application and click submit.

After a few more minutes of searching, nothing else catches my eye, so I give up and head down to the kitchen for some lunch. While

I'm making a sandwich, Ali comes in and steals a piece of turkey from the pile. She pops it in the microwave for a few seconds, then stuffs the steaming meat in her mouth. I just shake my head and keep assembling my food.

"What?" she says, her tone defensive. "I'm not supposed to eat deli meat unless it's warmed up." She wraps her hands under her stomach and sighs. "I'll be glad when this one's born and I can go back to eating whatever I like."

My heart pangs in sympathy. Ali's a foodie, so I know it's been hard having to change her dietary habits this past year. "I'm sorry. But I'm sure it'll be well worth the inconvenience."

She rubs her belly affectionately. "I'm sure, too."

"What brings you by? Have the day off?"

"No, I'm just stopping by on my lunch break to pick up some baby stuff Mom got. She didn't say where to look. Have you seen a pile anywhere?"

I press my lips together in thought. "Maybe in the front room? I saw a medium-sized box there earlier this morning."

"Thanks. What have you been up to today?"

Finished with my lunch preparation, I turn and open the fridge to return everything to its proper place. "Doing some job hunting. I applied for an opening at the Biltmore."

"That's exciting! Oh, I talked to my friend in New York and they have management positions available. He's supposed to email me the listing and I'll forward it on to you."

Thankfully, my back is to her, so she can't see the face I make. I don't want to live in New York. It's so big and loud and busy. And so far away from my family. I'm going to be an aunt soon and I can't imagine having to get to know my little nephew or niece over video calls. How am I supposed to sniff their sweet baby head or snuggle their warm, squishy body through my phone? Still, I know she's being supportive and it may be the only thing that works out. "Thanks, Ali. Send it to me and I'll fill out the application form."

When I turn, she's beaming at me. "I'm so proud of you,

Meredith. I hope you know that. It couldn't have been easy completing the MBA program, but it seems like you've made it your own. And you've made our parents happy."

Seems like my sisters and I are all in agreement that pursuing my MBA was the right call, even if it felt like wearing an old sweater—a little scratchy and too tight in some areas. I can only nod in response because my throat is choked with emotion. Something that happened eleven years ago shouldn't affect me so much now, but grief is its own machine and doesn't play by any rules. Ali seems to read the turmoil in my face because she comes over and hugs me against her, rubbing up and down my back. I feel silly. We both lost our brother, yet she seems to have dealt with it better than I have. But then I hear her sniff and realize that we all must manifest our feelings in different ways. I wrap an arm around her back and squeeze briefly before letting go and clearing my throat.

"Whoa, sorry about that."

I notice Ali's smile is a little watery, and she wipes under one of her eyes. "This pregnancy has made me more emotional than usual. Sorry I started it."

I shake my head. "No, I appreciate your kind words. You're nothing but supportive of me and I appreciate it. You're going to be such a great mom."

She smiles wider, this one strong and sure. The heavy mood between us evaporates. "Thanks. I'm sorry to interrupt your lunch, but would you mind carrying the box to my car? I don't know if I can manage." She looks down at her bulging belly for emphasis.

"Of course!"

❄❄❄

After lunch, I head downtown to do some Christmas shopping. I find some cute shirts and earrings for my sisters. My dad's getting a "World's Best Grandpa" hat. I wonder if he's going to be called Grandpa or something else. I grew up with a Granddad and a

Grimm. Not sure how my mom's father got that name, but it seemed to suit him. I guess we'll find out what my dad's new name is in January.

My next stop is the bookstore, so I can find the book on female inventors I heard Mom mention a couple of months ago. I also want to get some books for Baby Fredrikson. My sister and brother-in-law have decided to wait until the birth to find out the baby's gender. It sounds like it'll be either Edward or Sophie, depending, though I've heard Rich mention Jordan a few times, which could work for either. Glad I don't have to decide anything as monumental as a person's name anytime soon. I want to be more situated with work and life before I have kids. Of course, I'd also need a spouse and I haven't been on a date in over a year. Not that I've met anyone that I've wanted to go on a date with. Brett comes unbidden to my mind, but it's probably just because I'm standing out front of the place where he works.

I shake off the thought and enter the store. I look around, realizing the layout has changed since I was here last. The front part is a Christmas explosion. The windows have fake snow and a gingerbread village, each building raised up on a stack of Christmas-themed books. Garland hangs from the ceiling and festive decor is swagged along the top of the shelves. Wait a minute. Is that *my* Happy Holidays banner over there? I walk over to the sign and flip up the triangle with the "S" on it. Sure enough, MerryDesigns is stamped in red on the backside. It's both weird and oddly pleasing to see my stuff out in the wild.

"Welcome to Page Turner Books. Are you looking for anything in particular?"

Goosebumps pebble on my arms at the sound of Brett's voice. I turn, my smile widening when I notice his red shirt has a picture of stacks of green books forming a tree, a little yellow star on top. I thought he wasn't into Christmas? He must see the question in my eyes because he rolls his eyes and says, "My boss makes us wear some of our shop merch once a week. She thinks it'll entice customers to purchase their own."

I nod slowly, taking in this information. "That sounds genius to me. I'm definitely more inclined to leave with a festive book-themed shirt after seeing yours. You know, you *could* wear this shirt at the Arboretum."

He gives me a skeptical look. "I think it's a little thin for working outdoors at night."

I concede his point with a tilt of my head. "To answer your first question, yes, I am looking for something specific, but I have a question for you first." I hitch a thumb up to the banner. "Who bought that?"

Brett's eyes widen slightly, and his lips twitch, but his face stays neutral otherwise. "My boss, Sarah."

"Huh. Wonder how she found my shop? I haven't been able to do much advertising, though I honestly don't know what would be the best way to get the word out."

He shifts his weight from one foot to the other and looks up at the banner behind me, an odd expression on his face. He definitely knows something. I put a hand on my hip and give him my best stern face. "Spill it, Brett."

He takes one look at my face and laughs. Guess my serious face isn't very intimidating. The smile that breaks out across his face feels like the sun emerging from behind a rain cloud. Why doesn't he smile much? It transforms his face. His very cute face, I notice. His beard has filled in and it gives him a rugged, manly look. One I realize I quite like. I meet his gaze and he quirks an eyebrow. Have I been studying his face for too long? My eyes dart down to my hands and I twist my fingers together.

"My co-worker told her about it. She must have stumbled upon your website and has been raving about it to everyone she sees."

Surprised, but also flattered that someone likes my stuff, I look back up at Brett. "That certainly explains the uptick in sales this past week. I just figured people were doing searches for Christmas decor on the Crafty website."

Brett nods. "That may also be true. What can I help you find?"

The change of topic draws me back to the reason I'm here. "Right. I'm looking for a specific book on women inventors for my mom." I hand him a slip of paper with the title written on it. "Do you have it?"

"Let's find out together."

He leads me through the bookshelf maze to the nonfiction section and locates it within seconds. I'm impressed by his knowledge of this labyrinth. The book is thick and weighs several pounds. I tuck it against me. "Thanks. I also want to get a few books for my nibling. Do you have any suggestions?"

"What's a nibling?"

The puzzled look on his face is oddly attractive. *Stop thinking about Brett like that. He's your employee.* I press my lips together to collect myself before replying. "It's a neutral term for niece or nephew. My sister's keeping it a surprise, so this is the easiest thing to say."

"Except that you spent more words explaining it than just saying niece or nephew."

I nod. "True. So, do you know much about kids' books?"

Brett's brow furrows, and I wonder if I insulted him somehow. Before I can ask, he turns away from me and begins heading back in the direction we came from. After a few stunned seconds of trying to figure out what just happened, I hurry to catch up with him. He makes a sharp turn and disappears from sight. I pick up my speed and nearly run into him when I round the corner because he's stopped at the entrance to a gorgeous children's book section.

Colorful rugs cover the floor and there are squishy foam blocks in the shape of a train, complete with openings where kids can sit inside the engine and two connected cars like comfy reading nooks. There's an oversized rocking chair to one side and a small table with four equally tiny chairs on each side.

"Wow," I breathe out.

Brett nods beside me. "Yeah, it's pretty awesome."

I look over at his face to see if he's joking, but his face has a serene, almost wistful look. I blink, and his face shifts back into business mode. He walks around the shelves, which make up the walls of the area, plucking a book from the shelves every few steps. He completes the circle and offers me half a dozen books.

"I don't know how many you were thinking, but these are all excellent."

He hands me the first one, an interactive book with doors to open and animals that pop out. "This one is for toddlers, but you can do the activities while you read it and babies are fascinated with it." The next one is a thin book with a weird texture that crinkles. "It's the perfect book for when kids are exploring their environment. Most baby books end up in mouths and this one is indestructible. Plus, the kids love hearing the animal sounds."

Brett talks me through each of the other books and, by the end, I'm convinced my nibling needs them all. "Wow, Brett. Your extensive knowledge of children's books surprises me. I never would have guessed."

"Why's that?"

I'm kept from responding by an announcement overhead. "Attention shoppers, our toddler story time will begin in five minutes in the children's section. Please make your way there and gather around the rocking chair."

Brett nods. "That's my cue."

My mouth drops open in shock. "*You're* in charge of story time?"

He nods, not seeming offended by my disbelief. "Yep. This is only the second one. It took me ages to convince Sarah to do it, but we noticed a decent bump in sales after the last one, so I hope it's here to stay."

I shake my head, trying to comprehend all this new and fascinating information I've just learned about Brett. He lifts his hands and ushers me out of the room and toward the front.

"Sorry to leave you hanging, but I have to get ready. Another staff member can help you with whatever else you need."

My hands are full of books and shopping bags that are only getting heavier. "Thanks for your help, Brett. I'll see you tonight."

He nods, then turns and disappears behind a shelf. I carry my books over to the counter and pay for them. I'm delighted by the reusable bag I receive with the Page Turner Books logo on it. It'll be easier to carry these books along with the rest of my purchases.

I turn toward the front door, but then I hear Brett's voice ring out across the store. "Hello, everyone! So glad to see you this afternoon."

I don't think I've ever heard him sound so chipper. Curiosity wins out over the ache in my arms and I return to the children's area. I peek around the shelf, not wanting to be seen. Brett is smiling wide, a stack of books in his lap. It's that same smile I saw earlier, and it's just as devastating the second time. Oh my heart. *Don't get any ideas. You are co-workers. Fledgling friends at most.* But a part of me is awakening to the desire for more.

I hover in my hiding place, watching Brett expertly engage the kids in the stories he's reading. The buzz that accompanies a group of toddlers fidgeting and making random comments doesn't seem to faze him. Before too long, all the kids are quiet and still, all eyes trained on Brett. He's using a distinct voice for each character and once again I'm stunned at this new facet of the stoic man I'm used to seeing.

I suddenly feel a little voyeuristic watching him from behind a bookshelf. I quietly return to the front and exit the store. My mind is so involved in working through everything I've just witnessed that I don't realize my feet have led me to my car until I'm standing in front of the trunk. I head back to the house, my brain still not computing how Bookstore Brett and Arboretum Brett are the same person.

13

Brett

MY BOSS, SARAH, approaches me at the register. She's smiling widely, so there's no need for concern. "Great job today. We sold out of our copies of *Llama Llama Holiday Drama* and only have one *If You Take a Mouse to the Movies* left! Your story time idea was genius. You're definitely at the top of the 'Employee of the Year' standings."

I smirk. "If only we had an 'Employee of the Year.'"

She gives me a conspiratorial grin. "Maybe we'll start one this year."

I can just imagine the look on Rachel's face if Sarah gave me that award. Actually, she'd probably be happy for me. She's not as competitive as I am. That doesn't mean she doesn't like to win, just that she's not the one issuing challenges of who can empty book carts the fastest when it's slow in the store.

Sarah's praise thrills me almost as much as catching Meredith watching my story time presentation. I saw her hovering behind the bookshelf. Only the top half of her head was visible, but my body sensed she was there and I've gotten used to her dark hair and piercing blue eyes. I used to hate women with black hair on sight, but she's slowly helping me to put that prejudice to rest. Not every woman with hair like Vicky's is a home wrecker. And, truly, I know she's not the one to blame. My father was the one who was married. No doubt she didn't know he had a family when they first got together. He's a charmer, just like Connor.

I search my brain for a more pleasant topic to ruminate on, not wanting to rehash the past, and settle back on Meredith. It was cute to see how excited she got about seeing her banner in the store. I was tempted to tell her the complete story of how it ended up there, but didn't want to sound like I was bragging.

When the scarf and gloves I ordered for my mom from Meredith's shop showed up, the quality and the super soft yarn blew me away. It's a good thing Mom and I don't live in the same town, because I'm dying to give them to her. I ordered a scarf for Rachel and gave it to her as an early Christmas present because I just had to let someone else in on Meredith's cute shop. She loved it just like I thought she would, wrapping it around her neck and snuggling into the softness. She came into work the next day, exclaiming about all the cute things on the site. When our boss mentioned updating the holiday decor, Rachel practically strong-armed her into checking out the stuff at MerryDesigns. Hence, the banner.

A puff of pride forms in my chest just thinking about it. I'm glad Meredith is getting new business, and that I played a small part in it. I'd love to purchase a bunch more of her stuff to support her, but my priority is my mom. The whole reason I'm working so much is to earn money to fix her car.

We spoke on the phone a couple of days ago. She was disappointed I have to work Christmas Eve and the night of Christmas, but I told her I'd drive up early Christmas morning and stay through mid-afternoon so we can celebrate together. She offered to come down, but that would require renting or borrowing a car and I don't want to burden my mom. I have this coming Saturday off both at the bookstore and the Arboretum so I'm going to spend the day with her.

It was hard to leave that day open rather than try to pick up another shift, but she's been asking when she's going to see me again and I didn't go up for Thanksgiving. If she wants to see me, then I'm going to do whatever is necessary to make that happen. If I don't have enough money to fix her car by Christmas, I'm tempted to give her mine and pick up a bicycle to ride from home to work. Plenty of people bike around Asheville. It'll keep me in shape, for sure. Though, if we get a lot of snow this year, I might regret the decision.

I've caught myself rubbing the scarf I got for my mom through my hands mindlessly while I watch television on my couch a few times. It's just so soft! Sure, it maybe reminds me of Meredith, but there's nothing wrong with that. I've thought about trying on the gloves, but I don't want to risk stretching them out. If I have a little money left over after dealing with Mom's car situation, I'll splurge on a pair for myself.

Rachel raps her knuckles on the counter in front of me. "What's that dreamy look on your face about?"

I straighten immediately, my mouth turning down, embarrassed at being caught out. "Nothing."

She gives me a knowing grin. "Did I see Meredith in here earlier?"

I roll my eyes in response.

"I thought so. I wish I'd thought to tell her how much I love the scarf she made. Did you tell her I wear it all the time?" She points to her neck. My fingers twitch, itching to reach out and touch it, but I keep my hand at my side.

"No. She noticed the banner, though, and was excited." The image of her giddy face flashes across my mind, and one corner of my mouth turns up.

"Aha!" Rachel says, gleefully.

I release a beleaguered sigh. "What?" I know what's coming,

but there's no way to stop it.

"You like her!"

"She's my boss. Nothing can happen, even if I want it to. Which, to be clear, I don't."

Rachel tilts her head, assessing me. "To paraphrase Shakespeare, 'The gentleman doth protest too much, methinks.'" She only grins when I narrow my eyes at her. "Besides, she's only your boss for another month. Then she's fair game."

She has valid points, but I don't think Meredith's interested. Though spying on me at story time might be something someone who likes me would do. Or maybe just someone trying to get to know their new employee better. It's a tricky dance and I don't want to risk my job by guessing incorrectly.

I don't have a response for Rachel, so she leaves, but not before hitting me with a smug, knowing look. Is this what it felt like for her when I was teasing her about Tom? Ugh. It's not as enjoyable from this side.

❄❄❄

Meredith's just finished her pre-event speech and people are dispersing to go to their assigned locations. I'm almost to the door when there's a hand on my arm. I turn, and there's Meredith, one arm behind her back. She isn't meeting my gaze. Is she nervous? I'm excellent at the waiting game, so I stand there quietly for a few seconds until she looks me in the eye. She swings her hidden arm forward and pushes a red gift bag into my chest.

"Here, I got you something."

My hands cup the bottom of the bag and she lets go of the handles, taking a small step back. "What is it?"

She chuckles, but it sounds forced. Not like her usual twinkly laugh. "I saw it and immediately thought of you." Her face pales slightly and her eyes widen. "Oh, I just realized. Please don't take it the wrong way. It's meant to be a silly gift."

I have no idea what all of that means. There's only one way to find out. I lift the tissue paper out and peer inside at some woven red wool. She got me clothing? Maybe she's tired of seeing my plain green sweater. I pull it out and open it up. It's an ugly Christmas sweater. A face stares back at me. A green face with yellow eyes and a wide, wicked smile. Surprise, amusement, and delight mingle together in my gut, and I bark out a rough laugh. "You got me a Grinch sweater?"

"Yes." The word hisses through her clenched teeth and the grimace of uncertainty twists my heart.

I smile, happy when her shoulders drop in relief, and pull her into a hug. "It's perfect." I'll probably never wear it, but it really is the thought that counts. Speaking of thought, my brain must have short-circuited because I plant a kiss on the top of her head before I realize what I'm doing. My muscles tense in awareness moments before the rest of me catches up and I quickly release her and step back. Maybe she didn't notice. The look on her face makes it clear that she did.

Well, European friends kiss each other on the cheek. This is like that, right? I'm sure the panic is clear on my face, but her eyes are also wide, so it looks like I'm not the only one having an internal freak out right now. Does she think I like her? Is she trying to figure out a polite way to let me down? Better claw my way out of this hole real quick.

"Sorry about that. I don't know what happened. That was inappropriate and won't happen again. I understand if you need to give me a warning."

She's quiet for a minute, studying me. I will myself not to squirm under her gaze. I deserve whatever comes next. She finally shakes her head, her arms crossed over her body. "You're fine. I'm just glad I didn't offend you. I might have had to give *myself* a warning."

She gives me an uncertain smile that breaks the tension. Relief sweeps through me. Hurray, I'm not getting fired today. "Thanks for the sweater."

Meredith waves a hand. "You don't have to wear it. I know it's not your thing. I just couldn't resist."

I feel oddly disappointed by her words. I should be pleased she's so understanding. What's going on with me?

An arm wraps around Meredith and the red sleeve with white trim informs me it's Connor. My hackles go up at the easy intimacy. Is something going on between them? "What's that in your hand, Jacobs?"

I close my eyes, stifling a groan. If Connor sees this, I know he's going to be a jerk, but I don't want Meredith to think I'm embarrassed by the gift, so I hold it up. Connor's laugh is tinged with malice. He slaps me on the back hard enough to sting, but I try not to flinch. "Ooh, burn! That's perfect. You *are* a grinch. Who got you such an epic gift?"

My face hardens into a scowl. I can practically feel the storm clouds forming overhead. I hate this guy. Connor points at my face, as if I'm emphasizing his point, but I don't care. I don't want to speak for fear of saying something that could get me fired. I just have to tough out working with him for one more month.

Meredith slides out of Connor's hold, easing the tension in my gut a little. "It was me. Just something fun between friends."

She shoots me an apologetic look, then heads out the door. I watch her for a bit. Connor clears his throat beside me. When I turn, I don't like the look on his face. He's grinning like he's got some clout over me. "I see how it is."

My stomach drops. I don't like the ominous sound of that. "I don't know what you mean."

His smile conjures an image of a serpent in my mind, sinister and dangerous. "Sure you don't. We both know how this is going to end. Might as well concede now."

Connor's definitely reading into a vibe that's not there. Nothing is happening between me and Meredith. Nor will it. But I know how his mind works. If he thinks I'm interested, then he's going to do whatever he can to get her for himself. I can't stand the idea of him playing with Meredith's emotions to prove he's better than me. The best thing I can do is ignore him and stay away from Meredith. I roll my eyes, then head out to the cocoa shack.

14

DECEMBER

Meredith

THE COUNTDOWN TO Christmas is officially on! I have most of my shopping done. I like to get it out of the way early. Though, I will still pick up a few little things for stocking stuffers because I just can't pass up things I know someone I love would enjoy.

Right now I'm focused more on what interviewers would love. Specifically, what I should wear to impress them. I have an interview for the position at the Biltmore later this morning and my room looks like my closet threw up. Slacks, blouses, sweaters, and dresses cover my bed, desk, and reading chair. I sink down on my heels and survey the options. I finally decide on black slacks and a matching blazer with a soft green blouse underneath. Plain silver hoop earrings go into my lower holes, and I keep the rest empty. I don't know how buttoned up I'm supposed to be, but I don't want to risk any sort of misstep today. It's too important.

I've pored over the job requirements multiple times, matching my classes and work experiences with each to prove my qualifications. I know I'm young, but I'm confident I can do the job. My parents held a mock interview for me with questions I gave them. They threw in a few of their own and I appreciated the opportunity to think on my toes.

I finish my outfit with low black heels. A check in the mirror confirms my hair and makeup still look good. I grab my leather tote bag and head out to the car.

After parking my car in the lot at the Inn at Biltmore Estate, the location of my interview, I head into the lobby. I stop and stare, taking in the warm wooden pillars, high ceilings, elaborate chandeliers, wall sconces, and shiny marble floors. It's as grand as I imagined. I locate the welcome desk and ask for Yasmine Garcia, my contact. The desk clerk picks up a phone, whispers something, then hangs up. "She'll be out shortly for you. Please have a seat."

He motions to a seating area of plush white couches and chairs to my left and I comply, sinking into the chair. I'm tempted to relax into it, but remember my purpose here and perch on the end, maintaining a straight back. A couple strolls through the lobby with their arms around each other. I bet they're here on an anniversary trip.

"Ms. Larson?"

I stand quickly and turn toward the woman, holding out my hand. "Yes. Ms. Garcia?"

She shakes my hand and gives me a warm smile. "Nice to meet you. Please follow me."

We walk down a set of stairs to the dining room. All the tables are empty except for one. Three people in suits are seated around a circular table. I brush invisible lint off my jacket pocket, thankful I opted for the blazer today. Nothing in the email said this would be a group interview, but I widen my smile, pushing down the nerves. *You can do this, Meredith.*

I'm introduced to everyone, and once seated, the interview begins. The knot in my stomach loosens after I answer a few questions. They're almost word-for-word the ones I gave my parents, so I'm ready with complete and concise answers for each of them. I'm completely relaxed and feel very confident that I made a good impression. There's lots of nodding at my answers and everyone is smiling at me by the end of our time together. I shake everyone's hand and thank them for the opportunity, then Ms. Garcia walks me back to the lobby.

"It was wonderful to meet you. We will contact you within the next two weeks to let you know our decision." She hands me an envelope. "Here are two tickets to the Candlelight Christmas tour."

I take the envelope, confused. "I didn't purchase any tickets."

She chuckles. "They're complimentary. It's our way of saying thank you to everyone who interviews for a position. Of course, when it's not Christmas season, the tickets are for the regular house tour."

I clutch the envelope to my chest, stunned and excited. "That's very generous. Thank you very much!"

I walk back to my car, feeling certain I made the best impression possible. If I don't get the job, it'll be because they chose a more qualified candidate. I hope that's not the case because I really want this job.

Squeezing the envelope, I feel giddy about this wonderful surprise. I've been on the daytime tour multiple times, but I bet seeing everything at night will be even more spectacular. Who should I take as my guest? Ali or Paige? My mom? I'll figure it out. I wonder if I'll get discounted or free tickets if I work here? *When* I work here, I amend. Might as well think positively.

15

Brett

WE'RE ALL GATHERED in the lobby, waiting for our illustrious leader's daily speech before we head off to our positions. A glance at the clock shows she's five minutes late, which is surprising, because Meredith seems very conscientious about respecting others' time. Joanne comes out from the office and delivers her version of the speech meant to get everyone excited about work. She isn't as skilled at infusing others with the Christmas spirit like Meredith is. Joanne's speech is delivered in a monotone and doesn't smile once. Meredith is grinning the whole time, using her whole body to spread her special brand of joy. My gut squeezes with concern about Meredith's absence.

It's very possible she has the night off. I don't know her break schedule. Just because ours lined up once doesn't mean they'll line up again. There are over fifty of us she has to take into consideration. Her off days are probably more sporadic, making sure we all get as many of our requested days off as possible. Though I must admit the thought of us not having another evening to hang out together is disappointing. I really enjoyed the trivia night and the things I learned about Meredith.

After two hours in the cocoa shack without sight or sound of Meredith, I've resigned myself to the fact that she's off for the night. I shouldn't feel disappointed. It's not like I have a right to know her schedule. Joanne checked on me about thirty minutes ago, reminding me to take my break when there's a lull in customers. No one's stopped by in a few minutes, so I decide now is as good a time as any. After closing the window and locking the door behind me, I head into the Baker building and down the hall to the breakroom. I pause at the door when I hear sniffling inside. I don't want to intrude, but it's not exactly a private room.

Cautiously, I peek around the door frame. An elf in a green and red dress and long black hair is hunched over in a chair, her face in her hands. My gut twists with concern. I hurry over to where Meredith's sitting.

"Here you are." I immediately wince, horrified by my words. It sounds like I've been looking all over for her.

Meredith jerks up, surprise on her face. "Brett, hi. What are you doing in here?"

I'm not sure whether I should be offended, but the noticeable distress on her face eliminates every other concern. "I'm taking my break."

"Oh."

Silence stretches between us until I feel a need to fill it with something. Anything. "We missed you at the meeting earlier."

Who's we? I suppose I'm speaking for everyone, though how can I possibly know how everyone else feels? *I* missed her at the meeting, but I can't say that. She smiles, but it doesn't reach her eyes. I bend down to see her face better, my skin tingling with concern. "You okay?"

She nods, but her lips press together, and her eyes are shiny. Is she going to cry? I wrap her hands in mine and pull her up to standing. She looks so small and vulnerable with her eyes downcast and her lips trembling that I pull her against me and wrap my arms around her. Her hands grip my sweater and her body shakes against mine.

After a few minutes, her shaking subsides, and her hold on my sweater loosens. I release my arms from Meredith and she steps back, her head lowered. She swipes under her eyes with her hands.

Meredith finally meets my eye. "Sorry about that." She chuckles, but it's forced.

"No problem." I didn't mind one bit having her in my arms, even if my body feels stressed and helpless against her sorrow. "Do you want to talk about it?"

She shakes her head, pauses, then nods. "It's silly, really. Just a rough afternoon."

My fingers itch to run a comforting hand up and down her arm. Would she interpret that as a friendly gesture or something more? I guess we'll never know because I'm a man of restraint. "I'm sorry to hear that."

She tilts her head back and forth and I wonder if that's going to be it. She releases a long breath, hugging her arms around her waist. "On my way to work, my car broke down on the highway and I was stranded for over an hour until my sister could come get me and bring me to work, which is why I'm so late. I hate being late. And now I have to figure out a ride home because my family can't do it. With my luck, I won't be able to get a ride share to come out here at eleven o'clock."

She looks up at me, and her troubled expression nearly rips my heart in two. "I'll take you home."

Her face opens in surprise and I'm sure mine is a mirror image. Did I really just say that? So much for being a man of restraint. I didn't even know that was going to come out of my mouth. Have I found my kryptonite?

"Are you sure?"

The hope in her eyes cuts through the last of my defenses. "Of course. It'd be my pleasure."

Come on, Brett. Are you working at Chick-Fil-A? It'd be YOUR pleasure? Meredith doesn't seem to notice how awkward my sentence was. Her face opens up, and she hits me with a genuine smile. It feels like the sun has just burst out from behind a cloud.

"Thank you, Brett!" She steps forward, wrapping her arms around my waist and giving me a quick hug. So quick that I don't have time to react before she pulls away again. "You're a lifesaver."

She wipes her hands over her cheeks and straightens her clothes, before taking a deep breath and releasing it like the world's suddenly been lifted off her shoulders. "Well, I'd better get over to the Education Center."

She heads for the doorway, turning back to send another glorious smile my way before she leaves. I straighten my shoulders, feeling like a million bucks. I'm suddenly full of energy and ready to get back to the cocoa shack.

I work the rest of my shift almost entirely on autopilot. The only thing my mind can focus on is the opportunity to spend some one-on-one time with Meredith.

At one point in the evening, Connor shows up with some friends and asks for beer on the house. I tell him it's not going to happen, that free admission on our days off does not also mean free food and beverages. Connor gives me a dirty look before leaving, but it rolls right off me.

After that, I'm flooded with customers until work's over. I tally up everything, confused when the tally of beer bottles remaining doesn't add up. Maybe everything's there and I just can't focus well enough to count properly. Better tell accounting just in case. I gather up the cash box and card reader before exiting the shack, locking the door behind me, and making sure the shutter's also secure, before heading into the Baker building. I'm now only minutes from being alone with Meredith!

16

Meredith

THIS HAS BEEN a roller coaster of a day. There was the high of acing the Biltmore interview, then the low of my car clunking out on me. I hope it's an easy fix. I don't have the money for a large expense. Though I have been making more than usual in my Crafty store. Plus, I know my parents would chip in if I asked. I've always felt weird about being in a family with money. It's my parents' money, not mine. I'd prefer to make my own way, just like my sisters are doing.

And now I'm sitting in Brett's truck, my heart beating out a staccato rhythm. It almost feels like I'm nervous, but it's probably just the ride my emotions have taken today. Brett's being a good friend. He can't help that whatever cologne he wears makes me practically salivate. I don't know what scent it is, but it's like my own personal catnip. I'm going to have to be very careful around him, or I'll end up with my nose pressed against his neck and forever be labeled a weirdo. Though I've been called worse. I don't mind people not getting my whimsical nature, but I'd hate to lose this friendship I feel forming with Brett. He's got a thick outer shell, apparently to keep people out, but I've slipped through a crack and am seeing more of his softer side. And I like it. A lot. Purely in a platonic sense, of course.

When Brett leans forward to start the truck, I catch another whiff of his cologne and have to swallow a groan. *Hold it together, Meredith.* Heavy metal music blasts from the speakers and I jump so high, my head hits the top of the cab. I wince and rub my head. Brett slaps a button and silence falls inside the truck. He touches my shoulder and I turn, one eye squinted closed as I try to figure out if I just lost some of my hearing. "Sorry. You okay?"

His words sound fine, so maybe my ears are okay. My head, on the other hand, is going to have a nice knot tomorrow morning. "I think the only thing damaged was my head."

His face scrunches up in sympathy, then he opens his door. "Be right back."

Brett dashes across the parking lot and into the Baker building. Did he forget his jacket or something? I haven't seen him wear anything other than jeans and his plain green sweater. Yes, I've noticed he's given himself a uniform. I wish he'd add a little fun to his wardrobe, but not everyone loves Christmas like I do, and I have to accept that.

He emerges from the building, running back to his truck carrying something in his hands. He walks around the back of the truck, opens my door, and hands me a ziplock bag of ice. My heart melts at his care and thoughtfulness. "Thanks. You didn't have to."

He shrugs. "I'm sorry about your head."

He closes the door, then walks back around to his side, stopping at the metal box in the bed to pull something from it. When he slides into the seat, he hands me a cloth. "To wrap the ice in."

Wow. I didn't expect this from Brett. Where has this sweet, sensitive guy been hiding? The cloth is a T-shirt, which I open simply because I'm curious. It's charcoal gray with what probably used to be a shiny silver knight's helmet. All that's left are a few semi-shiny patches in the black helmet outline. A faded red plume over the helmet is the only splash of color on the shirt. I turn to Brett. "Are you into the renaissance or something?"

He shakes his head. "It's the logo of my favorite band, Metalhead."

I motion to the dashboard. "Is that who that was?"

Brett nods.

"What other bands do you like?"

He studies me, and I suppress a shiver that threatens to run up my spine at his penetrating gaze. "Probably none you've heard of."

I lift my chin, challenging. "Try me."

He lists half a dozen and all I can do is shake my head. "You're making those up. There's no way a band exists that's called Giant Rats of Reno."

Brett smirks, then scrolls through the music app on his phone, tipping the screen toward me with a photo of one of their albums. Well, color me surprised. I hold up my hands. "You win."

He clicks open the maps app and hands the phone to me. "Type in your address so I can get you home."

Oh right. He's my ride. This isn't a date or anything. We drive in silence for a bit until Brett asks what my favorite bands are. It feels embarrassing to admit to him I prefer the top forty radio station, but I've never hidden who I am or what I like.

"I bet you and my friend Rachel would get along. She loves that music and is also pretty cool."

I blink a few times, surprised by Brett's comment. Did he just call me cool? I must be reading too much into his statement. I'm probably a super annoying little sister to him. Time for a new subject. "How is it working at the Arboretum? Does it offend all of your anti-Christmas sensibilities?" I make sure my tone is teasing.

Brett rolls his eyes. "I'm actually really enjoying it. The staff is nice and I can see how much the crowds enjoy it. Especially the kids.

Their faces light up when they enter the gardens and I have a front-row seat to their joy."

I hadn't even thought about his vantage point from the shack. He now has a small smile on his lips and it reminds me of watching him at story time. "You really like kids, huh?"

He glances at me briefly, then returns his eyes to the road. "Why do you say that?"

"I, uh, sort of spied on your children's time at the bookstore the other day. You were like a whole different person—open, animated, happy."

"Yeah, I saw you peeking around the bookshelf."

I press my lips together and look away. Guess I wouldn't make a good undercover agent, not that it's an aspiration of mine. "Why do you enjoy working at the bookstore?"

We're stopped at a light and Brett turns his head toward me, his forehead creased and his mouth in a straight line. I meet his eyes, determined to hold up under his scrutiny. I see the traffic signal change out of the corner of my eye. Brett must as well, because he breaks eye contact and presses the gas pedal. The quiet stretches and I wonder if I've stumbled upon a sensitive matter. I'm on the verge of asking a less personal question when he opens his mouth and speaks.

"Books have helped me get through challenging times in my life. And Page Turner Books specifically has a wonderful, supportive staff. It's a great work environment where the owner welcomes ideas and suggestions for new programs. Like the story time. Sarah's let me make it my own and I enjoy sharing my love of reading with the younger generation. It's also an opportunity to be silly, which I don't do a lot of these days."

Those might be the most words I've ever heard Brett speak at once. The warmth in his voice lets me know he's sincere. I'm happy that he loves what he's doing. I want to have a job that fills me with passion like Brett. As much as I want to make my family proud, I also want to feel like I'm fulfilling my purpose. But nothing says those goals are mutually exclusive. Not if the right job comes along. Like maybe the Biltmore?

"Why can't you be silly?"

"I guess I'm just out of practice. I've felt responsible for my mom ever since we lost my father, so it doesn't feel like fun is something I have time for."

My hand reaches across the bench and squeezes his forearm. I keep it there to convey my sympathy. "I'm so sorry, Brett. When did he pass away?"

Brett barks out a sardonic laugh. "Oh, he's not dead. He left us for another woman."

To a kid, that probably feels worse than a parent dying. At least then there's little chance of you feeling like it was your fault or that something was lacking in you that kept him from staying. Not that I know any of this from experience, but I had several friends growing up whose parents divorced. "That had to be tough. And I guess you felt like you had to be the man of the house, even though you were just a kid?"

"I appreciate your concern, but I wasn't exactly a kid. I was sixteen. And Mom and I have done just fine without him."

A memory of something Brett said a while ago makes its way to the forefront. It makes more sense now. "You took this job to help your mom. You're still taking care of her."

He keeps his eyes on the road, but nods.

"Losing people is hard, no matter how they exit our lives." I squeeze his arm once more before pulling back. The conversation has turned my mind to my own loss. Thankfully, Brett seems to be too caught up in his own thoughts to press me on my last statement. I spend the rest of the ride home thinking about Oliver.

17

Brett

I TURN ONTO a quiet street and pull up next to an enormous house. Meredith lives here? How in the world? Didn't she just finish school? "This is your house?"

She nods. "Well, not exactly. It's my parents' house, but I'm living here. Just until I find a full-time job. It seems pointless to find my own place if I end up moving away for work."

The idea of her leaving Asheville doesn't sit well with me, but I realize this is the reality of today's job market. You go where the job is, and often it requires relocating. "How's the job search going?"

She unbuckles her seatbelt and twists so she's facing me. "I had an interview with Biltmore Estate earlier today that went well. The position is for managing their hotel properties."

Maybe she'll get the job and be able to stay in Asheville. I don't want to think too hard about why I want her to stay. "That sounds like something you'd be good at. I hope you get it."

"Thanks. I have to admit, part of my emotional outburst earlier was probably because of my nerves about the job prospect."

"That's understandable." I look past her shoulder and get another glimpse of the mansion where she lives. "Do you have a big family?"

She looks over her shoulder before turning back to me. "I have two older sisters, but my parents bought the house before they had any of us."

"Guess they were planning ahead. How does your dad feel about being surrounded by women?"

Meredith's smile dims and her expression turns sad. "I also had an older brother, but he died when I was a teenager."

Her earlier comment about loss suddenly makes sense. I want to reach out to her, but something holds me back. Probably the concern that if I have her in my arms, I won't want to let her go. "I'm so sorry, Meredith."

She shrugs. "It was a long time ago, but I still miss him."

I understand her feelings all too well. Should I share my experience with her so she knows I understand? I've already told her about my father, so why not? "I lost my uncle a few years ago to cancer. He was like my surrogate dad after my real one left."

Meredith gives me a grateful look, then slides across the bench seat, grabs my hand, and lays her head on my shoulder. "I'm sorry about your uncle, but glad he could support you through a tough time."

All the points where we connect are lit up with heat. My shoulder, my fingers, my palm, my wrist. I stay stock still, afraid that if I move, Meredith will return to her side of the truck. I opt instead for sharing more information. "Uncle Kevin took me to my first Metalhead concert. It was his favorite band."

Meredith lifts her head and removes her hand from mine. My body involuntarily leans toward her, hoping to reengage with some part of her again, even though I know I should be keeping distance between us. She uses her left hand to pull up the right sleeve of her coat, revealing a small blue and black butterfly tattoo.

"Oliver used to call me his little butterfly because, as a kid, I followed him all around the house. Part of me wanted him to play with me, but another part just wanted to be near him. He didn't seem to mind my presence and was such a loving big brother. Just before he went off to college, he got this butterfly tattoo. He said it was so I'd always be with him. He died a year later in a car accident. I got this in memory of him."

I now feel terrible for assuming her tattoo was a rebellious act or just for show. It shows how big her heart is. Before I can think twice, I lift up my shirt to reveal the small knight's helmet with a red plume I have tattooed on my ribs. "Uncle Kevin and I got matching tattoos when I turned eighteen."

Meredith reaches a hand out, but then pauses, looking at me for approval. I nod and she traces the outline with her index finger. Fire trails along my skin underneath her touch and I shudder at the intensity. She draws back, dropping her hand. "Sorry. That was weird, huh?"

I release my shirt and touch the back of her hand. "It's fine."

She shakes her head; her furrowed forehead smoothing out. "How did we get on this topic, anyway?"

I think back through the last few minutes. "I asked about your family."

"Right. Yes, the big house. My parents bought it for the basement."

I'd be concerned about this revelation, wondering if there's some strange hobby that requires the secretiveness a basement provides, except Meredith's about as intimidating as a baby bunny, so I doubt her parents are much different. Still, who buys a house for the basement? "That's kind of weird."

Meredith chuckles. "My mom's an inventor and was looking for a place where she could have a research lab. The basement was unfinished, so she turned it into the perfect space for her. She still uses it, too."

"Has she created anything I use?"

"You may have without knowing it. She invented the spill-proof sippy cup."

I shrug, having no idea.

She continues ticking things off her fingers. "She created a cup with a built-in silicone brush to wash dog paws and those silicone disks that pop up into water and food bowls for campers and pet owners. As you may guess, silicone is her primary medium."

I'm impressed, though I rarely think about where useful tools come from. "That's pretty cool. What does the rest of your family do?"

Meredith sits up, her mood brightening with the more pleasant subject. "My dad was a commercial pilot for thirty years, but recently retired. He's now waiting impatiently to be a grandpa."

I chuckle. "No pressure, right?"

"My oldest sister, an accountant, is due in January. Dad'll be set for a while with him or her."

"Oh, right, the baby books."

Meredith nods. "My other sister is a journalist."

What would it be like to be part of a big family? I suppose I could have found out if I really wanted to, since my father and Vicky have three kids together. Of course, the oldest is only in middle school, so we'd have nothing in common besides half of our DNA.

"What does your mom do?"

Her question draws me back out of my thoughts. "She works at Griggs Hauser, helping the sales team with quotes. Though she's applied for a promotion, which would turn her into a salesperson. Which means she needs money to fix her car so she can visit customers."

"And that's why you're working at the Arboretum," Meredith says. "So you can help her achieve her goal."

Something about the way she immediately understands pleases me. I feel like she and I could be good together, that we'd complement one another.

"Can I ask you a personal question?"

The uncertain look on her face has me curious about what she wants to know. "Sure."

"Why'd you shave your beard?"

I'm not sure what it means that she noticed. Did she like how it looked? I'm not brave enough to ask. "The actual story is why I had it in the first place. There's an annual fundraiser challenge called No Shave November where people let their hair grow all month in honor of cancer patients who lose their hair during treatment. I've participated the past four years in honor of my uncle, donating money to several cancer foundations."

"Oh, Brett, that's so noble and generous." The look in her eyes warms my chest.

"I don't know about that."

"I think that's who you are, though you do a pretty good job of hiding it. Speaking of generous, thank you for driving me home tonight."

She'd better stop with the compliments or I won't be able to stay on my side of the truck much longer. The urge to wrap her up in my arms is strong, which is why I haven't removed my seatbelt. Thankfully, or regretfully, she opens the door and gets out.

I lean over to her side. "Do you need a ride to or from work tomorrow?"

"My mom can bring me in, though I may need a ride home. It really depends on what the mechanic says about my car."

I grimace, understanding all too well the frustration of having car issues. "I'm more than happy to bring you home. Just let me know." *More* than happy? Could my eagerness to spend time with her be any more obvious?

She hits me with a heart-stopping smile that removes all doubt about my growing feelings for Meredith. I'm definitely in trouble, especially because her kindness is probably just standard Meredith and not a sign of reciprocal interest. *Button it up, Brett, so you don't embarrass yourself.* Thankfully, she shuts the door and walks up to the house, leaving me alone with my thoughts and emotions. When the front door closes with her inside, I drop my head into my hands. What am I doing? I can't get involved with my boss, no matter how remarkable she seems.

Besides, despite what my body thinks, I'm firmly in the friend zone. Meredith is a naturally friendly person, so I'm obviously interpreting her kind words and gestures more deeply than intended. I've got to get this crazy notion that we could be together out of my head. I pull away from the curb, doing everything I can to convince myself that friendship with Meredith is all I want.

18

Meredith

I'VE LOOKED THROUGH the paperwork from accounting multiple time, convinced I'm misreading things, but keep ending up with the same conclusion. The alcohol purchases and inventory are not balancing out. Because of pouring discrepancies, there's bound to be a difference of one bottle of wine or so, but beer is a one-to-one transaction. One purchase, one full bottle poured into a cup. It makes no sense for half a dozen beers to go missing on multiple occasions. And one evening the wine discrepancy was four bottles which doesn't seem right even with the amount of receipts for purchased glasses. Something's not right.

Joanne has tasked me with talking to Brett about it since all the off counts have been from the shack on evenings he worked. He seems like a man of integrity, but that could just be a bias I've formed. Seeing new sides of Brett has changed my thoughts about him. I've definitely started having more-than-friendly feelings for him, but I'm not sure how he feels. He hasn't rebuffed me when I've gotten close to him, and he pulled me into a hug the night I was overwhelmed, but it could just be because he's a nice guy underneath that gruff exterior. Or maybe he's just doing whatever he can to make sure he keeps his job. Not that I'd abuse my power like that. It really complicates things not being on equal footing with him in the workplace. Technically, there isn't a rule against us dating, but I understand if he's hesitant because he's worried about what people will think. I must admit that I've had the same thoughts.

Will the other staff think I'm favoring someone I'm dating? Will they think I've scheduled our breaks off on purpose? I didn't intentionally line them up like that, though I can't say I'm sorry that's how things have worked out. Just like I'm not sorry that Connor and I have different break schedules.

Connor's been getting more brazen with his flirting and side hugs. I thought he and Genesis were seeing each other, but maybe not. Regardless, I'm not interested in Connor. He seems solely focused on himself and what he wants. The thought of him using other staff members makes my skin crawl. He's still doing great as Santa and is very professional during the hours we have guests, but outside of performance hours, there's just something about him I don't trust. I'm going to suggest starting the hunt for next year's Santa right after the new year. And get a second one, which we'll rotate, just as an extra precaution. Zach, our s'mores expert, has the right personality. Maybe he'd be interested.

After our post-work meeting, I look for Brett in the crowd, but don't see him. After inquiring about him, someone says they saw him heading toward the cocoa shack. I hurry out there and try the handle. It turns easily, and I open the door to find Brett working on his inventory.

"Hey, Brett."

He turns, startled. "Oh, hey. Just double checking inventory. Everything's fine tonight. I can't understand what's been happening lately."

The concern in his voice makes me want to reach out and offer him reassurance, but I'm here on professional business, so I don't. "Is this about the missing drinks?"

He meets my eye. "Yeah. I just don't get it. It's happened a few times, but only about once a week and on different days. I promise I haven't been over pouring or giving away drinks. Has accounting figured anything out?"

My body straightens, surprised by his question. "What do you mean?"

"I told them about the off counts and they said they'd look into it, but I've heard nothing since then."

So Brett's the one that brought the issue to our attention? There's no way he'd do that if he was responsible. There has to be something else going on. Maybe some punk kids are sneaking into the shack when he's busy with customers? It's not out of the realm of possibilities. "No, unfortunately, we don't have any answers. I appreciate you bringing this to our attention, though. I'd just suggest making sure you keep the door locked at all times and maybe look out for suspicious people."

Brett frowns, and it takes me a second to realize he's focused on something over my shoulder. At that exact moment, an arm wraps around my waist and I flinch. I step further into the shack to break the contact and turn. "Connor, hey. Do you need something?"

He gives me a wide smile. "I was coming to see if I could walk you to your car."

He's never offered before. Why now? "That's kind of you, but I still have work to do."

"I can wait. It's late. I just want to make sure you're safe." He punctuates his words with a wink accompanied by a smile that reminds me of the big bad wolf.

Instinctively, I take another step back and bump into Brett. The warmth of his body against mine is oddly reassuring and I don't move away. Brett shifts behind me. His fingers brush against mine down by my side and I suck in a breath at the electric touch. I resist the urge to look down, instead clearing my throat and meeting Connor's gaze.

"I don't want to keep you. Besides, it's plenty safe here at the Arboretum. Thanks, though."

Connor's eyes narrow slightly, but he's looking behind me. Suddenly, his face relaxes into nonchalance. "No problem. See you tomorrow."

He leaves, and my body relaxes. I hadn't realized I was so tense. Realizing I'm still leaning against Brett, I take a step forward and turn, my body protesting when I lose all contact with Brett. "Sorry about that. Not sure what that was."

Brett's frowning more than usual, his forehead a ripple of troubled thoughts. This obviously has something to do with whatever issue Brett has with Connor. His face looks almost exactly the same as it did when he came for his interview after passing Connor in the hallway. Do I want to know? Yes, but because I'm the boss, I ought to leave it alone unless it starts affecting their job performance.

However, Brett and I can still be friends and chat outside of work. That's not inappropriate. The subject of friendship reminds me of the other reason I wanted to talk with Brett. My stomach swirls with nerves, but I'm determined to ask, even though I know there's a strong possibility of rejection. A look at his face tells me he's still lost in his thoughts, so I touch his arm to get his attention. When his gaze meets mine, I blurt it all out.

"I have an extra ticket for Biltmore's Candlelight Christmas tour this Thursday evening and wondered if you wanted to go. I know Christmas isn't your thing, but none of my family is free and I really don't want to go alone. I completely understand if you say no, but—"

"I'll go."

I'm floored. He actually said yes? I squeeze my hands together to keep from clapping them in delight, but I realize I'm bouncing on my toes so my attempt at playing it cool has been ruined already. I manage to get the soles of my feet back to the ground. "Great, thank you." I pull out my phone. "What's your address? I'll pick you up." Belatedly, I realize I could just get it out of his employee file, but that seems a little weird.

"I don't mind driving."

I shake my head. "I invited you, so I should take care of everything."

It's Brett's turn to shake his head. "Please let me drive. You live closer to the Biltmore so I can pick you up on the way."

I don't have any idea where he lives, so I can't argue with his logic. It's really not a big deal who drives, anyway. "Okay, yes, you can drive. Thank you."

One side of his mouth quirks up. "You're welcome. Though, maybe I should be concerned you're so knowledgeable about my schedule. I might almost think you planned our days off to line up on purpose."

My eyebrows shoot up and my mouth drops open. I was *just* thinking about how employees might think something like that if Brett and I dated. Now there's no doubt in my mind that's what would happen.

He notices the shock on my face, because his smile disappears and he takes a step toward me. "Hey, I was just joking. Sorry if it sounded accusatory."

I shake my head vigorously, taking small steps backward toward the door. "No, you're fine. I overreacted. Anyway, I'll let you finish what you're doing. See you tomorrow."

When my feet hit the ground outside the door, I turn and hightail it back to my office to wrap up the rest of my evening, wondering about the bewildered look on Brett's face when I fled. I won't be surprised if he reneges on his agreement to accompany me to the Biltmore. I also won't blame him, though disappointment pulses in my gut at the thought.

19

Brett

THURSDAY EVENING AT five, I'm standing on the doorstep of Meredith's house. I roll my shoulders a few times to loosen up my body. A large portion of today was spent trying to imagine how this evening might play out. I thought about bringing flowers, but I'm not sure whether this is a date or just an activity between two friends. My heart definitely hopes it's the former, but my brain is more realistic. I take a deep breath, then ring the doorbell.

The door swings open and I'm startled when I'm met by a woman with shoulder-length brown hair and the same blue eyes I've grown quite fond of. She scans me from head to toe, then smiles in a way that makes me think of a hunter assessing its prey.

I clear my throat. "Uh, hi. I'm here to pick up Meredith."

The woman gives me a wink. "You must be Brett." Her voice is syrupy. Is she flirting with me? She opens the door wider. "Come on in."

When I step inside, she puts out her hand, palm down, like she's expecting me to kiss it. "I'm Paige."

I take her hand with mine and turn it, shaking her hand like normal people do. I have to tug a little to extract my hand from hers. She just grins at me, her eyes running over my body again. I know I look good. I took extra time ironing out the wrinkles in my slacks and button-down shirt, but I didn't do it for her. "Is Meredith ready?"

Paige rolls her eyes, apparently disappointed in my lack of interest. She turns toward a staircase and hollers. "Mel, your hunky date is here!" She turns back around and gives me another wink, this one making me as uncomfortable as the first one did.

Movement on the landing above draws my attention. Meredith comes down the stairs in a sparkly red skirt and a black fitted sweater. Her hair has some curl to it, a marked change from her usually straight style. She pauses at the bottom, her eyes taking in my outfit, then smiles and all the discomfort I was feeling disappears. Now that's the approval I was looking for. I want to comment on how great she looks, but we have an audience in her sister, so I remain silent. The only hint of my thoughts is the small smile on my lips.

Meredith steps into a pair of black ankle boots, then grabs her purse from the railing. When she comes closer, I have to fight back a laugh when I realize the purse is a gingerbread house. It's so perfectly her.

"Are you ready?" I say.

"Yep, let's go."

She grabs my arm and pulls me to the door. Paige follows us, calling out just before I shut the door. "Hope to see *more* of you soon, Brett."

I catch Meredith glaring at the door, and her cheeks flush slightly. "Sorry about Paige. She's having a rough week and is not acting like herself."

I open the truck door for her and watch as she slides in, careful not to catch her skirt in the door when I close it. I get in on the other side, then type in the address of our destination. "You look really nice," I say, meeting her gaze.

"Thanks. So do you."

Why didn't Meredith take her sister tonight? She'd said everyone in her family was busy, but was that just an excuse? I suppose it doesn't really matter. Even so, I'm curious.

"Is it rude of me to ask what's up with your sister?"

Meredith sighs, her smile dropping. "No. Paige was supposed to be on a date with her boyfriend tonight, but they broke up this afternoon. She's been nursing her heartache with a few strong mimosas. And by harassing handsome guys. Again, sorry about that."

Did she just say I'm handsome? Maybe this *is* a date. "It's fine. That's probably why she called you Mel instead of Meredith, huh?"

"No, Mel's my family nickname." When she sees my puzzled look, she explains. "My initials are M-E-L. Paige's middle name is Archer, so we sometimes call her PAL. My big sister Ali used to be ALL, but then she got married. Now she's ALF."

I chuckle. "That's kind of cool. My initials are all consonants, so they don't spell anything. Though a few of my friends in high school called me J.B."

Meredith studies me, her lips twisted to the side. "You don't really look like a J.B. to me. I think Brett fits you better. Though, I think you could also pull off Josh. Is there a reason you go by your middle name?"

I'm surprised she didn't figure it out when she read my application. Not that I really care. "My full name is Joshua Brett Jacobs, Jr. I grew up being called Joshua, but when my father left, I decided I wanted to be called Brett. It took a bit for my mom to make the switch, but now everyone in my life calls me that. And, like you said, it suits me."

"I'm sorry I brought it up."

I shrug. "Don't be. It is what it is. I've moved on. Speaking of moving on, we should probably get going unless you'd rather just sit out in front of your house all night." Which wouldn't bother me in the slightest.

She smiles. "Take us to the Christmas magic!"

I groan, but smile to show I'm just teasing. I start my truck and steer us toward Biltmore Estate.

❄❄❄

When we step inside the house, I'm amazed by the size of the foyer. I'm struck even more by the enormous poinsettia plants on the table in the center of the room. Red velvet ropes and staff usher us to the right where we can pick up audio guides to listen to while we tour. I forgo one, but Meredith accepts hers from the attendant.

Our first stop is the atrium, where someone is playing holiday instrumentals on a grand piano. The windows above are dark, the room lit by candle stands placed around the room. Meredith listens to her guide and I look at the other guests around us. Some are dressed in holiday sweaters and dresses. Others are wearing clothes that make me wonder if they came straight from work. It's what I look like in my khakis and blue checked shirt. I had the fleeting idea to wear the Grinch sweater, but thought that might make it too obvious that I'm beginning to have feelings for Meredith.

She lowers the audio guide from her ear and inclines her head to the right, indicating she's ready to move on. I nod and we walk to the Billiards room. It's quite remarkable with its two tables and lots of leather seating. There's a large Christmas tree near the doorway we're looking through. Meredith has the guide near her ear again, her attention on the room. My attention is drawn to the jewelry on her ear. She has a silver hoop in her bottom lobe. Above it is a small diamond stud. The top of her ear is empty. The more subtle choices are oddly disappointing.

But her lips are anything but subtle. They are bright red and shiny, obviously lipstick. She turns toward me, and my eyes travel up to hers. They seem even bluer than normal, despite the soft light in the house.

I shrug a shoulder in question and she nods, leading us on to the next room. We enter the banquet hall and I stop in my tracks, awed by its grandeur. It's a gigantic room with a vaulted ceiling so high I have to lean back to take it all in. My eyes travel over everything in the room—the enormous Christmas tree at one end, the organ pipes partially hidden behind it, the table that seats over twenty people. Giant circular chandeliers hang from the ceiling, and the other end of the room has a fireplace with three separate hearths. It's spectacular.

Despite living here for years, this is my first time taking a tour of the mansion. The opportunity to see what all the hype's about is one of the reasons I accepted Meredith's invitation. Though her distress at not having a companion was obviously a bigger tug on my heart.

Meredith nudges me. "First time inside the house?"

I turn and look at her. "That obvious, huh?"

She shrugs. "This is my favorite room."

I look around more slowly, taking in the details. I'm not really one of those people who like architecture, but this really is a sight to behold. As is the gorgeous woman next to me. I glance down and notice our hands are only inches apart. I'm tempted to grab it, but until I can figure out for sure if this is a date, I'm not going to risk screwing things up.

"Are you sure you don't want to listen to the guide?" She holds it out to me. "I've been here a bunch of times."

I wave it away. "No, I'm good. But if *you* want to share things you know about the house, I'd be happy to hear it."

She perks up, her eyes sparkling. "Challenge accepted."

I didn't mean to sound like I was issuing a challenge, but if she takes it that way, then so be it. "What do I need to know?"

"That thirty-five foot Fraser fir is from Andrews Nursery in Newland. They've provided trees for Biltmore since the seventies.

There are sixty-seven hand-decorated trees throughout the house and one thousand poinsettias."

It shouldn't surprise me Meredith knows so much about the Christmas decor.

"Who's in charge of counting the poinsettias?" I say, a joking tone in my voice. "Will that be one of your responsibilities when you work here?"

She hits me with a pleased smile, and my heart flops in response. "I appreciate your confidence in me, but no. There's an entire staff in charge of Christmas. I wouldn't even get to choose decor for the hotel properties, unfortunately."

Her words make me wonder about her responsibilities at work. "Have you gotten to choose any of the designs or decor for Winter Lights?"

She shakes her head. "No, but whoever fills the position permanently will get some say."

"Why can't that be you?"

She tilts her head to the side, her brow creased. "Huh. I hadn't really considered it. Joanne hasn't said anything to me about applying for it. Maybe they want someone with more experience."

"Who else has worked Winter Lights for eight years in a row?"

Meredith rolls her eyes. "The job is more than this one event. We have programs throughout the year."

"So? You could do it."

She waves away my words, apparently finished with this conversation. "The job hasn't been posted yet. Maybe when it is, I'll fill out an application."

I'm not convinced she's really heard me, but I let it go, opting to keep the rest of our tour pleasant and on the topic of the house itself. Meredith shares more facts as we go along. What interests me the most is the chess set Meredith points out in the library that was once owned by Napoleon Bonaparte. If I had to choose a favorite room, the library would be it with its giant fireplace and two-story shelves stuffed with books that look hundreds of years old.

If Meredith doesn't end up working here, I'll be shocked. She's a perfect ambassador for the estate.

❄❄❄

When we finish the tour, I drive us over to Antler Hill Village. We buy hot cocoa and chocolates from one of the outdoor shops and walk around, checking out the various light displays. There are two open Adirondack chairs at a large fire pit and we commandeer them. Meredith offers me a chocolate, which I pop into my mouth while trying to come up with something to ask her. It hits me right as I'm swallowing.

"Where did you end up getting your MBA?"

She moves her gaze from the roaring fire over to me. "I did Appalachian State's online program, so I was mostly here, but had to go up a few times for in-person activities."

"I went to App State. Boone is a great college town. It's actually where I grew up."

Her face lights up. "Oh yeah? It looks cute. Definitely seems like a place for younger people and outdoor enthusiasts."

"There are a lot of fun things to do. I could take you snow tubing. One of my high school friends runs a place."

She nods, her smile widening. "That would be fun. Though, is it something we could do after the new year? I'm kind of booked with work."

I chuckle. "Yeah, me too. We can definitely plan to go in January. Let me know when you're available and I'll make it work."

"Will you also take me to all your favorite places from growing up?"

I really like the idea of showing her around. Though Boone's small enough that, if I wander around town and go to my friend's tubing park, word will make it back to my mom. I'd hate for her to know I was there and didn't visit. "I can, though I'll also need to stop in and see my mom, at least for a few minutes."

Meredith lowers her head, looking at me through her lashes, something flashing in her eyes. "Brett, are you asking me to meet your mother?"

My eyes go wide with panic until she snickers and I realize she's teasing me. I choose to lean into this possibly flirty conversation. "Yeah, I guess I am. Is that a problem?"

"No problem that I see. I'm sure she has loads of embarrassing stories about you she'd love to share."

Ooh, this woman. Beautiful and feisty. It's official. I'm smitten. I've been trying to fight my attraction, but it appears to be a losing battle. Especially if I'm reading the vibes I'm getting from her correctly and she *is* flirting with me. If only the whole *me needing this job to help my mom out* thing wasn't in the way, then I wouldn't be worried so much about getting these signals mixed up.

We tentatively have plans for January. If I can hold out until then, maybe I'll have a clearer understanding of what's going on. *Good luck with that.* Yeah, yeah, Brain, thanks for the vote of confidence.

20

Meredith

TOURING BILTMORE ESTATE with Brett was a blast. I think he enjoyed himself despite his aversion to Christmas. I still haven't heard the full story about that, but I suppose it's enough to know it reminds him of his dad's abandonment. His facial hair has returned. Is he doing that for me? Might that mean he sees me as more than a friend? I can't ask him outright because of the whole boss/employee thing. If anything is going to happen between us, he'll have to make the first move. I don't want to create an awkward work environment if I'm misconstruing his behavior toward me.

I've noticed him watching me at meetings, though I'm usually the one talking so it could just be polite respect on his part. It's not like every employee who pays attention must think I'm cute. My ego's not as big as Connor's. Who, by the way, has increased his flirting with me at work. It appears things between him and Genesis seem to have cooled. I've been ignoring his show of interest, but may have to tell him outright I'm not interested soon. However, Brett's eyes on me feel like a different level of attentiveness than the others. One I'd gladly invite more of. Of course, I could just be seeing what I hope is there.

A shadow falls across my face, interrupting my thoughts. I look up from my spot against the wall in the Education Center. Connor's standing right in front of me, grinning like he has a secret. It makes my stomach twist with unease.

Before I can push away from the wall, Connor leans toward me, bracing himself on the wall with a hand near my head. There's a gleam in his eye that I don't like. His closeness makes goosebumps rise on my arms, but I mask my discomfort with a smile. "Connor, what's up?"

"I was thinking we should go out for drinks one night. You look like a margarita girl. Maybe Naranjas downtown?"

Now he's straight up asking me out. Here's my chance to dash his hopes. Kindly, of course. Glancing around the room, my eyes find Genesis's. Her eyes are shooting daggers into Connor's back. Uh oh. There's the downside to allowing employees to date. Hopefully, I can avoid adding to this drama.

"I'm busy most nights, as you're aware. And the nights I *am* free, you aren't." Thank goodness for my unconscious scheduling. Some part of me must have known I needed to put up as many barriers as possible between me and Connor. I shift a little to the side, but he only leans in closer. His breath is warm against my cheek. And does it smell like peppermint? Is he eating the candy canes meant for the kids? I'm not surprised.

"How about we turn it into an afternoon drink?"

"Don't you have work during the day?"

He waves his free hand, like my question is irrelevant. "Eh, I work for my old man. He doesn't care if I skip out now and then. As long as I show up to the office for thirty minutes or so and make myself seen to the higher ups, I can pretty much work wherever."

"Sounds like a cushy job. What do you do?"

"I'm VP of marketing."

A schmoozing roll, most likely. Fits him to a T, though I'm not impressed. Enough beating around the bush.

"While I'm flattered by your invitation, I'm really not a 'Margarita Girl,' nor am I interested in being anything other than friends with you. I hope you understand."

When I turn my head, I catch sight of Brett on the other side of the room. His eyes are saucers and he's frozen like a deer in headlights.

Our eyes meet and he blinks out of his stupor, his face morphing into something like hurt or anger. He turns and leaves, but not before I catch the scowl on his face. Connor notices that he's lost my attention because he turns, then smirks at Brett's retreating back. I don't have time to analyze this because my heart has already kicked up in speed. I use Connor's distraction as an excuse to slide out from under him, and my feet take off after Brett. My stomach roils with a combination of worry and panic. *What is Brett thinking? Why did he run off like that?*

My legs are moving as fast as they can, but my elf slippers are thin and the pavement is hard beneath my feet. Maybe I'll make some covers to go over tennis shoes so I don't have this problem again. Though, how was I to know I'd be chasing someone through a parking lot tonight?

His legs are longer than mine, plus he had a head start, but I manage to catch up with him at his truck. I yank the door open and stand in front of it so he can't back out of his parking spot. I then take a minute to catch my breath, as I'm not used to sprinting at full speed, holding up a finger to let him know I have something to say. My breath returns, but my heart is still beating a mile a minute.

His face is blank, except for a line between his eyebrows. Is he trying to work out what he just saw? I take a few more gulps of air. "Brett, that wasn't what it looked like."

He shrugs, staring straight out the front windshield. He hasn't looked at me once since I've arrived. His voice is monotone when he speaks. "Co-workers are free to date, right? You're both consenting adults."

I sigh, frustrated at his behavior. "Yes, but I'm not interested in *Connor*." I want to tell him who I *am* interested in, but I've promised myself I'd let him make the first move. It's the right thing to do as someone in authority.

His lips are pressed together in a firm line and I can't stop staring, hoping they'll tick up just the slightest, letting me know he understands what I'm not saying. The silence between us grows, but I'm determined to wait him out. Finally, he releases a breath and my heart races wildly in nervous anticipation of whatever he's going to say.

"Would you please move? I need to go."

My heart plummets. He's dismissing me? Reluctantly, I step back. Brett reaches out and pulls the door closed. The loud thud feels like the death knell on my hope that something was growing between us. I watch him back out of his space and drive away.

❄❄❄

A few days later, while I'm wallowing at home before I have to go into work, my phone rings. It's Ms. Garcia from Biltmore Estate. I'm briefly buoyed, grateful for any scrap of good news.

"Meredith, thank you for your interest in working at Biltmore. We all enjoyed speaking with you during your interview."

Okay. That sounds positive. My heart picks up pace as hope flutters in my chest. "I appreciate the opportunity to be considered for the position. I love Biltmore Estate and would love the chance to help visitors enjoy the property's many amenities and feel welcomed and pampered while there."

"That's exactly the attitude we hope for from our employees."

Is she counting me among the ranks of a Biltmore employee? I cross my fingers and toes, holding my breath while my heart hammers in my chest.

"You were an outstanding candidate," Ms. Garcia continues, "but, unfortunately, the group has offered the job to someone else."

My breath hisses out of me like a deflating balloon. My shoulders slouch forward with resignation. I didn't get the job. She gives a few more conciliatory statements, but I barely hear them. I thank her for her consideration and hang up.

My first thought is to text Brett, but he hasn't spoken to me since that night in the parking lot. Instead, I drag myself to the kitchen to find something salty, since that's how I'm feeling. Paige's head pops out from behind the open refrigerator door, and I jump. I didn't think anyone would be in here. Switching course, I travel around the island in the middle of the kitchen until I reach my final destination—the pantry. A bag of Baked Lays draws my attention. I open the bag and stuff a few into my mouth. The salt delights my tongue and I get a small hit of dopamine. Hoping to experience more of this feel-good hormone, I carry the bag over to the island and hop up onto a stool.

Paige sits down next to me, the bowl in her hand clinking loudly when it hits the counter. I look over and see her food of choice is mom's homemade macaroni and cheese. My mouth waters. I snatch a noodle from her bowl with my fingers and toss it into my mouth. Mmm, delicious. Paige gives me a disgusted look, sliding her bowl away from me. "I just wanted one," I say, aware I'm being rude but not particularly caring.

"What is up with you, Mel? You've been sulking all week."

I roll my eyes, fully immersing myself in angry, angsty teenager mode. "You're one to talk, Pal. You haven't exactly been a ray of sunshine since you and Elliot broke up."

I know it's a low blow bringing up such a tender subject, but she's been moping around since whatever happened between them. She hasn't told me the details and I haven't asked, afraid she'd yell at me for invading her privacy. Yet she isn't afraid of invading mine. Surprisingly, she only sighs.

"Want to tell me what's wrong?"

The gentleness in her voice makes my foul mood waver a bit. Paige rarely shows vulnerability, so she must see how bothered I am.

"The Biltmore called. I didn't get my dream job."

She places a hand on my shoulder, squeezing lightly, and I yank my body away from her sympathetic touch. I'm not in the mood to be comforted right now. She sighs, but doesn't comment. We eat in silence for a few minutes. Well, not silence exactly. The crunch of chips between my teeth seems deafening compared to the quiet clink of Paige's fork against the bowl. I shove the bag of chips away from me, cross my arms on the counter, and drop my head onto them.

A hand lands on my back, and soothing circles are drawn on my sweatshirt. I tense at the initial sensation, then force my muscles to relax. I hate that I'm being such a brat. Paige is being unusually sympathetic. I roll my head to the side so I can look at her. The concerned look on her face twists my heart.

"I'm sorry they didn't hire you, but there are more opportunities out there. Don't let one setback derail you completely."

I blow a steady stream of air through my lips. "I know."

Paige chuckles. "No offense, but you seem pretty brokenhearted for just losing a potential job opportunity. You and I could be two peas in a pod right now." Her smile turns sad and I immediately feel like a terrible person for comparing our situations. She and Elliot dated for almost two years. Of course, she'd be so broken up about it. Paige probably thought they'd get married.

Her words sink in and I realize it's not just the job that's put me in a foul mood. It's that I've also lost my friendship with Brett. And whatever else we had the potential to be. I guess I liked him more than I realized, but it doesn't matter now.

Paige is right. I can't let two bad things ruin the rest of my week. There are more opportunities out there—both for jobs and relationships. If I can just tune into my normally positive frame of mind, surely things will get better. I mean, my Crafty shop is seeing a higher volume of orders than I've ever received. Speaking of which,

I have some custom-order scarves I need to work on.

That's the spirit! Positive thoughts and gratitude will help turn things around. The freezer door snags my attention. But maybe also a few scoops of Peppermint Stick ice cream.

21

Brett

WORKING AT THE Arboretum has been a little awkward since I walked in on Connor and Meredith getting cozy up against the wall. So much for not being intimate at work. Though I suppose the boss can do whatever she wants.

She denied that anything was going on with Connor, but I saw the truth pressed against that wall. I didn't have any claims on her, even if I'd kind of hoped the attraction was mutual. I really can't be mad at her for falling for Connor's charm. He's very good at wooing the ladies. Especially ladies I'm interested in. I guess I didn't hide my interest in Meredith from Connor well enough.

It surprised me how visceral the response was to finding Santa and a dark-haired woman dressed as an elf in almost the same position fourteen years later. Of course, in the first instance, the pair had their hands all over one another and were making out like there was no tomorrow. I bet when you're sneaking around, every encounter is exciting. Until your sixteen-year-old son accidentally catches you in the act.

That's right, I caught my father cheating on my mom in Boone Mall on Christmas Eve. He and I had made plans to meet up after his Santa shift for some last-minute shopping. I guess he forgot or lost track of time.

They jumped apart when I called his name, but there wasn't any remorse on his face. He tried introducing me to Vicky like nothing was amiss, but I turned and left without another word. She didn't seem surprised to see me either, so maybe he hadn't been hiding the fact that he had a family.

My father wasn't more than two minutes behind me getting home and confessed everything, admitting he'd been seeing her off and on for the past few years. Mom gave him an ultimatum, us or her, and he chose her. I wouldn't have even given him the opportunity to reject us, just kicked him out, but that's just more proof of Mom's generous heart.

All those memories flooded my brain when I saw Connor and Meredith, and, once again, getting far away from the situation was my first recourse. I couldn't do anything else. Now that it's been a few days, I feel a little bad about not hearing Meredith out, but I can't risk my heart getting any more invested in a relationship that isn't going to pan out.

I've already lost one woman I cared about to Connor. It devastated me when my college girlfriend, Lindsay, chose Connor over me. We'd been dating for almost a year when she dumped me like a hot potato at the first sign of interest from Connor. They only dated for a month before Connor moved on to someone else. Lindsay apologized and wanted to get back together, but I won't be someone's second choice. I deserve someone who has eyes only for me. I've learned to cut my losses and run before it's too late.

Which means I've been keeping to myself at work. I've continued to engage with the customers at the shack, but haven't been spending extra time with any of my co-workers, not that anyone seems to have noticed my aloofness. Zach invited me to trivia on our last night off, but I declined, not wanting to risk seeing Meredith. Or worse, Meredith and Connor together. Though, I know he doesn't have the same nights off as she and I do because he always seems to show up at Winter Lights and tries to mess with me while I'm working. Doesn't he have anything better to do? Maybe he actually comes to see Meredith, and tormenting me is just an added bonus.

There's a knock on the shack door and I unlock it, pulling the door open. Joanne peeks her head in and my heart sinks. Part of me hoped it would be Meredith, though she hasn't come by to check on me since our falling out in the parking lot. I should be glad she's giving me space, but I kind of miss her nightly visits.

"Brett, will you please come with me to the office?"

My brow furrows and I look between her and the customer at my window. "Now?" She nods. "What about our customers?"

Joanne opens the door wider and I see a guy in a Darth Vader Christmas sweater next to her. "Tony here will fill in for you."

My gut twists as an ominous feeling makes the hair on my arms stand up. I haven't done anything wrong, so I'm not sure what's going on. Maybe customers have noticed my sullen demeanor. Still, I'm providing excellent service, so whatever this is about, it shouldn't take long.

I follow Joanne into the building and back to her office. Meredith is in there, sitting in one of two chairs behind the desk. Joanne takes the one next to her and I drop into a chair on the other side of the desk. I risk a glance at Meredith, but she's studying her hands, which are fidgeting in her lap. I feel bad if I hurt her, but I refuse to be involved in a love triangle again. When it's me versus Connor, he seems to know how to come out on top. I continue to stare, willing her to meet my gaze so I can try to read her expression. Her lips are a thin line, which doesn't tell me much.

"Brett, you're being terminated effective immediately."

My gut twists at Joanne's words. "What? Why?"

"Beer and wine have gone missing from your station on multiple occasions. More than what could be chalked up to liberal pours."

My neck feels warm and sweaty. Surely, this isn't happening. The truth is on my side. "I know. I reported it to accounting myself."

Joanne's eyebrows go up, like this is news to her, but then her face hardens into conviction. "An excellent cover-up to throw suspicion off of you."

"Who would rat on themselves?" My gaze swings to Meredith, but her eyes are on Joanne. We talked about this not that long ago. She knows I'm a trustworthy guy. Right?

"Who indeed, Mr. Jacobs?" Joanne says. "Normally, I'd be inclined to believe it wasn't you, but we found three six packs of beer and a case of wine in your truck."

I turn to face Joanne. "When? Where?" This is not making sense.

"Just a few minutes ago, actually. In the bed. You really should have covered it up with a tarp or something. That was just sloppy work."

I'm seeing red, but take a deep breath to hold it back, speaking slowly and deliberately so I don't say something inappropriate. "Anyone could have put something in the bed of my truck. I swear it wasn't me. I need this job. Why would I take such a risk?"

Joanne shrugs. "Maybe you thought you could make a little extra selling inventory on the side. I don't know. You're the mastermind behind all of this."

"I didn't do it."

"We have evidence that says you did."

I grit my teeth, frustrated that she's not listening, and that Meredith hasn't lent me any support. I fist my hands at my sides but quickly spread my fingers wide so I'm not accused of being physically aggressive. "Evidence that someone else must have planted."

Joanne raises an eyebrow. "And who would want to frame

you?"

One name flashes in my head, but I don't say it out loud. I know who might do something like that, but without proof, I'd probably just look like someone who's still bitter after all this time.

Meredith's continued silence stings. Does she think I would do something like this? She looks troubled, but she still won't look at me. There's nothing I can do. I can't prove my innocence.

Defeated, I stand and tug my lanyard over my head, dropping it on the desk. "It looks like your mind is made up about me. I'll see myself out."

"Actually," Joanne says. "Security will escort you to your vehicle."

I cast one more look Meredith's way. She's actually looking at me now, her face pinched with what looks like regret mixed with something else. Incomprehension, maybe? Yeah, same here. This has blindsided me.

A security officer waits for me outside the office door. Are they really worried I'll steal something or make a fuss? I walk slowly to my truck, ignoring the man following me. Another person in a security vehicle follows me all the way to the entrance gates. Way to make me feel like a real criminal.

I suppose I should be glad they're not pressing charges for theft, even though I didn't do anything wrong, but that's the lesser of my worries. What am I going to do for extra money to afford Mom's car repair bill now? At least I don't have to worry about seeing Meredith every day. The disappointment in my gut reveals that's not exactly a pleasant fact, though why I should want to see someone who chose Connor over me is confusing. Of course, I didn't exactly declare my interest in her, so I can't justifiably be angry at her. I sigh, knowing it's myself I'm mad at.

I let Meredith go without even allowing for the possibility of something to form between us. She might not have been interested, but I could have at least had the courage to find out. Or even just warn her about Connor. Instead, I'm faced with the knowledge that

Connor won again. I know he sabotaged me, even if I can't prove it. He definitely did everything he could to make sure I'm no threat to him. I just hate that someone as sweet as Meredith fell for his charm. It's only a matter of time before he gets bored and moves on, leaving her with a crushed heart. The thought makes my temper flare, but there's nothing I can do now.

22

Meredith

THE WINDOW OF the cocoa shack doesn't have any customers standing in line, so I approach, startled when Tony's smiling face peers out at me. "Hey, Meredith. What can I do for you?"

"I was just checking on you, seeing if you need anything."

He shakes his head. "Nope, everything's cool here."

"Okay. Keep up the good work."

I wave, then turn and continue my route to the Baker building, where I check on the staff working inside. There's a crowd over at the photo counter, and I walk over to see what's going on. People are laughing at a photo of a woman being kissed on the cheek by Santa, her eyes wide with surprise. I smile, amused at Connor's ability to throw himself into the role. He hasn't been as flirty lately. Not nearly as blatant since Brett left. I guess he got the message I'm not interested.

I finish my round of the building, then head back up toward the

Education Center, my eyes darting over to the cocoa shack as I pass by again. My stomach twists, reminding me how disappointed I felt when I saw Tony in the shack rather than Brett. I hate how things turned out with him. He doesn't seem like he would do something so sneaky. I argued as much with Joanne, but how was I to prove his character to her? Still, the whole situation seems fishy to me. His argument that anyone could have put the drinks in his truck was solid to me, but I could tell Joanne just wanted to close the case and move on. I guess we'll see if any more goes missing now that Brett's gone.

He wouldn't say who he thought might be behind this, but I'm pretty sure I know who he was thinking of. I still don't know what the deal is, but there was obvious friction between Brett and Connor whenever they were in the same room. Connor trying to get rid of Brett doesn't seem like such a far-fetched prospect to me. While I don't owe Brett anything, I know he was counting on this job, so I'll keep my eyes and ears open in case the real culprit reveals himself. Or herself. Gotta keep all possibilities open.

❄❄❄

The next morning, I receive an email from Ali with a link to a job posting. It's the New York City position she's been talking about. The company is an international hotel chain, but the job is to work for their New York branch. There's a line in the listing about the potential for travel as employees move up in the company. That would be pretty cool. I'd love to see other parts of the world, though living there might be a different story. I'm not too keen on relocating seven hundred miles away from my family, but I promised Ali I'd apply. Besides, I haven't found anything local that's promising. My Biltmore dream's been dashed. For now, at least. I've been obsessively checking job listing sites, hoping they'll have another opening for a management job. So far, no luck. I just know I'd be a perfect fit, but I obviously didn't prove that to the interviewers.

Out of curiosity, I search the hotel chain's other job listings to see if they have positions available in other parts of the country. There's an opening in Los Angeles. Um, no thanks. The other side of the country is way too far. Ooh, a spot in London. More enticing, but across an ocean, so even farther away. Though, I could probably convince my family to visit me in England. Ali would come for a potential royal sighting. She loves that stuff.

I spy an opening in Chicago, which is the closest city so far, but winters there sound brutal. A quick internet search tells me the flight time from Asheville is about the same as to New York City, but about forty minutes closer to drive. Eh, why not? I fill out applications for both New York and Chicago and send them off.

Just for fun, I check out flights to London. Yeesh, it's faster to drive to New York. Maybe I should become a flight attendant, then I can travel all over and visit my family whenever I want. While that sounds fun, it would require extra training and wouldn't put my MBA to use. Well, a fun flight of fancy while it lasted. Get it? *Flight* of fancy? No one in my family appreciates word play like I do.

A glance at the clock tells me I need to get dressed and head into work. I shut down my computer, discouraged that I'm no closer to finding a full-time job I'm excited about.

My life's not all doom and gloom, though. My Crafty business has been going crazy this month. I've had so many custom orders I can barely keep up. I'm not sure where all the customers are coming from, but that's not a complaint. It's been so exciting seeing others share my love of Christmas and helping them create special gifts others will love. It warms my heart to know that people will receive Christmas presents I made. Even if I never get to see their happy faces, I know I helped make someone's holiday a little more festive.

My joy once again restored at the thought of cheerful people, I bound upstairs to my room and go in search of my most festive Christmas sweater. I don't have to be an elf tonight, so I settle on my red Rudolph top with the light up nose. Checking the battery pack, I grin at myself in the mirror as the nose blinks on and off. I know just the earrings to pair with this. The words to "Holly Jolly Christmas" fill my head and I sing at the top of my lungs while putting in my reindeer and sleigh earrings that climb the whole side of my ear. I grab my green Arboretum Santa hat and I'm off, a spring in my step.

23

Brett

MY LUNCH BREAK has been an hour of scrolling job websites while mindlessly shoveling food into my mouth. I didn't pack anything and am too lazy to go out in this wintery mix so I'm eating very nutritious potato chips and cookies from the vending machine. Who am I kidding? It's one of my favorite on-the-fly meals.

I don't know why I'm even looking for a new job. If I get an interview, by the time I receive an offer and start working, the holiday season will be over. Frustrated by this realization, I set my phone screen-down on the table and put my head in my hands. But only for a moment, because I remember I'm not doing this for myself.

Picking my phone back up, I type "earn money fast Asheville" in my browser's search bar. I'm obviously not the only person who's done this search because lists pop up with titles like "Best Side Hustles for Extra Cash." That's definitely what I'm looking for. The first link is a dud, but the second mentions things like donating plasma, focus groups, surveys, and ride share driving. Being a taxi for others in a truck would be a little weird and cramped. Though maybe I could hire myself out to help move furniture or something. Or deliver food. That's a thriving service in this culinary town.

On my way back to the front after my break, I pause at the bulletin board to see if there are any advertisements for cash jobs. There's a piano instructor advertising their services. I'm not a musician, so that's a no. Someone's looking for a babysitter. I'm good with kids, but most parents are wary about leaving their children with men who are strangers. Nothing truly promising. I'm resourceful, though, so I'll figure something out.

I distract myself from my problems helping customers find books for themselves and loved ones, but my discouragement from losing the perfect gig through no fault of my own is a steady hum in the background of my mind. It still bothers me that Meredith thinks I could have done something like this. I thought we were making progress in our friendship, and she had a good idea of who I am. Sure, I can come off a little antisocial, but I'm not a criminal. I sigh. I've got to let this go. There's nothing to be done now, and ruminating on the unfairness of the situation will just tank my attitude even more.

Rachel rounds the corner of a bookshelf and I see there's something white stuck to her black pant leg. Is that a sock? A chance to tease my favorite co-worker will help drag me out of my funk. I walk toward her, snarky comments blossoming in my mind.

❄❄❄

I park in front of my childhood home and walk up the driveway, overnight bag in hand. My shift tomorrow starts at eleven, so I can make the drive in the morning. No one needed their shift covered today. Extra weekend hours have become scarce the closer we get to Christmas. I can't blame anyone for wanting more money.

Using my key to let myself in, I find Mom in the kitchen, stirring something on the stove. I drop my bag at the end of the hall leading to the bedrooms, then kiss her on the cheek. "Hey, Mom. That smells mouthwatering."

Her eyes crinkle with her smile. "Thanks, Brett. There's plenty to share, thankfully, since you didn't tell me you were coming." She hits me with her accusing mom look, but I just shrug. I didn't tell her on purpose because I didn't want her running to the store and having to carry extra groceries home on the bus.

"Sorry, Mom. How about I drive us to the store after lunch *and* cook dinner for you tonight?"

Her face relaxes back into a smile, and she pats my cheek. "That sounds lovely. You're so good to your momma."

The words slash my chest, knowing I'm failing her right now. I know she wouldn't see it like that, but I've promised myself to do whatever I can to make her life easier to balance out all the hardship my father caused. I turn away and get two bowls down for the homemade chicken noodle soup on the stove so she won't see my conflicting emotions. Then I look through the pantry and fridge, removing all the ingredients for grilled cheese sandwiches. I pull a large pan from the cabinet next to the stove and set it on a free burner.

The pan warms while I assemble the sandwiches, the bread sizzling pleasantly when the mayonnaise side hits the pan. I used to have grilled cheese showdowns with roommates in college whenever they tried to tease me about not using butter. They all came over to my side after trying one of my sandwiches.

Mom and I used to make soup and sandwiches all the time when I was growing up. It was our favorite Saturday tradition when the weather got cold. The soup would change from week to week and sometimes we'd add in turkey or ham to the sandwiches depending on what was available in the fridge.

When the sandwiches are golden brown and yellow cheese oozes out of the middle, I transfer them to plates and cut them into triangles. I carry them over to the dining room table where I used to do my homework and talk about my day with Mom while she made dinner. I place Mom's in front of her, then sit down in the seat that faces the kitchen, the one that's always been mine.

We tuck into our food and the first taste of soup on my tongue brings with it a flood of memories. Playing card games at the table with my parents when I was a kid. My father helping me with school science projects. The year I wanted to do a baking soda volcano and red bubbles ended up covering the table and dripping onto the floor. The white linoleum underneath still has faint pink stains from the food coloring.

I let myself bask in these pleasant memories until one surfaces of Mom and I at this same kitchen table, staring uncomprehendingly at my father in his Santa suit, minus the hat and beard. His large padded belly made him look larger than life in that tiny kitchen. A fitting image, since that's how I saw him my entire childhood. He was my hero, and I didn't think he could do any wrong. Boy, was I mistaken.

I shake my head to dispel the unwanted memory, and turn my attention to Mom. "Any updates on that sales job?"

She smiles at me and my heart twists at everything she's endured over the years. She's so loving and kind and generous. My father never deserved her. I don't deserve her, either, most of the time. I just want her to be happy and not have to worry about anything.

"I have my interview on Monday. It sounds like they want to have their person chosen by the end of the year so they can train them and send them off."

I smile, but the pressure to make more money feels even heavier. "That's great. I'm sure you're a shoo-in."

Mom pats my hand. "I appreciate your confidence."

She stands suddenly, goes to a drawer in the kitchen, then comes back, dumping envelopes next to my plate. "I almost forgot. Here's the stuff that's come for you since your last visit."

I sift through the mostly junk mail, pausing when I uncover a thick, creamy envelope. My name and address are written in pretty calligraphy. It looks like a wedding invitation. I pick it up and flip it over, but don't recognize the return address. Curious, I open the flap with my finger, then pull out the card inside. My eyes zoom in on the large names in the center of the page and the card drops from my fingers like I've been burned. It lands face up and I quickly turn it over, not wanting my mom to see.

She shakes her head at my antics. "Brett, I know what that is. You don't have to protect me so much. I'm fine."

I frown. "You're *fine* that Josh is renewing his vows with the woman who broke up our family?"

She reaches for my hand, but I quickly slide it away and under the table. "I've had a lot of time to process everything that happened. Was it an awful time and a terrible thing for your father to do? Yes. Do I wish you hadn't been the one to discover his affair? Also yes. But do I want to hold on to bitterness and hurt over something that happened nearly a decade and a half ago and let it affect my present and future? No. I'm responsible for how I let others' actions affect me and I have chosen to let go of your father's mistakes."

I scowl and open my mouth to respond, but she holds up a hand to stop me. "My life is great now. I have you because of your dad and I'd never wish you away. Believe it or not, I'm happy he's found happiness with Victoria and I'm glad their kids have a positive example of love."

"Unlike me," I grumble.

Mom pins me with another no-nonsense look. "You know very well your dad tried to make it up to you and stay present in your life. It was your choice to close him out, which I don't begrudge you, but you can't have it both ways. If you want him in your life, you have to let him in. He's not going to force you to have a relationship with him, though I know he'd love you to spend time with your brothers."

"*Half* brothers," I respond.

She shoots me an exasperated look and sighs.

My shoulders drop. She's right. I rebuffed all his attempts to be involved in my life. I was just so angry. Truthfully, I'm still angry. How could anyone hurt a woman as wonderful as my mom? Do I wish I still had a relationship with my father? I don't know. But I know I haven't been fair to him by keeping him firmly on a pedestal of villainy. We all make mistakes, though some are bigger and more devastating than others.

Still, the idea of him getting off scot free and living a picture-perfect life rankles me. Doesn't he have any regrets? About hurting my mom? About betraying me? Abandoning us? But Mom's right. My anger only seems to affect me. It hasn't kept Josh from enjoying his life.

"It's not too late to fix your relationship. Look at this invitation as an olive branch."

It feels like an invitation for him to rub his happiness and his new family in my face, but I won't tell Mom that. I suppose I'm glad the past doesn't weigh her down anymore, but she's a better, more forgiving person than I am. Still, I don't want to burden her with my issues.

"I'll think about it, Mom." I'm not going to think about it. There's no way I'm going. I punctuate my words with a smile that I hope she doesn't see through. Then another thought occurs to me. "Are *you* going?"

She chuckles. "Of course not. Technically, I wasn't invited, but I wouldn't have gone, anyway. This is your father's new life. I'm not part of that, nor do I wish to be. I like my own new life just fine."

The afternoon passes with much less drama. We stock up at the grocery store. I get everything I need to make lasagna, a hearty meal for a wintry day. I got the recipe from Rachel, who learned it from her grandmother. At the house, I put Christmas lights around the door and windows outside while Mom tackles the bushes. When we're finished, we go inside and warm up with some hot apple cider before tackling the artificial tree.

I've assembled her tree and strung the lights every year since my father left. It was his job, but someone had to take over in his absence. I don't begrudge Mom her cheery decor, though I draw the line at putting ornaments on the tree. I'll add the star to the top because I don't want Mom to fall off the ladder, but it's hard looking at ornaments from my childhood. They bring up a lot of memories, mostly of our family of three, which no longer exists.

When my tasks are finished, I sit back on the couch, keeping Mom company while she decorates. Nat King Cole is playing on my phone and I've put a fake crackling fire on the television. The lights are dim, making the multicolored lights on the tree glow. Mom sings along to the music.

Maybe I should get her some new ornaments and decorations for the tree, something without connections to the past. I know she'd love me to help with this part, but she understands my refusal and hasn't pushed it. I could get some of the cute things from the MerryDesigns store. I know Mom would love the hand-painted ceramic ornaments depicting the twelve days of Christmas.

My stomach pangs with regret at how I left things with Meredith. I probably could have talked to her after I saw her with Connor, given her a real chance to explain, but my past took up too much of my brain to properly consider my actions at the time. If I could go back and act differently, I would. She's such a sweet person. She reminds me a lot of my mom.

Mom's words from earlier ring in my mind. Do *I* want to let something that happened so long ago affect *my* present and future? Well, the past has definitely been in charge of my actions lately. Do I want to continue to let it? Certainty settles in my gut. No, I don't. I've given my father and his transgression too much power in my life. That needs to end now.

24

Meredith

MY PLANE LANDS at LaGuardia Airport in the early afternoon. After taking the private car to the hotel where Sanders Hotel Group is putting me up—Trinity Tower in Midtown near Times Square, one of the properties I'd be managing—I drop my bags off and head out for some sightseeing in the city that never sleeps. I sleep, however, which means I'd better cram in as much as I can before getting some shuteye to prepare for my interview tomorrow.

My first stop, of course, is Rockefeller Center to check out the tree for myself. It's still light out, so I make a mental note to wander back this way after dark. I meander past gorgeous storefront windows, all advertising gifts in a way that I almost feel compelled to step inside and pick one up for a loved one.

I grab a slice of pizza on my way to Grand Central Terminal and eat while I wait for the train to carry me to the New York Botanical Garden in The Bronx. The concierge at the hotel wrote instructions for me, so I find the gardens easily. There's no way I could pass up their Glow event. I'm curious to see how Winter Lights compares to big city garden lights.

The displays are phenomenal and the lit up buildings are incredibly stunning; the designs changing from time to time. It's a lot like our displays, only bigger. At least if I live here, I'll be able to come somewhere that reminds me a little of home.

A sign for a train show in the Conservatory makes me eager to discover if it's anything like the little Rocky Cove Railroad at the Arboretum. They probably have at least four trains. I'm pleasantly surprised to discover replicas of the buildings here at the Botanical Garden, but also iconic buildings and locations around the city. Everything is made from plant and organic materials and trains run through the various scenes. It reminds me of a similar display Brett and I saw at Antler Hill Village recently, only those were Biltmore and Asheville buildings.

I sigh, as my mind turns over my last few interactions with Brett. I hate that he caught me in such a weird situation with Connor and still don't understand why he wouldn't listen to my explanation.

One good thing about potentially moving away from Asheville is that I wouldn't risk running into Brett. It's bizarre how often I see someone I know when I'm out running errands or eating at a restaurant. It'll be impossible to avoid him if I stay in Asheville and thoughts of him are still a little tender. We didn't even go on a real date and I can't say for sure whether he even liked me, but I've never been brave enough to make the first move with a guy. Flirting to show interest was a big step for me and now I'm expected to just move on? Seems a little unfair.

I wrap up my visit to the Botanical Garden and make my way back to the train station. While I wait, I order a to-go cup of hot chocolate from a stand to warm up my hands and my insides. It's definitely colder up here than at home. The beverage is delicious. The plain stand did not give me high hopes for the quality of products, and I mentally apologize to the man behind the counter.

Back in Midtown, I return to the tree, in awe of its ginormous glory. I snap a few photos to add to my growing collection of New York Christmas sights. The city is doing an excellent job of wooing me, though right now is probably when it looks its best. I bet in February it's gray and dreary. Though, to be fair, Asheville isn't exactly a rainbow of color then either.

If I moved here, where would I live? There are plenty of stories about the astronomical rent prices. I looked online at a few near the hotel I'm staying at just for fun and the cost for a shoebox of an apartment was outrageously uneconomical. I may have to learn the subway system and commute. My parents would gladly help me with a deposit and first month if needed, and I could always pay them back once I was situated, but it's not my first choice.

I'm acting like living here's a sure thing and I haven't even interviewed yet. Still, it's good to compare everything, including costs. Like flights home to visit my family. There are daily flights from Asheville to NYC that cost less than the gas it'd take to drive the distance. I could feasibly go home for long weekends, or my family could come visit me. Though I'd definitely miss a lot of Baby Fredrikson's life. There's always video chatting, I suppose.

My sightseeing has led me back to Trinity Tower and I walk through the pristine lobby, marveling at its thirty-foot ceiling and shiny white marble floor on my way to the two golden elevators. One carries me smoothly up to the twelfth floor, dinging pleasantly just before the doors open. The thick red carpet of the hall dampens the sound of my footsteps.

The staff has already completed the turndown service and there's a chocolate on my pillow in the shape of the hotel. I unwrap it and pop it into my mouth. The chocolate feels velvety on my tongue, a sign of quality chocolate. These tiny service details raise the profile of the company in my eyes. I'm sure I'll know even more tomorrow after my interview.

❄❄❄

I settle comfortably into my seat for my return flight. Sanders Hotel Group spared no expense with this interview process. First-class seats for my flights, a driver holding a board with my name on it when I arrived, and a delicious breakfast buffet complete with made-to-order omelets and a carving station at the restaurant on the top floor of the hotel. The floor-to-ceiling glass windows provided gorgeous views of the surrounding city.

The interview was conducted in a conference room on the floor below the restaurant, also with large windows that showcased the view. My interviewers were the woman who would be my boss and the general manager of Trinity Tower. They were both very warm and friendly. I felt at ease with them almost at once. They seemed impressed by the level of responsibility I currently have at the Arboretum. After we wrapped up, they escorted me to the lobby where my bags had already been carried, and put me in another private car back to the airport.

I spend the flight home thinking about my time in the city. I didn't feel overwhelmed by the size like I thought I would. Pride fills me at the memory of navigating my little sightseeing escapade the night before with no issues. Everyone here seems to have a lot of energy, which I appreciate. The hustle and bustle certainly appeal to me, plus people don't seem to care if you're a little quirky.

The cost of living is a big downside, so the offered salary will be a large factor. Along with what I really think about managing several hotels. I wouldn't have much face time with customers and it's the people part of hospitality I really enjoy. Though I suppose that's the fate of managers—training those who interact with the public and only getting involved when absolutely necessary.

That thought depresses me a little, but I remind myself that my family will be proud of me if I get this job. I know Oliver would be. He'd talked about moving to a big city after college. This feels like just the thing he'd have done. I can imagine him and a bunch of his new city friends visiting all the cool spots, like password-only bars and hole-in-the-wall comedy clubs where big names randomly show up. He was always the life of the party, with big ideas that ended up being a rowdy, but terrific, time. I still can't believe a drunk driver took him from us.

A tear slips down my cheek and I wipe it away, turning toward the window so my seatmate doesn't notice. There's nothing to see out the window except blue sky over blankets of clouds. I lower the shade and rest my head against the back of the seat.

It might be nice to get a fresh start in a new place. I've lived in western North Carolina my whole life. My wings could use an opportunity to spread and maybe soar. The idea of moving to New York is growing on me, especially because I'm sure I'd get along with the people I'd be working with. Of course, there's still one major hurdle. Actually being offered the job. Well, we'll see what happens.

25

Brett

I'VE MANAGED TO make some money doing odds and ends since I was fired from the Arboretum. Not enough to equal what I was getting paid, but something's better than nothing. I'm now donating plasma twice a week, which is beneficial not only for myself, but for those who receive this "gift of life." Even after Christmas is over, I think I'll continue with this practice, knowing an hour of my life, and part of my blood, can help others.

While delivering food wasn't as great as I'd hoped, I found a new way to use my truck as a moneymaker. Who knew so many people would pay for me to haul unwanted items to the landfill? I suppose it saves time for other people. I learned a lot with my first customer. For instance, it costs money to use the dump. More if you're getting rid of old televisions or paint. After the first trip, I let customers know there would be additional charges if their items fell under one of the "extra expenses" listed by the landfill. It didn't seem to affect business. It's a dirty, smelly job and people don't want to do it.

I doubt I'll continue this service once I've earned enough for my mom, but it's nice to know there's something to fall back on if I ever need it. And it might be nice to pad my income since Bookstore Clerk is not a high paying position. But it's hard to put a price on happiness and that's what this job provides.

I've just finished another rambunctious story time session. The kids loved the snowman-themed books, *Snowmen at Night* by Caralyn Buehner being the favorite by far. Not that I was surprised. Who doesn't love searching for hidden cats, bunnies, and T-Rexes? We, of course, sold out of our copies afterward.

Once the toddler and preschool crowd has dispersed from the store, I head back to the break room for some water and an energy bar. Being gregarious for half an hour while receiving all that little-kid energy requires a refuel and a few minutes in a quiet room. Retrieving my phone, water, and snack from my locker, I plop down in a chair at the table.

There's a missed call from a local number on my screen. Whoever it was left a message. Unknown numbers don't get returned without one. And even then sometimes I still don't call back. I hit the play button and Meredith's voice in my ear makes the hair on my neck stand up. What does she want? Her message only asks me to call back to a specific number. The monotone of her voice gives nothing away and I call the number, mostly out of curiosity.

I hadn't expected to hear from her again and wonder why she'd contact me now. Especially sounding so serious and professional. Did I forget to return something to the Arboretum when I got fired? The hat! That stupid green Santa hat is somewhere in my apartment. If she wants that back, she'll have to come get it herself.

"Hello, this is Meredith Larson."

Hearing her voice again, my heart thuds loudly against my rib cage. Settle down, Brett. This is just a work-related call. It's not like she's about to ask me out or anything. Though, technically, there's nothing to stop us. She's not my boss anymore. Of course, she also fired me, so that's bound to make things awkward between us for the foreseeable future.

"Hello?"

There's a hint of concern in that one word and I realize I haven't yet responded. "Hi, sorry, this is Brett Jacobs."

"Brett, hi. I'm so glad you called." Her tone immediately warms and my body perks up at that detail. "We discovered the true culprit responsible for the missing beverages, and we've fired them. I'm so sorry you were falsely accused. Please accept my sincerest apology for all your troubles."

I'm glad that my name's been cleared, but it doesn't help with my money situation. Still, it feels good to know at least Meredith knows the truth.

"Thanks."

"So…I don't want to be insensitive to the delicate nature of the situation, but I'm also wondering if you'd consider coming back to work at the Arboretum. We'd love to have you for the rest of the season."

Disappointment thuds in my chest. Mentally, I knew this was a work call, but a tiny part of me had hoped maybe it wouldn't be only about business. There are only two weeks left in the year, but working there would be better than hauling junk. Plus, I could still do that and donate plasma in any windows of free time I have. I've scraped together almost twenty-five hundred dollars, but I don't know if that's enough to cover everything Mom's car needs. A little more cushion wouldn't hurt. Speaking of hurt, I can't resist making a dig at my old employer.

"I don't know. Are you sure you can trust me to work in the cocoa shack?"

As soon as the words are out of my mouth, I regret them. I can't fault them for following the evidence they had at the time.

"Joanne was adamant that the wrongdoer be dealt with

immediately. I didn't think you were guilty of stealing, but I didn't have any proof to back it up. But since you brought it up, we're hoping you can fill a different position that was recently vacated."

Her belief in my innocence is refreshing. It *was* Joanne who accused and fired me. I guess Meredith was the needed HR witness for the event. That must have been extremely uncomfortable for her. But my mind hones in on her last sentence. The way she said it gives me a bad feeling.

"Which position is that?"

"We'd like you to be our Santa Claus."

My stomach drops, but so does the penny. "Connor was the one who sabotaged me, right?"

There's a beat of silence. "Legally, I'm not allowed to say anything about the incident."

That's all the confirmation I need. Who else would have done it? But why? Probably just because he's never liked me. Why did he steal my girlfriend in college? I've never figured it out. He's just a selfish person, I guess. It's one of the reasons I've been worried about Meredith. Though, I suppose if he got fired, they're probably not seeing each other. If they ever were. Which means my return to Winter Lights would be much more pleasant. No Connor *and* lots of time working with Meredith since she plays an elf? Sounds nearly ideal.

Still, it was a blow to my ego when I was unceremoniously fired. Part of me wants to do whatever I can to help Meredith, but the other part is holding a grudge that she didn't fight for me.

"I can't do it."

"Please, Brett. You'd be doing me a huge favor. I know you explicitly asked not to be placed in that role when you interviewed, but I've seen how good you are with kids. You're the only one I trust to jump right in and do a good job."

Wow. Okay, I didn't expect to be flattered like that. It's a good thing Meredith doesn't know how much she affects me. I've noticeably missed her bubbly personality and quirky sense of humor these past couple of weeks. Her smile sort of burrowed itself into my memory and now it's like I need to see it just to have a good day. But it doesn't escape my notice that I'm being asked out of desperation. I bet if she had any other avenue, she'd pursue it. This thought gives me fuel to stick by my refusal.

"I appreciate the compliment, but I have to pass. Sorry."

I hang up before my resistance is worn down by Meredith's sweet voice and enthusiasm. I haven't heard from her since I was let go, which makes me think we were nothing more than co-workers in her eyes. Which is fine, but returning to work with that knowledge would only make things more difficult for me. While I would have liked the opportunity to make more money for my mom's car fund, sometimes self-preservation is more important.

❄❄❄

My conversation with Meredith has been stuck in my brain since we hung up a few days ago. I know my response to her inquiry was made hastily, my emotions doing most of the deciding. After several days of thought, though, I'm no longer satisfied with my flat refusal to help Meredith out.

Yes, Connor got me again, but not filling his position does nothing to balance the scales between us. The best thing I can do is just forget about him and move on. His deceitfulness finally caught up with him and I should be satisfied with that, though I doubt it'll have any lasting effect on his character.

No, the only person who may have been stuck in a hard spot by my rash decision is Meredith. She's the one responsible for staffing Winter Lights and the successes and failures will reflect on her. The thought that my grudge-fueled decision may jeopardize her opportunity to go after a job she wants has been a constant thorn in my side. I know I said we're only co-workers, but I feel like we'd at least crossed the bridge into friendship, and a genuine friend wouldn't let someone down if they could help it.

I've had a vendetta against Santa for a long time, but my mom's words about not letting the past dictate my present seem to have been working their way into my heart. Filling the Santa role doesn't mean I'm following in my father's footsteps and it certainly doesn't predicate me becoming an unfaithful jerk as well. Okay, so maybe I still have a ways to go on the forgiveness front, but this is a step I can take for myself.

I pull up Meredith's work number from my call history and press the button. While it rings, my stomach twists with nerves. Will she be happy to hear from me? Grateful for my change of heart? Or am I "out of sight, out of mind?"

"This is Meredith Larson."

"I'll do it." The words rocket out of my mouth before I lose my nerve and change my mind.

The line is silent for a few seconds. "Who is this?"

I close my eyes and shake my head. Brilliant, Brett. "Oh, sorry. This is Brett Jacobs."

"Hey, Brett. How can I help you?"

"I'm calling to say that I'll fill in as Santa." The silence on the other end makes my heart race. Did they already find a replacement? "That is, if you still need a replacement."

"We've been using Jerry, the guy who filled in on our regular Santa's days off."

Oh. They don't need me. I suppose that's a relief, but it doesn't explain the pang of disappointment in my gut. "Okay, great." Time to get off the phone and end my humiliation. "I guess you're all set, then."

"Brett?"

"Yes?"

"Why are you volunteering to be Santa now?"

"Uh…" Do I tell the truth? Maybe one part of the truth. "I felt bad about refusing, knowing it might be challenging to find a replacement this late in the game. I want your tenure at Winter Lights to be a success, so I thought I'd try to ease your burden, but I guess I don't have to."

"Actually…"

My heartbeat pounds in my ears at the hesitation in her voice. "Yes?"

"Jerry doesn't seem to be a good fit for full-time Santa work. Once a week, he's great with the kids. He's patient and understanding and jolly as all get out. But interacting with kids four days in a row has worn him thin. I'm worried he's teetering on the edge of a mental break."

"Yikes."

"I know. So, really, if you're willing to replace him, I'd be very appreciative."

The hope in her voice spurs me on.

"Of course, I'll do it. It's why I called, right?"

I have to yank the phone away from my ear when Meredith squeals with joy. My mouth curves into a wide, pleased smile. "Thank you, Brett. You're the best!"

"I don't know about that." *But you're more than welcome to keep telling me that. Perhaps at dinner one evening?*

Reality slams into my chest. We're co-workers again. Nothing about this conversation has given me hope she sees me as anything more. Better rein it in for another couple of weeks until we're officially free of a potentially prickly situation. I can use the time to show her who I am, find out more about her, and possibly even convince her to give me a chance on the dating front. Time to turn on the Jacobs charm. Wait, do I have that? Well, I'll try to smile more around her. Maybe that'll work.

26

Meredith

MY BODY DANCES with nervous energy. I'm trying to keep it under wraps, but I'm just so excited about seeing Brett tonight. I was thrilled when he called and offered to play Santa. His initial refusal was understandable. Even I would have been hesitant to return to a place where I'd been unceremoniously fired. It shouldn't have been that surprising he changed his mind since I know he's kind and generous just from the little time I've been around him. He talks so much about his mom that I know he's a good person.

It's still hard for me to believe that Connor set him up, even with the indisputable evidence. I knew he was a little too self-focused, but still. Why would he actively try to get rid of someone he hardly interacted with at work? I'm still thankful for Genesis's quick thinking. I know it wasn't completely altruistic, as she was obviously hurt when things with Connor fizzled out, but I'm not complaining about the motive.

She approached me after work one evening, saying she'd overheard Connor bragging to a few guys about what he'd done. I told her that word of mouth wasn't enough proof to take action. She then pulled out her phone and showed me the video she'd recorded of the conversation. Not only did Connor admit to stealing beer on his days off, but that he'd also put the alcohol in Brett's truck. I had her send the video to me so I could show Joanne.

The most interesting part of the video, to me at least, was when he revealed his motive. Apparently, Connor thought Brett was interested in me and didn't want Brett dating me after I'd turned him down. It's unfathomable to me that a person would ruin someone else's reputation because someone they liked might be into someone else. Some people's consciences work differently than mine, I suppose.

Connor initially denied the allegations until we showed him the video. Then he just shrugged, like it didn't even matter. Curiosity got the better of me and I asked him why he'd go to all that trouble when there were plenty of other people interested in dating him. His answer floored me. He said it was a fun challenge for him to steal women away from other guys, even bragging that he'd been successful with one of Brett's girlfriends in college and wanted to see if he could still do it. What a jerk.

We're definitely not hiring him ever again. Not that he even needed this job. I guess it was just something fun to do. Probably a new way for him to meet women.

I get now why Brett didn't care for him. I wouldn't either if someone interfered with my relationships. Especially now that I know what happened with his parents. It's the reason he's so fiercely loyal to his mom. They've both been in the same boat. I bet whoever Brett ends up with will benefit from his unwavering devotion. Could that person be me?

I'm definitely interested in applying for the position of Brett's girlfriend, though I still can't read him well enough to know what he thinks of me. Connor obviously thought Brett liked me, but I can't trust anything that comes out of Connor's mouth or goes through his misguided brain. Luckily, I don't have to see him again.

Brett enters the lobby of the Baker building and I pick up the plate of cookies I baked to welcome him back and thank him for saving my rear by taking over the Santa job. I realize that's a lot for one plate of cookies to represent, but it was the first thing I thought of. I rush over toward him, the foil-topped plate cradled in front of me.

"Hi, Brett. I baked you my famous white chocolate macadamia cookies, complete with sugar glaze and a cranberry garnish."

I whip off the foil and extend them toward him, marveling at how cute they look. Brett's eyes widen and he takes a step back, his hands coming up as a shield. I quickly pull the plate back, confused.

"Uh, thanks, but I'm allergic to macadamia nuts."

"I'm so sorry. I didn't know."

I spin around so my back is to him and try to re-wrap the foil around the plate.

"It's okay. I'm only in trouble if I ingest one. I appreciate the effort, though. Normally I really like cookies."

He walks around to face me and expertly fits the foil back over the plate. I look up at him, grateful for his kindness.

"What cookies are your favorite?"

"You don't have to bake me cookies."

There's warmth in his eyes, like he's humored by me.

"I want to."

He nods. "I can never say no to kiss cookies."

Did he just say something about a kiss? My eyes zero in on his mouth, thoughts of what it would feel like against mine drowning out everything else. One corner of his mouth quirks up and I wonder if it's because I've been quiet too long. What were we talking about again? Oh right. Kisses. I mean, cookies. "What's a kiss cookie?"

"The ones with the Hershey's Kisses on them. Is that not what you call them?"

"I assume you're talking about peanut butter blossoms, which

I'd think you wouldn't be able to eat."

He shakes his head. "I'm not allergic to *all* nuts, just macadamias."

Huh. Food allergies are interesting. I would have assumed all nuts were off limits. I make a mean peanut butter blossom, but I kind of like his name for them better. My eyes wander back to his lips. Definitely kissable. I dart my gaze away, hoping he didn't notice.

"I'll bring you some tomorrow."

"Thanks. Nice outfit, by the way."

I look down and am startled by the bright red fabric of the dress I'm wearing. I'd forgotten that I'd put on a red dress instead of my usual green elf costume. That Brett noticed makes me feel good, but also self-conscious. Will he figure out I did it to match the Santa suit? I sure hope not. It's my subtle attempt to show Brett I think we'd go well together.

I suppose I should just tell him, but I don't want him to feel pressured to date me so he can keep his job. Not that I'd fire him if he turned me down, but I need to know that he *wants* to date me and not worry that he's only doing it out of some sense of obligation. I'll focus on laying more groundwork, see if he makes the first move. If not, maybe I'll straight up ask him out when Winter Lights ends. My eyes widen at the thought, my heart beating faster. I've never asked a guy out before. Okay, so technically I invited Brett to the Biltmore, but that wasn't really a date. The panic fluttering in my chest makes me sympathetic toward all the guys who've asked me out in the past. Who knew it was so nerve-wracking? Yeah, a couple more weeks to gather my courage can't hurt.

After the pre-work meeting, we all head to our spots. I walk up to the Education Center with Zach, Genesis, Ava, and Brett. The two women help me get Brett into costume.

My stomach twists with nerves, wondering if this is going to work out like I hope. Brett settles into the sleigh seat, the parts of his face not covered by the beard conveying a feeling of doubt. *Yeah, I feel the same, Brett.*

When the first child enters the line, Brett's face brightens, and he transforms into a warm, jolly Santa. The tension in my gut eases, and I marvel at how he just jumps right into character. An hour flies by and I haven't stopped being amazed at how great he is in this role. He's even better than Connor, probably because he seems much more genuine in his interactions with the children. It's so obvious he loves kids. Definitely a necessary quality in a Santa Claus. *And in a potential marriage partner.*

The thought makes me freeze. Who said anything about marriage? I can't even ask a guy out. How can I tell him I want a big family? But I do. I have no idea if that's something Brett might want, but it doesn't really matter at the moment. Though it would be pointless to date someone who doesn't want kids. Maybe I can find a way to bring it up in conversation. If he says he doesn't, then I can stop worrying about it and concentrate on getting rid of my growing feelings for Brett.

I force myself to focus back on the task at hand, but my concerns continue to play in the background of my mind. *Surely only someone who wants a family would champion starting a story time at the library. And volunteer to run it.* Wow, I guess I know which way my mind hopes Brett falls.

27

Brett

MEREDITH TEXTS ME just as I'm getting home from my day at Page Turner Books.

Meredith: It's trivia night! Are you in?

I had fun the last time I went. There's no chance Connor will be there. It might be nice to spend some more time with my co-workers. A specific person's presence is obviously an added incentive. Sure, we see each other every evening at work, but we're busy making sure the guests have fun. There's not much time for small talk amongst ourselves. Plus, Meredith did bake me some out-of-this-world kiss cookies. It'd be rather rude of me to turn down her invitation.

Brett: I'll be there.

She responds with a bunch of emojis that I take to mean she's happy I said yes. I change out of my bookish Christmas shirt and into my favorite black hoodie with Metalhead's logo on the front. I squirt my chest with cologne, knowing I may sit close to Meredith tonight.

When I arrive at Nothing But Wings, it takes two laps around the parking lot before I find an open space. Heading inside, I spot Meredith at the same table, but she's all alone. I wave and make my way over, dodging people and scooting past tables until I reach her. I slide into the curved booth.

"Where's everyone else?"

Meredith shoots me an apologetic look. "Everyone else has plans tonight. Apparently, it's a popular Christmas party night."

"You can't tell from the looks of this room."

She giggles, and my chest puffs up from being the cause. Not that what I said was particularly witty. Still, I'll take it. I settle back against the booth's cushion.

"If you want to bow out, I understand."

I shrug. "No way. My mouth's been watering for garlic wings since you texted."

Her shoulders relax. Guess I gave the answer she was hoping for. "Okay, cool."

A server appears, and I order a beer. Meredith asks for a ginger ale. I take the opportunity to ask her something I've wondered since last trivia night. "Do you not drink at trivia nights to stay sharp or…?"

Meredith flinches, surprising me. What did I say? I quickly backtrack. "You don't have to answer that."

"No, it's fine." Her voice wobbles a little. "You remember me saying my brother died in a car accident?"

I nod. It was the night I learned about her tattoo.

"Well, what I didn't say was that his car was hit by a drunk driver."

Her chin trembles, and I reach across the table, covering her hand with mine. She lifts her free hand to brush a tear from her cheek and my heart hitches at her emotion. She stares at our hands for a beat before pulling her hand from under mine, blinking and shaking her head. "Sorry about that. It seems ridiculous that I still get emotional."

I shake my head. "It's not. You're allowed to feel any way you want. Loss of any kind is hard, but I don't think you ever really get over losing someone you love."

She gives me a grateful smile. "Yeah, I think you're right." She clears her throat. "Let's talk about something else."

"Sure." I cast around for something new to talk about. "Anything new on your search for a full-time job?"

"I had an interview in New York City about a week ago."

I don't like the idea of Meredith moving so far away, but I'm sure it's a wonderful opportunity for her. "Oh yeah? How did it go?"

"I liked the interviewers and was impressed by the company itself. And seeing the big city during the Christmas season was outstanding."

It sounds like there's something she's not saying. "But?"

She grins, like she's been caught out. "*But* it's really expensive to live there and I've never lived away from my family."

"Sounds like you need to make a pro-con."

"A what?"

"You know, a list of pros and cons."

She rolls her eyes. "I don't even know if I'm going to be offered the job."

I shrug. "Still, it's good to be prepared."

Retrieving my phone from my pocket, I quickly create a spreadsheet, typing Pro and Con at the top of two columns.

"Alright, hit me with a pro."

She gives me a skeptical look. I challenge her with a raised eyebrow, and she slumps back against the booth in reluctant acceptance.

"Fine. Uh, nice people."

It's generic, but she's new at this, so I let it slide. "Normally I like to go back and forth, but we can do pros first and then cons if you prefer."

"Let's stick with pros. Let me think. Christmastime in New York is exceptional."

I roll my eyes, but it's not my list, so I add it.

"I'd be using my degree, which would make my family happy."

This strikes me as an odd thing to say, but maybe they paid for her schooling and she wants them to feel it was worth it. I can understand that. I type it in, keeping my fingers poised over the keyboard for her next entry. When Meredith's quiet for a bit too long, I look up at her. She shrugs at me.

"Okay, let's move to the Con side. We can come back later. Obviously, it's outrageously expensive." She nods and I type it in. "You also said it's far from family which, depending on the family, could be a pro or a con."

She chuckles, and my heart thumps its pleasure at the sound. "Yes, that's a con. Another con—it's colder and gets more snow up there."

I add it, then pause. "You seem like someone who would like snow. I can see you making snow angels and building snow families. Wouldn't that be a plus?"

She shoots me a challenging look. "You're supposed to be on my side."

"I am." *I'd really love for you to stay, but I can't sway you selfishly.* "The Pro-Con list helps you be unbiased in your decision making."

"Humph."

She extends her hand toward my phone, and I set it in her palm. She turns it so she can read the list. "There's an even number on both sides."

"Did you finish with the con side?"

"No. I'd have no friends up there. I'd never see my new nibling. No more Winter Lights or trivia nights." She waves her hand around the room for emphasis, her voice rising with emotion. "No family dinners on the weekends. No one to go sightseeing with. I'd have to learn the transportation system—"

"Whoa, Meredith." I slide around the bench, grab her hand, and squeeze it in what I hope is a reassuring gesture. "It's okay. If you'd hate living in New York City, you don't have to take the job if they offer it."

She swings her gaze to me, distress etched clearly on her face. "But I *do*. My sister got me this interview and my brother always talked about moving to New York after he graduated. My parents are so excited about this opportunity. I can't let them all down."

Her reasoning doesn't make sense to me. There's something she's not saying and I can't get all the pieces to fit together. "Meredith, what's going on?"

"What do you mean?"

"I know you love your family, but why are you making decisions about *your* life based on what *they'd* like?"

She opens her mouth, but then closes it again, her forehead crinkling in thought. Finally, she shakes her head, tugging her hand from my grasp and hunching over my phone. I lean over her shoulder in time to see her text the list to herself. She places the phone down on the table. "You wouldn't understand, but thanks for trying to help. I'll figure it out." She looks around like she's searching for a way out of this conversation. "I'm going to visit the restroom. If our server comes by, will you order me some ranch garlic wings and calamari?"

She slides out of the booth and disappears before I can respond. I'm stunned, wondering what just happened. When fifteen minutes go by and there's still no sign of Meredith, I start to worry. I'd be more concerned if her purse wasn't still at the table. The Quiz Master gives a last call for teams to join the trivia game. A quick look at the television screen shows me Meredith didn't sign us up yet, so I quickly download the app and add Merry Quizmas to the list of competitors, though it pains me to use her groan-inducing team name. Meredith slides into the booth just before our server appears with our food and right as the Quiz Master starts his welcome speech.

She smiles at me, though it doesn't reach her eyes. Thankfully, things loosen up between us once the game gets going. Between the two of us, we get most of the answers correct and earn another gift card which more than covers our tab since there are only two of us. We seem to be back on solid ground again, so I venture back into personal question territory.

"Does your quiz team only play during Winter Lights, hence the name?"

"I play year-round. The rest of the year my team name is Never Gonna Quiz You Up." My groan elicits a genuine smile. "Sometimes I can convince my sisters to join me, otherwise I put out a call to friends to help fill the table."

There's no doubt she'd fare just fine on her own, so I suspect she just does it to spend time with people. "Are you open to other team names?"

She quirks an eyebrow and there's a twinkle in her eye. "Why? Are you interested in becoming a regular member?"

Is she flirting with me? "Maybe."

"Maybe, huh? You definitely know your trivia, so I'd consider giving you a standing invitation, depending on your name suggestions." She's leaning forward on the table, absently swirling the straw in her nearly empty glass. Her relaxed posture and teasing smile beckon me closer. Her voice drops to a conspiratorial whisper. "The rule is the name has to be punny."

She's definitely flirting with me. I ache to slide around the bench, but my thoughts are definitely veering into the more-than-friends category and, if I act on the desire to be closer to her I don't know that I'll be able to stop myself from doing more. Instead, I try to concentrate on coming up with something that fits her punny rule.

"How about Skilli Vanilli?" I laugh as soon as I say it, hearing how terrible it is out loud. "No, never mind. Ignore that. Let me think. Oh, I know! Risky Quizness!"

Meredith grins. "I'd be willing to consider that one. Not bad, Jacobs."

Her use of my last name serves as a reminder that she's off-limits to me. For right now, at least. I realize I'm staring at her mouth. Her lips are moving, but it's suddenly gotten louder in here. Music is playing over the speakers and chair legs scrape across the floor. I motion to my ear and shake my head. She slides around the bench and my chest pulses with the rapid beat of my heart at her closeness. She leans in, her lips brushing the shell of my ear, and heat shoots up my neck at the contact. "It's too loud in here."

She pulls back and I nod, motioning that I'm ready to get out of here if she is. The doors shut behind us, cutting off most of the noise. Outside is refreshingly quiet. And also chilly. I flip up the hood of my sweatshirt and stick my hands into my pockets. "Where are you parked?"

"I'm around back. You?"

"Same." We walk behind the building and find we're parked right next to each other. I stand next to my truck, looking over the hood of her car to where she stands at her driver's side door. I search for something to say because I'm not quite ready to end my one-on-one time with Meredith. She beats me to it.

"Can you believe Christmas is only two days away? It got here fast."

"Yeah, I guess working two jobs really made the time fly. Maybe I'll have to do Winter Lights every year."

Meredith perks up, her whole face shining with delight. "You really should. It's such a wonderful experience." She sighs. "I think that's one of the things I'd miss most if I moved away."

Uh oh, we're back to that minefield of a conversation. I stay quiet, not wanting to ruin the pleasantness of the last hour. Thankfully, she asks another question.

"Does that mean you don't mind working Christmas Eve and

Christmas night? A lot of people turn down the job when they realize they have to work on holiday nights."

I shrug. "It's fine with me. I'll spend Christmas morning with my mom and head back in the afternoon."

She smiles. "We'd be happy to have you next year. In any position you prefer." She pauses. "Well, I'm sure the Arboretum would. I can't exactly speak for them since I won't be working for them."

"Have they found someone to fill your position?"

Her smile fades. "No. Joanne has hinted that they might be getting close, but I still haven't seen the job posted anywhere."

Meredith brings her hands to her mouth and blows into them, her breath forming a white cloud. It reminds me we're standing out in the cold, though I haven't noticed the chilly temperature. "Sorry for keeping you standing out here. We should get home."

She blows into her hands again. "Yeah, you're right. Thanks for coming tonight, Brett. It was nice not being all alone."

Her cheeks are pink from the cold, and she looks even prettier than usual. She turns her head and the light above us glints off of her earrings.

"Not a problem. By the way, I like your punctuation earrings. I always look forward to seeing what's on your ears each day."

Meredith touches one of her question marks in her lower lobes. There are exclamation points on her upper ears. "Oh, thanks."

She smiles at me one more time before saying goodnight and ducking into her car. I get into my truck, but just sit there until she backs out and drives off. Wow, what an interesting night. I definitely learned more about her and, with each new piece, my attraction continues to grow. Of course, there's also the mystery of why she feels like she has to take the job in New York if she's offered it. As bad as this sounds, I really hope she doesn't get it. It'd put a cramp in my plans to ask her out. Only nine more days of Winter Lights and then whatever happens, happens. I hope she'll say yes.

Unless she gets the job in New York before then, in which case

I'll keep my feelings to myself. I don't think long distance would work for me. I mean, I couldn't even keep a girlfriend when we lived in the same dormitory at college. How could I expect to keep a woman happy when she's in such an impressive city hundreds of miles away? I'm sure there are tons of good-looking guys in New York who'd be all over Meredith the minute they saw her. Not that I could blame them, but the fear of getting attached to someone and then losing them again is almost too much for me to handle. I've had enough rejection from people I care about for one lifetime.

28

Meredith

THE PHONE RINGS, breaking my flow. I'm tempted to let it go to voicemail until I recognize the area code for Manhattan. My stomach knots with instant nerves. "Hello?"

"Hello, this is Tara Bridges with Sanders Hotel Group. Is this Meredith Larson?"

She sounds very chipper. Does that mean it's good news? "Yes. Great to hear from you, Ms. Bridges."

"Please call me Tara. I'm delighted to be calling you to say we'd like you to be the Hospitality Manager for our Manhattan trio of hotels."

My heart sinks, which is odd because job offers are usually fantastic news. I try to infuse my voice with enthusiasm I don't feel. "Wow, that's great. Thank you!"

"I'm sorry to call you on Christmas Eve, but we wanted to give you time to look over the offer and make a decision. I'll send you an email with the offer details. Please let us know your answer by the first week of January."

At least I have time to mull it over, though I don't really have a choice in the matter. Once I tell my family, they'll be over the moon and I'm not willing to break their hearts. They've experienced enough suffering. "Okay, thank you, Tara. Happy holidays."

"Same to you. I look forward to working with you!"

We hang up, and I sprawl back on my bed, devoid of holiday spirit. Who knew getting a job could kill my Christmas joy? Bringing my phone up toward my face, I see that Tara's already emailed. The first attachment lists the responsibilities I'll have. Lots of computer screen time. A couple of weekly meetings with staff will make up the bulk of my interaction with co-workers. Unless we get a high-profile guest, in which case I get to be their point of contact for the duration of their stay. How frequently does that happen? And what's the protocol if there's more than one high-profile guest? Or VIPs at each of the three hotels under my supervision? Probably the hotel manager, duh.

I move down the page to the list of benefits. Excellent health insurance. A gym membership. Child care services. Very nice starting salary. There's even a stipend for the first year to help offset the cost of housing. I'm impressed.

It's clear that if I do a good job, there are opportunities for advancement. I can't find anything in the email that would be a reason not to take the job. I sigh, resigned to my fate. At least the family will be happy. I'm sure they'll be thrilled that I've apparently figured out my future. It'll be one of my Christmas gifts for them tomorrow.

Speaking of gifts. I sit up and reach for a glove on the bedspread in front of me. Using a small needle, I adjust uneven rows of stitching until the metallic gray glove with flame-red fingertips looks as perfect as if it were machine-manufactured. I do the same to the other glove until I'm satisfied with how it looks. I carry them over to my desk, which has turned into a gift wrap station, sealing them into a small white box. Mulling my paper options, I settle on the buffalo plaid pattern. I cut a piece and tape it around the box, then add red twine and two tiny pine cones. It looks as perfect as what you'd see in a fancy store display. I hope the recipient likes it.

There's a knock on my door before Ali barges in and waddles over to my bed, dropping onto the mattress and using my pillows to support her back against the headboard.

"Make yourself at home," I say, shaking my head.

She rubs her belly. "I can't believe I still have three more weeks of walking like a penguin. I don't think Baby Fredrikson has any more room in there."

I sit next to Ali and rest my hand on the apex of her abdomen. Something pulses against my palm and I look up to Ali in surprise. She grins at me. "See? I think the baby is ready to come out and meet everyone, too."

I smile, leaning down and pressing a kiss to my sister's stomach. Then I rest my cheek there, smiling when I feel something slide across it. Is that a foot? "We're all ready for you, Little Fredrikson. We love you already."

"You're going to be such a great aunt, Mel. Babysit whenever you want. Rich and I will probably welcome some time alone once we're a family of three."

My stomach twists, dreading having to break the news to Ali that I won't be around to offer free babysitting. I'd love nothing more than to steal my nibling away for some one-on-one time, but it'll be impossible from seven hundred miles away. I'm not ready to shatter this idyllic image just yet, so I keep quiet. When Ali yawns, I sit up, a question popping into my head.

"Not that random pop-ins from my sister are bad, but is there a reason you came upstairs?"

She yawns again. "Oh yeah. I'm supposed to tell you it's lunchtime, but I think I'm going to stay up here and take a quick nap before I tackle the stairs again."

Ali slides down the headboard until her head hits the mountain of pillows she made. She turns onto her side, cradling her stomach. I grab the blanket off of my desk chair and drape it over her. "I'll fix us both lunch and bring it up to you."

She waves me off. "I'll come down soon. You go ahead."

I turn off the lights and shut the door behind me. Down in the kitchen, Rich and Paige are already sitting at the table with steaming bowls of chili. I kiss Dad's cheek on my way to grab a bowl for myself. "What's the Scoville rating for this one, Dad?"

"Not too bad. I'd say three. Just jalapeños and poblanos today."

Three thousand units are still pretty hot for my timid taste buds. After doctoring my chili with cheddar cheese, sour cream, and corn chips, I take a bite. My tongue tingles with the heat from the peppers. "Pretty good, Dad." I turn to Rich. "You might want to fix something else for Ali, or she might end up having the baby tonight." I pause. "Though she might like that idea."

My dad's the last to sit down at the table. When he does, he fixes his warm gaze on me. "We're looking forward to seeing you tonight at Winter Lights."

I perk up. "You're coming tonight? Yay!"

"Well, your dad and I will certainly be there," my mom says. "It depends on how Ali's feeling later. She may be too exhausted to walk around."

I nod. "Completely understandable. She's napping in my bed right now, by the way."

"Where can we find you?"

"I'm an elf tonight, which means I'll be in the Education Center. You should definitely come see Santa. We've got a great one this year."

Should I formally introduce Brett to my family? It's not unusual for me to introduce my parents to new friends. Though they might try to read something into it since it's a male friend. Especially Paige. Though I remember the first time Paige met Brett. *That* was an awkward interaction. I wonder if her behavior embarrassed her the next day or if she doesn't even remember practically throwing herself at Brett. She hasn't brought it up to me, so I'm guessing it's the latter. Seeing him again might jog her memory, though. On second thought, maybe I won't introduce everyone after all and save Paige's dignity.

29

Brett

MEREDITH PULLS ME aside at the Education Center a few minutes before work and hands me a small red and black package. I can tell she's trying to suppress a smile, but she's bouncing on the balls of her toes, giving away her excitement. "Should I open this now or wait until tomorrow?"

"Open it now!" She clasps her hands together, pressing them to her chest.

Oh boy, I better prepare myself to show some enthusiasm for whatever this is, so I don't kill her joy. I untie the string, then stuff it in the pocket of my Santa suit. It feels kind of weird opening a gift while dressed as the Head Gift Giver. I shake my head to get rid of that thought and carefully unwrap the gift. Meredith takes the paper from me, leaving me with a small white box. I open the lid and remove two super soft gloves. They're made of gray yarn with red at the ends and black rectangles near the middle. Kind of a strange pattern, but I suspect she made them herself. The thought of her working on something specifically for me breathes new life into the hope that she'll say yes when I ask her out next week. The smile I give her is genuine.

"Thanks, Meredith. These are so soft. I can't wait to wear them."

"Try them on. I want to make sure they fit."

She takes the box from me, and I slide my hand into the first one. The yarn feels like a warm hug around my hand. I put on the second one, bending my fingers.

"They fit perfectly."

"Now put your index fingers together."

I give her a puzzled look at her odd instructions. She tucks the paper and box under one arm, then grabs my hands and positions them just so. My mouth drops open as I realize what she's done.

"You made me Metalhead gloves?"

Her smile is suddenly shy. "I did."

I look back down at my hands. The black rectangles together form the eye slit for the knight's helmet and the red fingertips are the exact shade of red of the plume in the band's logo. My heart thumps wildly as implications for such a thoughtful gift swirl around in my mind. There's no way she'd do something like this for someone who's just a friend, right? I didn't see her with gifts for anyone else at work. Maybe she's being cautious like I am. She has more to lose than I do because of her position.

"Meredith, these are amazing. Thank you so much."

I pull her into a hug, though it feels awkward with the stuffing in my coat between us. I release her after a few seconds, even though I really don't want to. But we have work to do. "By the way, I have something for you too, but it's at home. I'll bring it tomorrow."

Her eyebrows lift like she didn't expect anything from me. I'm not crafty enough to make something like she did, but I put thought into the gift and I hope she'll see that. Will it be obvious I'm falling for her when she opens it?

The doors open and a family comes in. The child immediately heads my way, so I quickly pull off the gloves and shove them into my pocket. I pull my official white gloves out of the other pocket and put them on, noticing how scratchy they feel compared to the others. Thankfully, my beard is already in place. I step over to the sleigh and settle in. The boy hops up and we chat about my reindeer, the workshop, and what he wants for Christmas.

I really have enjoyed filling the role of Santa. Seeing children light up while we talk has been almost as gratifying as my story times at the bookstore. Being near Meredith for most of the night is also a bonus. More than once I've caught her staring at me, which gives me added confidence for what might happen between us when we're no longer working together.

Three boys are next in line. Two look like they're elementary school age and the third has the too-cool-for-Santa vibe of a teenager. When they're right in front of me, I get an odd feeling of familiarity. They all look alike, so maybe that's what it is. We talk about what they're doing for Christmas and what they hope to find under the tree. When I ask the older kid, he just rolls his eyes.

Jim, the photographer, motions for the kids to turn around for a picture. He calls to the parents to join in. I didn't notice any parents, but it makes sense they aren't here alone. From the corner of my eye, I see two people squeeze in next to the boys.

"Alright," Jim says, "everyone say 'Christmas cookies!'"

A voice to my left makes me freeze, goosebumps rising on my arms. The light from the camera flashes and I wonder if my surprise will show up in the photo. Hopefully, the beard will obscure my expression. The boys step away. Genesis hands a paper to the father, who then turns and holds out his hand to me to shake. Not wanting to alert him, I grab it firmly. We lock eyes and the smile on the man's face morphs into shock. His hand goes slack in mine and I let it go.

"Joshua?" He looks like he can't believe his eyes.

My lips press together and I hold a gloved finger up to my mouth, motioning with my head to the line of kids waiting to see

Santa. He turns to look over his shoulder. When he faces me again, his eyes are crinkled in mirth and he barks out a laugh. "This is rich." He turns to his waiting family and I see Vicky with an arm around each of the younger boys. "Vic, you and the boys go get s'mores. I'll be there in just a minute. I need a word with Santa."

"Okay, Josh. See you in a bit."

When they've gone through the doors, my father turns back to me. "So, Santa, huh? Never thought I'd see you following in your old man's footsteps."

I shush him and beckon him closer, not wanting to alert the kids to what's going on. "I'm nothing like you," I hiss through gritted teeth.

"Still haven't forgiven me, huh?" At least he has the presence of mind to whisper.

"Still don't feel sorry about abandoning us, huh?" It's a cheap shot, but I'm not feeling particularly charitable at the moment, regardless of what I'm wearing. It seems strange to be whispering angry words, but I will not let Meredith down by ruining Santa for the waiting kids. Especially not because of *him.*

Josh winces, and I feel a sting of remorse for retaliating. I should be better than this, not sink down to his level.

"I *am* sorry that I hurt you, but I can't change the past. I'd still like to be a part of your life. Can we have dinner together sometime?"

I'm so mad, all I can do is scoff in response.

"My phone number's the same if you change your mind. It'd be great if you came to the ceremony next week. I know the boys would like to get to know their big brother."

I cross my arms and just resist rolling my eyes. Why does being around my father cause me to revert to a rebellious teenager? "It's a hard pass on the ceremony, but I hope for the boys' sake this vow renewal means something to you."

He frowns. "I suppose I deserve that, but I hope you'll work through your anger. It's not healthy to hold on to negative emotions."

Meredith comes over to the sleigh and puts a hand on my sleeve. "Is everything okay over here?"

My father looks Meredith up and down, then turns to me with a smug smile. "Looks like we have at least one thing in common."

I bite my tongue to keep from saying something I might regret later. Instead, I pick up a candy cane and hand it to him. "Have a wonderful Christmas, sir."

He takes it, nods, and leaves. I stand up from the chair. "Santa needs ten minutes to go feed his reindeer," I announce, then head down the hall, pulling open a door at random, stepping inside, and shutting the door. I yank off the hat and beard and bend over, my breathing rapid and shallow. I pull open my coat, suddenly feeling overheated. I shrug it off my shoulders, letting it drop to the ground, then yank off my gloves.

Bright light pierces the dark space and I realize I'm in a broom closet.

"Brett, are you okay?"

I grab Meredith's hand, pull her inside, and yank the door closed again. I try to step back when I feel her breath on my cheek and realize how close we are in this small room, but my leg hits something solid a few inches behind me. In the dark, I feel her fingers slip into my left hand. Her touch grounds me and my breathing slows and deepens.

She touches my right arm, her hand sliding down my forearm until she's holding my other hand as well.

"Brett, you're sweating. Are you having a medical emergency? Do we need to call the paramedics?"

The concern lacing her voice helps calm me even more. I squeeze her hands with mine. "No, I'll be fine."

"What happened out there?"

I sigh, not relishing the way this conversation is happening. "That was my father and his other family."

She releases my hands, then pulls me into a hug. "I'm sorry.

That must have been quite a shock."

I allow myself to melt into her embrace, my arms wrapping around her waist and drawing her against my chest. Something about her is just so reassuring. She's like my own personal weighted blanket with the way she affects my nervous system.

"Do you want to go home? Maybe I can find someone to take your place."

We both know there isn't anyone else. And I can't let my issues with my father affect my work. "I'll be fine. I just needed a couple of minutes."

"Are you sure?"

Her breath puffs against my neck again, and a shiver runs through me. Even though I'm drenched with sweat, I still feel the warmth of her body pressed against mine in this tight space. I tilt my head down and, with the crack of light coming under the door, can just make out her outline. She's tipped her head up and our faces are only inches apart. A floral scent wafts up to my nose. I didn't know Meredith wore perfume, but it's immediately my new favorite smell. Automatically, my arms flex tighter around Meredith, and she gasps as our bodies press even closer together. I swallow the groan that threatens to escape my throat. All of my nerves are on fire right now. I know I should release my hold on her, but the feel of her in my arms is too strong to resist.

My eyes have now adjusted to the darkness, so I see the moment Meredith's eyes dart down to my mouth. Does she want to kiss me? My brain stutters at the thought. This isn't how I saw things playing out. I've imagined asking her out after our last day of work, making sure nothing looks unprofessional, but I'm now desperate to find out what her mouth tastes like. I close the distance between us, pausing when our lips are millimeters apart to give her a chance to say no. Her breath hitches and her eyelids fall shut. That doesn't seem like a rebuff to me. I close my own eyes; the tension fizzing between us.

Someone bangs on the door, and Meredith emits a strangled

scream. She buries her face in my chest, her arms squeezing the breath out of me.

"Everything okay in there?"

My body tenses. It's Ava. I'd completely forgotten where we were. My head drops back in frustration and I hit it on the wall behind me, groaning. I let go of Meredith to rub the throbbing spot on my skull.

"Brett?" Ava says. "Do you need help?"

My first thought is annoyance at being interrupted by what was to be our first kiss. But my second one, the one telling me it looks like I'm making out with my boss at work, causes a riptide of panic to roar through me.

"No. Thanks. I'm fine, Ava. I'll be out in a sec."

"Okay."

I hear her retreating steps and let out a relieved sigh. There's a loud click and then I'm blinded by light. I throw my hand up to cover my eyes and feel it brush Meredith. Oh, man. This is going to look bad if someone finds us.

Meredith bends down to retrieve my coat, but the space is so tight that her face hits my sweaty torso. She rockets back upright, her eyes scanning from my flushed face down my body. Her hands fly up over her wide eyes and she spins around.

"I'll, uh, let you put yourself back together. I'll wait out here to make sure no one comes in."

She opens the door a crack and squeezes through without a backward glance. I look down. My white T-shirt is plastered to my body. Sweat has turned in translucent, leaving nothing to the imagination. I don't know what Meredith thought, but she left in a panic, which doesn't make me feel great. No one would mistake me for a professional athlete, but I keep myself in pretty good shape. Still, her quick dismissal is a kick to the ego.

I quickly gather my things and put them back on, silently berating myself for being so stupid and letting my emotions get the best of me. I bet she was relieved by the interruption. *So much for the*

Jacobs charm. I open the door and step out, clicking off the light before shutting the door.

A young couple walks by and the man nudges the woman, whispering loud enough for me to hear. "Looks like someone's gotten into the Christmas spirit." She giggles, and he gives me a knowing wink before they turn the corner.

Meredith turns to me, a surprised look on her face and I'm transported back fourteen years. It's the same face Vicky had when I caught her and my father. His words about having something in common rings in my head. Except I don't want to hurt the people I care about, including Meredith.

Rumors of us in closets could affect her career. The only way to ensure she's safe is to stay away from her. We still have over a week of working together left, but if I really care about her and her future, then I should keep her at arm's length until Winter Lights is over. It's the best way to protect her.

"Stay here for a few minutes so it doesn't look like we were together. We don't want rumors spreading about us."

She gives me a confused look. "What?"

"We can't risk people thinking we're making out when we're supposed to be working."

Her mouth opens, confusion turning to shock before settling into an expression that makes my chest ache. Better a little discomfort now than a lot later, right?

"I'd better get out there before the parents and kids get cranky."

I don't wait for a response, not wanting to see the pained look on her face any longer than I have to, instead walking away from her down the hall, fixing a smile on my face before turning the corner and reappearing to the crowd as the jolly old elf himself. Inside, I feel anything but jolly because I've just hurt Meredith with my actions. Even if I'm looking out for her, I still hate the suffering I'm causing her. If only she knew it's because I care about her. I paste on a smile and “ho ho ho” like I’ve got nothing to lose, even though it feels like everything is on the line.

30

Meredith

THE EVENTS OF last night are still swirling through my mind early the next morning. I feel bad about Brett's run-in with his father, not that I was responsible. Still, I know he was blindsided. Their conversation didn't look pleasant, not that I could hear any of it, but Brett's body language told its own story. Who knew foreheads, shoulders, and mouths could say so much without uttering a word? I'm amazed he could recover himself enough to finish the evening. The crowd had no clue he was troubled, though I've been around him enough to recognize the cracks in his cheery facade.

What astonishes me even more was how kind he was to my family when they showed up. Ali made it, but Paige was absent. Rich whispered to me that she got a phone call and disappeared. Ali insisted on getting a photo of their almost family of three with Santa, the start of a new tradition.

When she took off her coat, she revealed a green, long sleeve shirt with a red and white Santa hat resting on top of her baby bump. I laughed out loud and couldn't resist pointing it out to Brett, so he knows I'm not the only Christmas-crazy person in my family. Rich rolled his eyes when Ali insisted he take his jacket off. Somehow she'd gotten him into a Christmas sweater as well, though it was one of those more tasteful ski sweaters, navy with a snowflake pattern around the chest. After the photo, Brett handed my sister a candy cane, which she immediately broke into pieces and stuck in her mouth.

It was great having my family come to support me at work. Mom insisted on a photo of everyone with Santa, including me, saying they'd edit Paige in later. Then they were off in search of the churro stand. Ali swore she could smell cinnamon from Santa's sleigh.

I think Brett and I both did an excellent job of pretending to be friendly, even after what happened in the broom closet. And boy, have I been thinking about that closet.

I followed him to make sure he was okay, but when we were in that small space with our arms around each other, something seemed to click into place between us. While it was dark in there, I don't think I misinterpreted the look on his face just a few moments before Ava knocked. He was going to kiss me and I wanted him to. When I turned on the lights and saw his toned torso through his sweat-soaked shirt, my attraction to Brett intensified. I didn't think muscles did much for me, but man, was I wrong. I wanted to run my fingers along his stomach to feel the ridges between his abs.

However, his bizarre behavior afterward left me confused and unsure of how to feel. Did he get cold feet because he remembered I'm his boss or was that a convenient excuse when the truth is that he's not that into me and just got wrapped up in the moment? His cold dismissal hurt me, but it's probably better to know for certain that my interest is not reciprocated. Just because it looked like he wanted to kiss me doesn't mean he thinks I'm girlfriend material.

With a little time, I could probably accept that we're just

friends, but what if he doesn't even want that? What if all this is just a job for him and, once it's through next week, he doesn't look back and forgets everything associated with Winter Lights? Including me.

Whatever the reason for the about face in his attitude toward me, I'm worried things might never get back to the easy friendship we'd developed after the last trivia night. We make a pretty fierce trivia duo. Doesn't that count for something? Maybe things will be back to normal this evening. I can only hope. It *is* Christmas, after all.

Which means today's the day I get to tell my family I was offered the job in New York. Womp womp. The clock tells me it's only six, but I've hardly slept and I'm way too anxious to fall back asleep. Might as well do something useful.

I head down to the kitchen, avoiding the squeaky stair near the bottom of the staircase, and flip on the coffee machine. Pulling a pot from a cabinet and milk from the fridge, I turn on a stove burner for my famous homemade peppermint hot chocolate. Most of the family prefers strong coffee on Christmas morning, but Ali has valiantly cut back on her caffeine consumption for the baby, so I'll drink cocoa in solidarity with her. Unless my lack of sleep catches up with me, in which case I may take a carafe of caffeine with me to work this afternoon.

While the milk warms up, I preheat the oven, then slide in the breakfast casserole and cinnamon rolls Dad made last night per tradition. With the rest of the house still quiet, I find a notepad on the desk in the kitchen and think about what I'd like the next year to look like. I definitely want to have a full-time job I love. Perhaps I can find some good things about the New York position. I could go to a Broadway show every week until I've seen them all. Of course, that may get expensive. Though I think there are places to get discount tickets. And, of course, that has nothing to do with my actual job. Maybe I can find ways to spend more time with people. Make the job more people-centric.

I pause my list making once the milk is heated to add the other ingredients until it tastes perfect, then pour some into my favorite

Christmas mug, a green and red design with Rudolph the Red-Nosed Reindeer from my favorite childhood Christmas movie. I'm definitely taking it with me when I move out.

By the time breakfast is ready, my parents have appeared in the kitchen for coffee and I've got a pretty respectable list.

Tasks for the New Year

1. Love my full-time job
2. One-on-one time with my nibling/babysitting for Ali and Rich
3. Go out on three dates
4. Create a new item for MerryDesigns (possibly something non-Christmas to determine demand)
5. Travel somewhere new (Santa Claus, Indiana?)

I look it over, hopeful that everything will come true. I'm ready for change and growth and my list reflects that.

Rich and Ali come through the door and I grin at my sister's bed head hair. "Sleep well, sis?"

She yawns and nods. "Yeah, actually. Best night I've had in a while. Didn't even feel Baby Fredrikson much."

She ladles herself some hot chocolate, then sits down at the table next to Rich.

"Well," Mom says, "who knows when Sleeping Beauty will join us? Let's eat while the food's still warm."

We've all gotten plates and sat down when Paige comes through the doorway. "Thanks for waiting for me," she says, heading straight to the coffee. She pours half a cup, then ladles some of the hot chocolate on top. She sees my puzzled face. "What? It's a homemade mocha."

I shrug, cut off a piece of cinnamon roll, and pop it in my mouth. When the warm cream cheese icing hits my tongue, I sigh. Now *this* makes it officially Christmas. My dad found a recipe for cinnamon rolls that taste just like the ones from that place in the mall and has made them every year for Christmas. It's the only time I eat them and I'm already eyeing the pan for seconds, even though I know I'll be stuffed after I finish what's on my plate. Maybe I'll have one for lunch or an afternoon snack.

Once everyone's had their fill, we move to the living room to open gifts. It's supposed to be Ali's year to pass out gifts, but we all know it'd be a struggle to get under the tree in her state, so I volunteer. It's kind of fun having the power of deciding who opens what.

It's no shocker that Ali and Rich get mostly baby stuff. I found something just for each of them so they don't feel like the baby's completely taken over their identities already. I got Ali a gift card for a spa day and a pencil holder for work with sayings on each side. My favorites are the ones that say *As long as everything is EXACTLY the way I want it, I'm totally flexible* and *I'm not bossy, I'm motivational.* She laughs when she reads them, which pleases me.

Rich opens my gift to him, homemade gloves in Carolina Panthers blue and two tickets to the last home game of the season. His eyes light up. "Awesome! Thanks, Meredith." He turns to Ali and leans down to her stomach. "Please don't decide to make your appearance on game day, little one." Ali's eyes go wide. His smile drops. "I'm just joking, hon."

She grabs his hand and squeezes, her face pinching closed. "You probably won't have to worry about that," she pants. "I think it might be time now."

"Are you sure? It could be Braxton-Hicks again."

Her body relaxes, and she motions for Rich to help her up. When she's on her feet, she looks down and we all follow her gaze to the dark stain on the inside of her red pajama pants. She looks behind her, then over to Mom. "Sorry about the couch cushion."

Mom smiles. "The cushion covers are washable. Rich, I think you need to take Ali to the hospital."

"But my bags! I thought we still had time."

I hop up from the floor. "I can pick them up and meet you at the hospital. Just tell me where they are."

"Behind our bedroom door."

After a quick change into jeans and a sweatshirt, I drive over to Ali's house, finding the bags just where she said they'd be, then continue on to the hospital. When I join everyone in the waiting room on the third floor, I text Rich to let him know I'm here and he comes out for the bags, disappearing back through a pair of swinging doors.

I sit down, setting a small gift bag beside me. I'd gotten a little red Santa hat for my nibling, which now seems perfect as he or she will be a little Santa Baby, assuming Ali doesn't labor all day. My plan to tell my family about the job obviously has to wait, not that I mind all that much.

After what feels like eternity, but is actually less than two hours, Rich comes out, a blissful look on his face. "It's a girl!"

I'm thrilled, though I'd have been happy no matter what he said. Rich takes the new grandparents back with him, letting Paige and I know that we're next. Paige has gone back to playing a game on her phone. She's never been a big fan of babies. I remember the hushed discussion about Paige's disappearance the night before and decide that now's the time to bring it up.

"Hey, Paige. I heard you got a phone call last night and disappeared. What happened?"

She looks up from her phone, surprised. "Oh, no big deal. I was offered a job at Global News Network."

"No big deal!" I yell, jumping up from my seat. The nurse at the desk shushes me and gives me a dirty look. I mouth sorry and sit back down, quieting my voice. "Paige, that's awesome. Are you going to take it?"

"I think so. Working at GNN would be a gigantic leap for my journalism career."

I'm excited for her. "Can you do it from here, or do you have to move?"

"They want me to move to headquarters in Atlanta."

The information sinks in. Paige is moving away. It makes sense for her. She's always been up for new things and lots of adventure. I'm much more of a homebody. Which is one of the reasons why, when I think about my job, there's no trace of the excitement that's written all over Paige's smiling face. I pull my sister into a hug. "Congratulations, Paige. I'm so happy for you."

"Thanks, but don't tell anyone. I was going to announce it today, but I think I'll wait a few days so Ali can enjoy the spotlight."

Yeah, same. Only now I have to figure out whether to give Paige her own time to shine or horn in on her celebration. All I really know is I have to tell them before New Year's.

My parents return to the waiting area so that Paige and I can meet our new niece. When I enter the room, a tired but happy Ali is holding a blanket-wrapped bundle in her arms. "Come meet Olivia Hope Fredrikson," she says.

My heart stutters at the name. They named the baby after our brother? My eyes instantly fill with tears. I don't bother to brush them away as they course down my cheeks. "Oh, Ali."

Her face scrunches up with emotion, and she waves at her eyes with one hand. "Stop, Mel. You're going to make me cry."

I wipe my cheeks with the back of my hand and suck in a deep breath to get my emotions under control. Olivia's eyes are closed and she looks so peaceful. My hands itch to grab her and cuddle her to my chest, but instead I hand the bag I brought to Rich. "Here. This seems super appropriate."

He pulls out the little knit hat, made from my favorite brand of super soft yarn, laughs, then exchanges it with Olivia's pink and blue hospital-issued hat. I pull out my phone and snap a photo of Ali and Olivia.

"Do you want to hold her?"

I shove my phone into my pocket, drop my purse, and lather my hands with the hand sanitizer attached to the wall. "Of course."

Rich takes the baby from Ali and sets her gently in my eager arms. Olivia is so precious, I fall instantly in love. I press a kiss to the hat on her forehead and inhale her sweet baby scent. "You and I are going to be best buds," I whisper.

I really don't want to move away now. Even in theory, I knew it'd be hard to put distance between me and my newest family member, but after officially meeting Olivia and cradling her in my arms, it now seems unthinkable. Who's going to teach her how to knit her first scarf? Who will take her out for ice cream sundaes and not make her eat lunch first? Who will share the joy and magic of Christmas with her? Her mother, probably. Still, aunts are important too. I wish there was a way to use my MBA *and* live close to my family. I don't want to let Oliver or my family down.

Now's not the time to worry about job stuff. I push my problem to the back of my mind so I can focus on the miracle in my arms right now. I don't care what may still be under the tree back at my parents' house. This right here is the best Christmas present ever.

31

Brett

JOANNE COMES OUT from her office and gives us a quick speech about focusing on the customers and making sure everyone has a great experience. It's not nearly as encouraging as Meredith's are. But Meredith is obviously not here. I'm pretty sure she's scheduled to work, so the underlying unease I've been feeling since I arrived increases in intensity. Did last night upset her? I know I was pretty gruff after the closet incident, but I'm only trying to protect her. Well, and maybe myself a little as well.

I head up to the Education Center and ask Ava and Genesis if they've heard anything. Genesis shakes her head and gives me a sympathetic look that makes me think she's figured out my feelings for Meredith. Does that mean Meredith knows too? She hasn't pulled away from me if she does. If I was reading her correctly last night, I think she likes me back. She at least seemed to like the idea of kissing me. My heart likes that idea, but I remind myself that I'm putting temporary distance between us for her sake. My feelings don't matter, even if thinking of our almost kiss makes my heart skip a beat.

What matters is not getting her into trouble at work. If only she wasn't my boss. *Just a week longer and she won't be.* But I could still share my feelings with her and say we should wait until after Winter Lights is over to act on them. If I'm wrong about her feelings, it will be a little awkward, sure, but I think she'd admire the way I handled things, my obvious respect for her job, and understand the trickiness of the situation. I'll tell her after she opens the Christmas present I got her. I don't know why I've been so reluctant to take a chance with Meredith. She's worth the risk.

Meredith shows up at the Education Center halfway through the night. She's dressed like an elf, but her mood seems somewhat subdued. There's a faraway look in her eye I can't interpret. She smiles at all the guests and chats pleasantly with the other staff, but I can tell her mind's not all here. She hasn't looked my way much this evening. Maybe that means my antics last night were effective. My stomach sinks at the thought. Now that I've admitted to myself how I really feel, I don't want to play it safe anymore.

I try to focus on connecting with the families, but my eyes keep checking up on Meredith, wanting to make sure she's okay. I feel bad that my behavior last night may be the reason she's off this evening.

By the time we're cleaning up, I can't take not knowing anymore. Meredith's returning brooms to the closet and I follow her, stopping her when she comes out. "Is everything okay?"

She looks around the empty hall. "You're not worried about other people getting the wrong idea?"

I wince. "I deserve that. I'm so sorry about last night. I was worried about compromising your job, but I handled the situation poorly. If I could go back and do things differently, I would."

She shrugs, her face unreadable.

I silently curse myself for causing the awkwardness between us. Still, I press forward. "I can tell there's something on your mind.

You can talk to me."

She frowns. The seconds of silence while I wait for her to respond feel like I'm dangling over a cliff. Will she shoot me down? Did I ruin our friendship with my self-preservation sabotage?

"It would be nice to talk to someone, but this isn't really the place to do it."

Relief courses through me. "What if we meet at the Waffle House nearby when we're finished? I can give you a more thorough apology for my behavior last night."

Meredith nods. "Some hash browns sound delicious."

We drive separately to the restaurant, taking the booth in the far corner from the door. Meredith orders an orange juice and hash browns all-the-way and I ask for a bacon, egg, and cheese sandwich and water.

"Okay, spill," I say when our server leaves.

She looks up and away as if gathering her thoughts, then sighs and her words tumble out. "I was offered the job in New York."

I jerk back like I've just been sucker punched. Meredith's moving to New York? This changes everything. I was going to throw caution to the wind and tell her how I feel, figuring I could endure a week of discomfort between us at work if she didn't reciprocate, but I don't think I could handle a long distance relationship. Losing Lindsay to someone else when we lived in the same city makes me doubt I'd have any chance of keeping a woman's interest when we're hundreds of miles apart. I try not to let any of these thoughts swirling in my head show as I focus back on Meredith.

"But I don't want to go so far away from my niece now that I've met her. Ali had the baby today, by the way. It's why I was late to work. Olivia Hope Fredrikson and she's perfect. And Paige told me *she's* moving to Atlanta for her new job and it feels like I'd be abandoning my older sister and I'll never see Paige because I can't visit Asheville *and* Atlanta and I just *know* I'm going to hate being stuck behind a desk most of my workday. But if I don't go, I'll be letting my family down and I can't do that either. I don't know what to do!"

Meredith drops her head into her hands and lets out an enormous sigh. The server appears and sets our drinks down. Meredith sticks a straw in her cup, then takes a big drink of her orange juice. She grabs the straw paper and tears it into small pieces, balling each one between her fingers until there are half a dozen tiny paper balls on the table between us.

I take a beat to process everything she's just said, deciding to start with the good news, even though the thought of her leaving is shredding my insides like the straw paper on the table between us. "Congratulations on your new niece. That's probably less confusing to say than nibling."

The corner of her mouth twitches and pleases me more than it should. "Also, congratulations to you and your sister on your job offers. Sounds like a bunch of good news at Christmas."

The server plunks our plates down in front of us and all I can do is stare at the mess that is Meredith's order. "What in the world is *that*?"

"My hash browns." She points to various parts of her plate. "Potatoes, onion, jalapeño, ham, tomato, mushrooms, American cheese, chili, and sausage gravy."

I make a disgusted face and she clicks her tongue. "Don't knock it until you try it. It's a delicious late night meal."

"Whatever you say." I am never trying that. "If you don't want to take the job, then don't. What's so hard about that?"

Meredith slumps against the seat, looking at me like I'm as thick as a brick. "The job is *in* New York City *and* requires an MBA."

She speaks slowly like the sentence explains everything, but I'm still clueless. "And that matters because why?"

"Because it was Oliver's dream."

This feels important, but the details are still fuzzy to me. "But why are *you* trying to do something *he* wanted?"

"It's my duty to make his dreams a reality. If I can do it, I should, since he can't. He and I were thick as thieves when I was little, despite our age difference. Neither of my sisters did anything to preserve his legacy, so it's up to me."

Something's still not adding up. "Is this what your family told you? They want you to take a job you seem like you don't want just because it's something your brother would have done?"

She looks down at her plate, picking at her food with her fork. "When I mentioned the idea of getting my MBA, my parents were so excited. They were thrilled about someone fulfilling Oliver's life plan, so I did it. I liked some classes in grad school and think I'd be great at management in the right environment. But this perfect opportunity is in front of me, one that Ali helped set up. I'd be letting everyone down if I don't follow through."

I've only met her family once, so I can't say for certain that they aren't putting this pressure on Meredith, but it doesn't seem like something loving parents would do. And there's no way someone as generous and kindhearted as Meredith would have been raised by inflexible, demanding people. If they knew how miserable this was making her, surely they'd encourage her to turn down the job. I know it's what my mom would do. I feel like I need to say something, but it takes a minute to come up with something that feels helpful and non-judgmental.

"I obviously don't know much about your family," I say, not wanting to make Meredith feel defensive, "but do you think being miserable in a city where you don't want to live while working a job you don't love would honor Oliver's memory? Would he be happy knowing you're unhappy?"

Her gaze shoots up to me, her eyes blinking rapidly, like she can't believe what just came out of my mouth. I kind of can't believe I just said that either. She looks away, sighs, and wipes a finger underneath one eye. "I don't know," she says after a minute of silence.

Way to murder what's supposed to be a joyful day. It's hard to believe it's still Christmas Day. A lot has happened in the past few minutes to fill a week. I ended up not driving up to see Mom this morning like originally planned. She said rather than hurry through the day, we'll celebrate after the New Year when I can come for a full weekend. It gives me a few more days to add to the car repair fund. I lean back, sticking my hand in my jacket pocket, and hit something. I pull it out, surprised that I'd forgotten about it. Like I said, it's been a busy night. Maybe this will help get rid of the morose mood that's settled over our table.

I plop the item on the table next to Meredith's plate. "I almost forgot. Merry Christmas."

She picks up the small gift wrapped in red and white striped paper. It's about the size of a matchbox, so not an impressive presentation. Still, her mouth quirks up into a small smile. "Thanks, Brett."

"Don't thank me until after you open it. You might hate it."

I doubt that's the case. And, even if it is, she'll probably hide her disappointment to spare my feelings because that's the type of person she is. Still, my pulse quickens when she removes the wrapping paper. I really hope she likes it.

Meredith opens the lid of the tiny white box and gasps. Inside is a pair of earrings. Six butterflies connected in a rainbow of colors that climb up the side of the ear. She looks from the box to me and back again. Suddenly she's crying and I don't know why. I slide out of my side of the booth and scoot in next to her, wrapping an arm around her shoulders. She turns her body, burying her face in my neck. I stay frozen like this, unsure whether to pull her closer. Is it something a friend would do or someone who wants to be more than a friend would do?

She lifts her head, grabbing her napkin to wipe under her eyes, and I drop my arm, but can't convince myself to move back to my side of the table.

"Sorry about that," she says, meeting my eyes again. "Brett, these are perfect. Thank you so much."

"You're welcome. I saw them and thought of you. And again, I'm so so sorry about how weird I was last night. I think you're great."

Her smile makes my heart thud with longing. I'm so torn. I really like her, but I don't want to hurt her. *Liar*, my mind interjects. *You don't want to get hurt.*

It's true. I don't want her to take the job in New York. I want her to stay here in Asheville so I can confess how I feel and see what happens, but that's me being selfish. On the other hand, I also want Meredith to be happy and, while I don't know that taking a job to please her family is the right move, I have no right to try to convince her otherwise. If I really care about her like I say I do, I need to get out of her way. Even if that means letting her move away without telling her how I really feel about her. This whole situation stinks. Merry Christmas to me.

32

Meredith

MY RECENT INTERACTIONS with Brett have my head spinning. It feels like I'm living out that Katy Perry song about someone who's hot, then cold. Everything was going well between us until Brett's father showed up on Christmas Eve. Whatever happened that night somehow infected our friendship. Despite the weird interaction in the broom closet that almost felt like the start of something until Brett jerked away, making me wonder if my feelings were one-sided, he seemed more like his normal self the next night at Waffle House. He was the thoughtful, kind, caring person I've seen more and more frequently. I mean, he gave me a beautiful gift—one that showed me he remembered our conversations and noticed my obsession with earrings. Yet, when I wore them the next night, he didn't even notice. Or, at least, he didn't say anything.

What is going on? He's still been polite, but the easy rapport and casual flirting between us has disappeared. I can't believe I actually thought there might be something real between us to explore once Winter Lights was over. At least not worrying about running into Brett around town will be one plus of moving to New York. Though every time I see my niece, my feet want to root themselves to Asheville soil so I can watch her grow up and be involved in all the highs and lows of her life.

I still haven't told my family about the job. There hasn't been a good opening. Paige told the family her news the day after Christmas and I wanted her to get her day. New Year's Eve is only three days away, so it's got to be today. We're all having a late lunch together at Ali's house. Not that she's cooking days after having a baby. Dad volunteered to make sandwiches, but thought it'd be easier if the new family didn't have to pack up to come visit. He practically lives over there right now, anyway. He's really enjoying the retired Pop-Pop life and I can't blame him. I still haven't heard the story of how he settled on that for his official grandfather name. Mom decided on Gram, which I like.

I click over to my MerryDesigns email and am surprised to find over two hundred new messages. Most of them are new orders. One is an alert that I've sold out of an item in my shop and should add more to capitalize on the demand. I've received quite a few custom order requests for scarves and gloves. The volume of traffic to my store is greater than ever. How are all the customers hearing about my store?

Better question, when am I going to find the time to pack and ship all these things? At least it's after Christmas, so there isn't a rush. I click open an inquiry email of someone asking if I can make a Metalhead scarf. That's a strange request. Did Brett show his gloves to a friend who also likes the band? I do an internet search for such an item, but it yields no results. Guess I'd have to figure it out on my own. I make a mental note to take some time to sketch ideas. It'll certainly be a fun challenge.

After making a list of yarn I need to order for custom items, I click over to my favorite website and place the order. I know what I'm doing after Winter Lights is over—lots of knitting. A groan escapes me when I realize that, no, I can't work on orders because I'll be packing up my stuff to move to New York. Will I even have time to manage my Crafty business when I'm working full time? Probably not. The thought of losing my creative outlet is depressing, and I flop onto my bed, despairing of all I'll have to give up in order to make my family's dream come true. Why can't there be a way for all of us to be happy and still honor Oliver? I shift all the pieces around in my mind, trying to make everything fit, but come up empty.

❄❄❄

Lunch has finished and I can tell Paige is itching to get back to her apartment, where she's busy packing up her things. The excitement of a new adventure is clear in her face. I wish I was as happy about my job situation. I take a deep breath, realizing this is the moment.

"Hey, everyone. I have some news. Sanders Hotel Group offered me the New York City job."

Ali squeals. "I knew you'd get it! Congrats, Mel."

At least someone's happy for me. "Thanks. It starts at the end of January, so I'll also be moving in a few weeks."

Ali's enthusiasm wanes. "Oh yeah. Forgot about that part." She snuggles Olivia closer against her chest, kissing her forehead, and my heart aches that I won't be here much longer to see these sweet moments.

"Congratulations, sweetie," my dad says. "We'll definitely miss you, but we don't want to keep you from following your dreams."

There's a hint of sadness in his voice, not at all what I expected. My gaze turns to Paige, whose excited face looks like how I thought everyone would look. "So awesome, Mel. We'll have to visit each other and show off the cool parts of our respective towns."

"Yeah, that'd be fun." My words are right, but my tone doesn't quite match.

"Meredith?" I turn to face my mom. Her eyebrows knit together, letting me know she's got her researcher's brain on. "What are you not saying? Do you not want the job?"

Part of me wants to admit the truth, but a bigger part doesn't want to let my family down. Better find out what she's thinking. "Why do you say that?"

"When Paige announced her big news, she practically deafened us with her announcement. But you're talking about this opportunity like it's a filling appointment at the dentist—something you feel you should do, but don't think will be an enjoyable experience."

Wow. She nailed it. How did I think I could get anything past her? "I'm nervous about leaving home. I'm going to miss being able to see Olivia whenever I want and I feel bad about not being able to be Ali's free babysitter, but this is an opportunity to use my MBA, *and* it's *New York*. If anything is a way to honor Oliver and fulfill his dreams, this is it."

My parents exchange a troubled look with one another. "Oh, Meredith," Mom says. "Is that what this is about? Trying to fill Oliver's shoes? We just want you to be happy."

My face scrunches up in thought. "But you said you hoped I'd turn out just like Oliver."

The furrows in my mom's forehead deepen. "What? Surely we didn't say that."

"I overheard you and Dad talking a few months after his death. You were discussing Oliver's plans for his future and what his life might have looked like after he graduated from college. You talked about him living in New York and excelling in the business world. Then Dad said I was the most similar to Oliver out of all of us kids and that maybe you'd get a glimpse of him through me."

"Meredith," Dad says, "we were grieving. We weren't trying to push you into Oliver's life. We want you to do what makes you happy. Don't squash your dreams for what you think other people want for you."

His words make me pause. I haven't exactly been squashing my dreams, but I've certainly been trying to force them into an Oliver-shaped box. "So you don't care that I got an MBA?"

Mom gets up from her seat at the table and comes over to hug me around the shoulders. "Honey, of course we're proud of you, but we thought you did that because you wanted to, not because of Oliver. You two were close, but you're your own person. If Oliver were still here, he'd want you to find work that lights you up."

Tears spring to my eyes, and I wipe them away. It's what I desperately want to hear, but I feel guilty about it. "But Ali used her contact for me. I just want to make you all proud."

"We love you regardless of what you do," Mom says. "You're part of our family and we want you to make life decisions that are right for you, not because you're worried about us. We'll be supportive of whatever you decide, but make sure it's what *you* want."

Feeling exposed, I slowly look around at the rest of my family, the same warmth and encouragement I feel from my mom reflected in their eyes. "Is that what you all think, too?"

Heads nod all around the table. I reach up and squeeze Mom's arm in gratitude. A weight I didn't realize I'd been carrying lifts from my shoulders. "Okay. Well, I guess I have some serious thinking to do."

33

Meredith

IT'S THE LAST night of Winter lights and I'm feeling all kinds of emotions. Sadness that my role as events director is at its end. Confused about whether I should take the NYC job even after what my family said. Guilt at the fact that I want to turn it down even as I'm grateful for all the help and support my family's given me to get this incredible offer. What if a new start in a new city is something I actually need and I'm just too scared to go for it? Too scared to make a change? But I also don't want to give up my Crafty business, which fills the creative spark inside me.

I've been thinking all day about what makes me happy. Olivia and my family, obviously. Knitting things for others. Winter Lights. A certain someone's face has popped up more than once during my musings. I'm thinking very hard about telling Brett I have feelings for him when work's over. My heart races every time I think about it, but if he's one of the reasons I'm considering staying in Asheville versus taking the job, then I want to know if there really is something between us.

My stomach lurches a little as consider what to say to him. *Hey, Brett. Remember that almost-kiss in the closet? I'd really like to have a do over.* Yeah, right. Whatever I end up saying, my plan is to talk to him at the end of the night. I haven't seen him since the opening meeting. Because Christmas is over and Santa has gone back to the North Pole, Brett is now helping Zach with s'mores. Joanne's had me looking over the finances to get a preliminary look at how Winter Lights has gone and work up a summary of what we can improve for next year. I guess she wants the new hire to know what to expect.

When the evening ends, the crew gathers in the lobby for the farewell speech. Joanne comes up beside me and gives me a smile. "We did it," she says. "Care to do the honors of officially closing Winter Lights?"

I'm momentarily stunned that she's handing this duty off to me. I don't have a speech prepared, but you don't say no to the boss. "Sure, but how do we get everyone's attention?"

The staff is giddy from their last night of work. Laughter and loud voices bounce off the walls of the room despite the late hour. Joanne puts two fingers in her mouth, emitting a sharp whistle that immediately stops all noise in the room. She then motions for me to take the floor.

I straighten my shoulders and smile. "Hey, everyone! You all were outstanding this season. Thank you so much for all your hard work and dedication to Winter Lights. You made it a wonderful success. We couldn't have done it without you!"

Someone whoops, eliciting a smattering of shouts and claps from the group. I find Brett in the crowd and give him a nod, hoping to express my appreciation for him specifically. His mouth quirks up on one side and my stomach somersaults with nerves. I still don't know what I want to say to him. I force myself to look away so I can continue my speech without distraction.

"I hope you will consider returning next year. I'm sure Joanne would love to have you." It hurts a little knowing I won't be part of this next year, but sometimes you have to move on from things that are good to receive something even better. It's just part of life. The thought makes me choke up a little and my next words come out strangled. "I'm so proud of all of you. Thank you for sharing your time and abilities with the Arboretum. Drop your lanyards off in the break room and you are free to go. Happy New Year!"

Ava and Genesis come up and give me hugs, promising they'll still come to trivia nights when they can. Zach gives me a high five and says he wants to do s'mores again next year. I search the crowd for Brett and see him heading for the door to the parking lot. I rush after him, calling his name after I burst through the door to the outside. He stops and turns, giving me the opportunity to catch up. Standing so close to him and looking into his eyes, all thoughts fly out of my mind. He raises an eyebrow, waiting for me to speak. *Think, Brain, think!*

"Brett, hey." So lame. My next words catch in my throat. "You weren't going to say goodbye?"

He swallows and looks away from me. "You seemed preoccupied. I didn't want to interrupt."

"I wouldn't mind you interrupting." I wish he'd look me in the eye again so I could see his reaction, but apparently there's something fascinating just past my right shoulder. Time to dig down and be courageous, despite the butterflies in my gut.

"So, I'm officially no longer your boss!" My voice ends on an excited note. Can he tell where I'm heading? His face is blank, reminding me of how he looked when I first met him. My stomach churns ominously, but I force myself to keep going. "Since we're no longer working together, I was wondering if you wanted to go to dinner with me sometime. Maybe this weekend?"

Brett's jaw ticks, the only movement in his face. What is he thinking? I wish I had telepathy and could know what's rattling around in his brain right now.

"I have plans this weekend. I'm sorry."

I wait for him to offer an alternate night for dinner. Or

something. Anything. That's it? That's all he's going to say? He has plans? ALL weekend?! Doesn't he know how big of a deal this is that I'm making the first move?

Maybe he does, and he's trying to spare my feelings. Oh, no. He's rejecting me? Oof. My face heats at the humiliation. "Oh, okay. I understand."

And I do. You can't help how you feel, or don't feel, about someone. At least he's being kind. It doesn't stop me from desperately wanting to get out of here and lick my wounds in private. But, in the off chance he does actually have plans and isn't just blowing me off, I make one last attempt. If I'm going to make a fool out of myself, might as well be thorough. "If anything changes, call me. I'm free and can also do weeknights. I'm flexible."

"Yeah, sure."

Wow, okay. Loud and clear, Brett. You are definitely not interested. Now thoroughly mortified, I'm ready to get away from this cringe-inducing situation. "I should get back inside. Happy New Year, Brett."

I don't wait for another lackluster response, but turn and rush back inside, my face a flame of humiliation and my heart battered from Brett's rejection.

34

JANUARY

Brett

ONLY A FEW more hours of work at the bookstore and then I'm headed up to Boone for my belated Christmas slash New Year's celebration with Mom. We'll drink mimosas and watch wintery movies, then I'll help her take down her decorations before coming back to Asheville. I'm excited to give her the money I've saved for the past two months. Surely it's enough to cover the repairs. I hate how estimates at car shops work. Supposedly, the repairs could cost less than expected, but that's never been my experience. At least I know the shop she uses won't take advantage of her. She's known the owner longer than I've been alive.

I'm also curious to know when Mom will find out about the sales job. I really hope she gets it. She could charm a leprechaun out of his pot of gold, so I know she'd be great working in sales.

Hopefully, her boss knows that, too.

Rachel is headed my way with a look in her eye that says she's on a mission. "What's up?" I say, when she reaches the checkout counter.

"Have you seen Metalhead's latest Photogram post?"

"You know I don't use social media. Anything I need to find out about them is on their website. Why do I need to know what other people ate for lunch or watch them open boxes of things they bought?"

"There's more than food and shopping on there." She pauses. "Though what I want to show you won't prove my point. However, I think even *you* would say this is an exception."

She hands me her phone, showing a photo of the awesome gloves Meredith knitted for me. I look up. "Yeah, you already showed me this photo. When you took it, remember?"

She rolls her eyes and moves her finger over the screen. "Read the caption. I sent the photo to the band's account, and they posted it!"

Looking back at the screen, I realize the photo was posted by an account called MetalheadOfficial. The message below praises the creativity of the artist and says the band is flattered by the tribute. They even mention MerryDesigns. I assume Rachel passed that information along. Scrolling further down, I'm agog at the hundreds of comments of fans saying they want a pair. "I wonder if Meredith's seen this."

"She's not tagged, so I doubt it. If you know her handle, I can put it in the comments so she'll see it."

I don't lift my head from the screen, but peer at her through my furrowed eyebrows, hoping my face tells her how silly her comment is. She must receive the message because she shakes her head. "One day I'm going to get you caught up with the times, Brett. I'll just screenshot it and send her a message through her business email."

I'm excited for Meredith and hope it leads to new business for her. She makes a quality product. My hands have never been warmer in the winter than they are this year. Yes, I've been wearing the gloves, even though they force me to think of her and remember what I want. It feels like a just punishment for the possibility of having hurt her even a tiny bit.

I was stunned when she asked me out to dinner, but it's my weekend with Mom and there's no way I could cancel on her after skipping Christmas with her. Meredith would understand that. I wanted to say yes so badly, but going to dinner with her won't change the fact that she's moving and I can't do long distance dating. It wouldn't be fair to either of us. Besides, she has a new life waiting in New York City, and I won't stand in her way. Having a long-distance boyfriend would be an anchor for her. Especially an insecure one like me. I know I'd be worried that one day she'd call to tell me it wasn't working out, and she'd found someone new. My paranoia and fear would probably sink our relationship before it really got started.

There's already a Meredith-shaped hole in my life after Winter Lights ended a few days ago and I know it'll grow into a black hole when she moves to New York. Who knew I'd come to enjoy my daily interactions with the spunky, Christmas-loving beauty with crazy earrings so much? She deserves everything she wants. I like her too much to hold her back.

❄❄❄

When I arrive at Mom's house, there's a car I don't recognize in the driveway. Does she have a guest over? I let myself in the locked door, wary of whatever I might find inside. Is she seeing someone and this is how she's going to tell me? As a precaution, I ring the doorbell before stepping inside. It'd be a little weird seeing Mom dating after all these years of being single, but she deserves all the love and happiness she can get.

There are streamers and balloons taped along the walls of the living room and all over the light fixture. Mom's nailed the party atmosphere. I hear scraping in the kitchen, drop my bag by the door, and head through the wall of streamers hanging down from the doorway. An artfully arranged charcuterie board is on the island next to two champagne flutes, a carton of orange juice, and an open bottle of Jacquart, our go-to mimosa champagne. A few years ago, we did a taste test with half a dozen brands and both agreed this one was our favorite.

I hear rummaging in the pantry and decide to announce myself in case she didn't hear the doorbell. "Hey, Mom. I'm here."

"Hey, Brett!"

The rustling and crinkling stops, Mom emerging with a couple of packages of crackers. She's wearing a nice, new-looking gray skirt suit. "Wow, you look nice." I motion to the counter. "Looks like I should have worn a tux instead. I'm definitely underdressed."

I unzip my coat, revealing the tuxedo T-shirt I wear every New Year's Eve. I paired it with black jeans, but Mom definitely has me beat on being fancy.

She sets down the crackers, then pulls me into a hug. "You look perfect. Do you really like my new work outfit?"

My eyes widen. I pull back enough to look her in the eye. She's smiling, her eyes sparkling with delight, and I let out a whoop, my arms wrapping even tighter around her. "Mom, that's awesome. Congratulations!" She pats my back, her signal to end the hug, and I drop my arms to my sides. "I'm so happy for you. When do you start?"

"Monday."

"That's fast."

She gives me a guilty look. "They offered me the job just before Christmas, but I wanted to tell you in person."

I can't be mad at that. I enjoy delivering good news in person as well. Speaking of news… "Whose car is that out front? I thought maybe you had a visitor."

"It's mine. The company gave me a Christmas bonus, which I used to buy a newer car! It's got heated seats and a backup camera. I never knew what I was missing!"

I'm speechless. So much for saving the day. She fills the flutes with champagne and orange juice, then hands me one. She clinks hers to mine and takes a sip. I do the same, still stunned that all my hard work, including my time as Santa, was for nothing.

"Will you take the food to the living room? You can decide which movie we're watching first. I'm going to change out of my suit so I don't spill anything on it before my first day."

Almost on autopilot, I follow her directions, but only get as far as turning on the TV before getting distracted by my thoughts. The couch cushion sinks next to me, but it barely registers. A hand on my shoulder makes me jump. When I turn, Mom has a concerned look on her face. "What's wrong?"

"Nothing, really."

She purses her lips, not buying my answer. "Something's obviously on your mind. Spill."

"It's dumb." She just looks at me expectantly. "When you said your car was in the shop, I was worried not having a reliable car would keep you from getting the sales job, so I got a part-time holiday job to earn extra money. And now it turns out you don't need it."

Mom squeezes my arm. "That was so sweet of you, but you know I'm a grown woman. I don't need you to take care of me."

"But I want to. You worked so hard supporting me through my rebellious high school period and helping to pay for college. I just want to prove that everything you've done for me was worth it."

"Oh, honey. You're my son. I love you. I'll always love you, but I want you to enjoy your life, not worry about me. It's so sweet of you to want to help, but maybe next time ask if I want help before just going ahead with your own plans."

I release a deep breath, knowing what she's said is true. She can take care of herself. I'm not supposed to be her protector or caretaker. "I'm sorry, Mom. You're right."

"Of course I am. Now, tell me, what else is on your mind?"

My brow furrows. "What do you mean?"

"You've been a little sad ever since you got here, and it's obviously not because I ruined your surprise. Does this have something to do with a woman?"

My eyes meet hers, shocked by her keen perception. "How did you know?"

She shrugs. "A mom knows these things. Do you want to talk about it?"

I slump deeper into the couch. "I met someone at work, but she's moving to New York soon."

"Okay…?"

Mom shrugs her shoulders like she doesn't see a problem.

"I'm worried that I won't be enough. That she'll find someone else and dump me."

She wraps an arm around my shoulders and pulls me against her. "Oh, sweetie. There's no way to know what might happen in a relationship. Maybe all the effort it takes to make it work will increase your feelings for one another. You might find that distance only highlights how much you care. Don't give up something potentially great just because you're afraid of something that might not even happen."

Being cuddled by my mom still feels comforting as an adult, but I find it hard to believe her words could be true. "I'm surprised you're still so optimistic about love after what Josh did."

"One bad relationship doesn't negate all the positive ones in my life. Like my relationship with you." She squeezes my shoulder one last time and kisses the top of my head before releasing me. "Since we're on the subject of your father, I heard you saw him."

My body jolts at the sudden change of subject. "What? How?"

She shakes her head. "I do still talk to Josh sometimes. Mainly to give him updates on you since you won't give him the time of day." I open up my mouth, my eyes already narrowing with anger, but she holds up her hand and I swallow my words. "I know, I know. He messed up big time, but I think you should give him a chance.

He'd really like you to get to know your brothers."

"I just don't know, Mom. It's hard to let go of the past."

Her smile is sympathetic. "It took me a long time to get to where I am now, but it feels so much better to forgive than to keep all that anger inside. What happened then is not your brothers' fault. Maybe don't punish them for their father's crimes. They're as innocent as you are."

Her words strike deep and I sit back, processing. I wanted siblings when I was growing up. I could be a positive influence in their lives. It might even be fun to be the cool big brother. "I'll think about it," I say finally.

Mom pats my arm. "Good. I know you'll do the right thing. You are a man of integrity, Brett, and I'm proud to be your mother."

I know she's my mom, but I also know she only says what she believes. It's where my conscience and loyalty come from. Maybe I should release my fear of being like my father when I've spent so long under my mom's influence. I should probably let go of some other fears as well. Like the one keeping me from opening myself up to the possibility of love.

35

Meredith

IT WAS A crazy Christmas and New Year's. I've seen my niece every day since she was born and am counting down the hours until I can visit today. She's not even two weeks old and doesn't do much besides eat and sleep, but I'm definitely wrapped around her pinkie finger. I had no idea how much I liked babies until now. Thinking I want a big family like the one I grew up in is one thing. Interacting with a new member of the family is making it more real and not diminishing my desire one bit. If anything, it's making me antsy to start my own. But then I remind myself I don't even have a boyfriend, and that settles down my hormones some.

I shared my New Year list with Ali and Paige and now they're both trying to get me to join a dating app. I'd prefer to do it the old-fashioned way and meet someone in person, which means finding places where guys I might be interested in would go. So far all I've come up with is trivia night, but it's hard to meet people outside your team. I have been approached by people trying to poach me over to their team, but I'll never defect from the team I founded. The compliment is nice, though.

I think part of the reason I've been slow to really start the dating process is that my heart is still a little wounded from everything that happened with Brett. We didn't date, but there was definitely something happening between us. I mean, those earrings felt heavy with meaning to me. It was one of the most thoughtful gifts I've ever received. Surely, someone who just wanted to be friends wouldn't put so much effort and consideration into a gift. Especially someone who claimed to hate Christmas. Though, maybe giving him the gloves put pressure on him to reciprocate. And boy, did he knock it out of the park!

I still can't believe Rachel sent that picture to the band. That post led to so many new orders. I gave her a knitted hat as a thank you, dropping it off to her at the bookstore. I was a little nervous about seeing another certain person at the bookstore, but he wasn't there. Part of me hoped if he saw me, it might get us talking again. Even though I told him to call me, my phone's been silent.

Rachel told me she shared the photo because Brett had gushed to her about how soft the gloves were and my creative design had impressed her. She also admitted to ordering a bunch of stuff from my site for her and Tom's families, which I found flattering.

The crazy part of all this is that the local news station contacted me about doing an interview to talk about my sudden spot of fame. I agreed, excited about the opportunity for some more exposure, even though I'm already swamped with orders. Maybe one day I'll rent out a space at Woolworth's or Kress and have a local presence in addition to my online store. Assuming the popularity continues. Already, MerryDesigns feels like a full-time business. I've wondered if maybe it could be. I'd get to stoke my creative side. Plus, running my own business would definitely make use of my MBA, though I'm not so worried about that now.

After talking to my family and working on another pro-con list,

I decided not to take the job in New York. I haven't had one pang of regret, so it was definitely the right decision. Knowing my family just wants me to find something I love has given me the freedom to really think about my future with wide open horizons. I'm teaching myself how to knit butterflies as an ode to my big brother and also to meet the non-Christmas item requirement from my list. I've learned from the Internet that lots of people use butterflies to remember family members and friends who have died. There may not turn out to be much of a demand for memorial butterflies, but if I can offer comfort to just one person, it'll be worth it.

It seems like so many things these days remind me of Brett. He's had a big influence on my life in such a short time. I never would have been honest with my family about what I want if he hadn't questioned my reasons for taking the job. Every Metalhead order that hits my inbox makes me think of him. Even butterflies now remind me of him.

I've been tempted to stop by the bookstore during story time hours so I'm sure to catch him, but he hasn't reached out on purpose and I know better than to set myself up for heartache again no matter how open-ended things feel with Brett. I'll never know if he was successful in earning enough money to help his mom, but my gut tells me he was. He doesn't seem like a guy to let things stop him from what he's determined to do. Which is another reason I haven't contacted him. If he was really interested in me, he'd have given me a reason he declined my dinner invitation or have texted me by now. Maybe time will help me get over my disappointment about how things turned out. Paige thinks going on dates with other men will help me forget Brett. I can only hope. At least I have knitting to keep me busy.

I haven't yet decided on a destination for the fifth item on my list—visit somewhere new. Since I still don't have a full-time job, it can't be too costly. I think I'd like to do or see something out of the ordinary. Online searches have yielded ideas like the Grand Canyon, Sequoia National Park, a tulip festival in Washington state, Lombard

Street in San Francisco, and manatees in Homosassa Springs, Florida. They all sound fun. My decision may all come down to the price of airline tickets, but that doesn't bother me. The idea of a small adventure gets me excited. I have a feeling checking off my list will lead to lots of fun and joy this year. I definitely need some.

36

Brett

I'VE THOUGHT A lot about my conversation with Mom and decided it's time to give Josh a second chance and see what happens. I really would like to have a relationship with my half-siblings, even if the way we're related isn't exactly Hallmark television material. It's unfair to punish them for our father's behavior.

My first meeting with them is at the Asheville Pinball Museum downtown. I figured doing an activity together, even if we're really just playing side-by-side, might be a good way to ease into things. We'll have lunch somewhere nearby when the kids get hungry and maybe try some small talk.

My hand slips into my pocket and palms my phone. I'm tempted to check the time again, but it can't have been more than a minute since I last looked. They're not late. I was just really early, wanting to make a good impression. I doubt Josh told them we unofficially met at Winter Lights, so this will be our real first meeting.

Shuffling my feet to stay warm in the cool, crisp, January air, I turn to look up the street. My heart beats faster when I see four guys of various heights headed my direction. Here they come.

Josh stops in front of me and holds out his hand. I shake it, feeling awkward at this impersonal greeting. Though he's right to assume a hug wouldn't be welcome. "Hey, Brett." He points at my brothers starting with the tallest, who is only about six inches shorter than I am. "This is Victor, that's JJ, and this," he drops a hand onto the head of the smallest boy, "is Fisher. Boys, this is Brett."

I wave, unsure what else to do. "Hey guys. Nice to meet you. Ready to play some video games?"

Fisher nods his head eagerly. "A friend had his birthday party here, but I was sick and couldn't go. I heard it was awesome."

"Good. Let's head inside and get our wristbands, and then you can play any game you want."

I usher everyone inside and pay for the group. Josh tries to hand me some cash, but I hold up my hand. "Today is my treat."

"Thanks. Fisher has been more excited than a fox in a henhouse since he heard he was coming here today."

We spend a few hours chasing high scores and cheering one another on. I try to spend some time with each boy, offering tips on games I know well and asking about their interests. At mid-afternoon, we take a break for sustenance. The boys request Big Bob's Burger Barn, so I treat everyone to burgers, onion rings, and milkshakes. Then it's back to the museum for more gaming action. We play until it closes.

Out on the sidewalk, I give the boys high fives. Victor rolls his eyes, but smacks my hand. He then says, "I have a basketball game on Tuesday night if you want to come or whatever."

This invitation feels like a test. One I don't want to fail. "Oh, yeah?" I say casually. "Text me the details and I'll be there."

He straightens up a little and there's a hint of a smile on his face. He lifts his chin in affirmation, but says nothing else.

"Alright, boys," Josh says. "We'd better get home. You've got school tomorrow."

They wave, then turn toward the direction they came from earlier. I wave back, heading in the opposite direction. That went much better than I expected. The younger boys were friendly right away, telling me all about school and what they like to do for fun. I received mostly grunts and silence any time I asked Victor a question. Not sure what prompted the game invitation, but I'll take it.

The evening has left me feeling more positive about Mom's suggestion. I have to admit I was nervous about spending time with Josh, but he hung back and let me connect with my brothers. Maybe he's giving me space to choose what our relationship will look like going forward. Releasing the anger and resentment I've carried for so long feels like a real possibility. What else have I been avoiding that I might need to reevaluate?

Meredith's sweet face pops into my head. I need to apologize to her. It's only been a few weeks since Winter Lights ended, but I miss her way more than I thought I would. Every time I see a butterfly, I'm reminded of her. It's overwhelming how many children's books have butterflies in them. I know I pushed her away out of fear, but maybe I'd rather be scared than sad. Sad is definitely my predominant emotion these days.

I know I've been totally unfair to Meredith, projecting past hurts onto her. First, I disliked her because she reminded me of Vicky and that awful time in my life. Then I worried a relationship with her would jeopardize my job, despite all the evidence of how professional she is. If that wasn't enough, I let the fear of what might happen in a long-distance relationship keep me from being honest with her about how much I care for her. Even after she was vulnerable with me, I still wasn't willing to look past my fear. Meredith's not Vicky and she's not Lindsay. She's Meredith—a fascinating, kind, big-hearted woman I like a lot. I've messed up so badly with her. Hopefully, it's not too late to ask forgiveness and receive a second chance.

I haven't seen or heard from her since our last night of working together, but I wasn't exactly subtle in rejecting her. *Stupid, scared, Brett, what did you do?*

Today has caused a tremendous shift in my thinking about relationships and it's now crystal clear that I'm one hundred percent responsible for torpedoing my chances with Meredith. I need to show her I care about her and it needs to be in a way that leaves no doubt about my feelings for her. I need help. And I know just who to call.

❄❄❄

When I knock on the door, it swings open to a grinning Rachel. "Finally came to your senses, huh?"

This may have been a bad idea. She pulls me into the house and Tom nods at me from the couch where he's watching the news. "Hey, man."

I lift a hand in greeting. "Hi, Tom. Thanks for letting me steal some of Rachel's time."

"No problem. I hear you need apology ideas. Have you tried lots of flowers and some chocolate?"

I try not to smile, remembering everything Tom sent to Rachel at work when he was trying to get her to forgive him. Now that I'm in his shoes, it really isn't that funny. I bet he had this same gnawing discomfort in his gut. "I'm definitely open to suggestions."

Rachel pushes me down into an armchair and then joins Tom on the couch. "You can almost never go wrong with flowers, but if you want to make the biggest impact, you really need to tailor your apology to something that's personal and meaningful for Meredith."

"That sounds good, but I don't feel like I know enough about her to do that. Does she have a favorite color? No clue. Favorite book? Who's to say? Does she have a sweet tooth? Okay, the answer to that is yes, because she likes to bake cookies."

Rachel perks up. "That's a start. Do you know what her favorite kind is?"

"No. I know she has a signature Christmas recipe because she tried to kill me with it." Rachel's scrunched face makes me elaborate. "I'm allergic to macadamia nuts."

"You are? How is this the first I'm hearing about it?"

"Probably because you've never offered me food with them in it. Not a lot of recipes call for macadamia nuts."

She tilts her head from side to side, considering. "Definitely don't try the Beach Nut at Little Shop of Sugar, then. Surely, you know more about Meredith than you think. How many siblings does she have?"

"Two older sisters and a deceased older brother. She has a butterfly tattoo on her wrist in his memory."

Rachel holds her arms out wide, hands up. "See? What else?"

Maybe she's right. Encouraged, I continue to scour my brain for more things I know about Meredith, spouting them out as they come. Rachel grabs a notepad and pen and starts jotting things down. Hopefully, they're grand apology ideas.

The sound of Meredith's name pulls my attention to the television and there she is, sitting next to one of the local reporters. What's going on? Rachel and Tom turn toward to the screen.

"Ms. Larson," the reporter says, "tell me about the incident that started the buzz around your MerryDesigns shop?"

She smiles and I can tell by the lack of crinkles at the corners of her eyes that she's nervous. My heart knocks against my chest, impotent of any ability to comfort her.

"A friend of mine is a big fan of the band Metalhead. I made him some gloves using their logo as a template and he raved about them to another friend." She holds up a pair that looks almost exactly like the ones currently in my coat pocket. "That friend took a picture and sent it to the band who posted it and the name of my business on their social media accounts. And everything snowballed from there."

Meredith called me a friend! It's better than I deserve, though maybe she's just making a good story for TV and actually hates me. What if I'm now a persona non grata to her? The thought prickles my skin with discomfort.

The reporter glances at the paper in her hand. "It says here that you've been inundated with hundreds of orders for Metalhead gloves and scarves since the photo was posted. You're a one-woman company. Will you be able to keep up with the demand?"

"I've contacted those who have requested custom orders and given them an expected timeline for when they can expect to receive their products, offering to cancel and refund their orders if the wait times are too long. Most people are willing to wait for the product, which means I'm going to have a busy couple of months ahead of me. I've temporarily disabled the custom order function until I get caught up, so if someone wants to order their own hand knit items, they can sign up for my newsletter to find out when that option opens up again."

I look over at Rachel, who's mirroring my own wide-eyed wonder. What did we do? She must feel so overwhelmed right now. I can't imagine how much stress she must be feeling with a mountain of orders on top of preparing to move to New York. Nothing short of learning how to knit so I can help her with her orders will come close to showing her how sorry I am. Which is pretty much impossible because, by the time I reach her skill level, she'll probably have all the orders finished. I feel bad for being responsible for anything that causes her discomfort.

What about my resolve not to interfere with her New York decision? If I'm honest with myself, that was just fear talking. I want not only to apologize for being a jerk but also to ask her on a date. Not spending time with Meredith has been torture. I miss her smile, her bubbly laugh, the way she bounces on her toes when she's excited, how she twists her earring when she's confident of trivia answers, the sparkle in her eyes when she teased me at work. Who am I kidding? I miss everything about her. I'm willing to trade some time with her over no time with her. If it means figuring out how to make a long-distance relationship work, so be it. I have some extra money since Mom wouldn't take the cash I saved up for her. Plane tickets seem like as good a use for it as any. My thoughts are flying way ahead of me, but it only hardens my resolve to set things right with Meredith.

"Congratulations on your business's success. I hope you've done something special for your friend who started this whole ball rolling."

I look back at the television in time to see her smile dim. "I haven't yet, but I hope to."

My heart squeezes, regret and longing mingling together. It kills me knowing Meredith's sad because of me. I want to do everything I can to make her happy again. An idea pops into my mind. It's something so very Meredith and I know she'll love it, but it's going to require some time and the help of other people. A smile unfurls across my face.

"Brett, are you okay?"

"Yeah, why?"

"Your smile reminds me of the Grinch when he steals Christmas."

I bark out a laugh. "Thanks, Rach. That was quite helpful, actually. I've got to go." I've got work to do.

37

Meredith

I KNOCK ON the closed door and wait. It opens and Joanne ushers me into her office.

"Thanks for coming, Meredith."

"Not a problem." She called me earlier in the day asking when I could come in to debrief about this year's Winter Lights. Since all I'm doing these days is knitting and hanging out with Olivia, my days are fairly open. Well, I'm also scouring the job sites for local positions that sound interesting. While I'm making more than enough to afford an apartment of my own from Crafty sales, I'm a people person and need daily interaction with roommates or co-workers. Since MerryDesigns is a one-woman business, my parents have become my social circle.

I drop into a chair and pull out my laptop. "I spent about an hour after you called typing out my final thoughts. Overall, it went well. We had a few unforeseeable hiccups, like having to find a new

Santa, but the changeover went surprisingly smooth. I created a dossier of this year's seasonal staff—their positions, job performance, attitude, and anything else I thought was relevant, like how many years they've worked here. There's a lot of good potential staff for this coming year. I'll email it to you after we're finished."

Joanne sits back, eyes wide with surprise. "Wow, Meredith. You've gone above and beyond in this position. I thought this year went as smoothly as previous years, if not more so. The staff morale was high throughout the season. I didn't field many complaints from them or guests. Mostly things like needing to make the Quilt Garden and Railroad more wheelchair accessible, which I'll have to discuss with maintenance, but that has nothing to do with you and your leadership. I've been very impressed with you."

I'd like to say I'm able to hide the pleasure I feel at her compliment, but I'm terrible at masking my emotions. My face is an excellent indicator of how I'm feeling at all times. Which means, if Joanne tells me they've found my replacement already, I may end up bawling in her office. I know I shouldn't be sad about it, but I really enjoyed being in charge of Winter Lights. It felt like a natural progression after all my years of working here. Of course, I'd like to apply for a position if I'm able, but I already know it'd be weird going back to being a seasonal employee. Still, I trust Joanne to find someone who will be a good fit for the Arboretum. She has good instincts.

"Thank you. It has been a joy to be the interim events director."

She smiles at me. "I'm glad to hear you say that because I'd like you to take the position permanently."

My jaw drops open. Say what? I blink a few times, my mind not quite comprehending. "I thought you had someone in mind already."

She laughs. "Yes, *you.* I thought you'd be perfect for the position, but wanted to make sure it would be a good fit for everyone involved. And I was right."

My brain swirls with excitement and I feel suddenly energized.

"Oh, Joanne, thank you! I joyfully accept. I have a few ideas to help next year go even more smoothly that I can't wait to share with you!"

"That's great, Meredith, but you're also in charge of our children's summer day camps and that's where we'll need your focus right away. Sign ups start next month and we need to decide which programs to put on and find camp leaders."

My smile widens. I love kids. I haven't ever led a camp group before, but wonder if that would be taking on too much. If I can pull double-duty at Winter Lights, it might be possible for summer as well. Though, maybe I should make sure I've gotten the hang of my new position first. Inside, I'm squealing with delight, which I'm sure my beaming smile gives away. "Yes, of course. I'll get right on that."

She holds up a hand when I stand up, indicating I should sit back down again. "You're welcome to get started on ideas, but your first official day will be Monday. I thought you might like a few days to prepare."

I nod. That's smart. I can't wait to tell my family! There's another person I'd like to tell, but we're not exactly on speaking terms. The thought dims my excitement slightly. Regardless of Brett not being romantically interested in me, I know he'd be thrilled about this news.

Even if it may sting a bit to see him, I have to share this awesome news with Brett. He's a big reason my Winter Lights tenure went so well. He saved my skin by filling in as Santa. It would feel wrong not to tell him. Oh, who am I kidding? I've been dying for an excuse to talk to him, but too chicken to just do it. This gives me the perfect intro to work up the courage to see if we can be friends again. I've really missed him. We had so much fun together and I hate to give it all up forever. Even if it takes a while to get over my feelings for him, I'm determined to see if I can restore the relationship we had before the broom closet incident. Sigh. That almost-kiss was one of the most romantic experiences of my life. Too bad everything blew up afterward. *Move on, Meredith. It's friendship or nothing with Brett.* Right. Friendship, it is.

Leaving the Arboretum, I drive straight to downtown. After finding a parking spot, I grab the package I've been carrying around in my car and walk to Page Turner Books. The door bell chimes when step inside. It's quiet, a stark contrast to the busyness when I was last here. I suppose many businesses see a slowdown in January.

There's no one at the checkout counter, so I wend my way through the maze of bookshelves until I reach the children's book section. It's empty as well. Unsure of where to look next, I make my way back to the front of the store and peruse the display shelves, hoping if I look like a customer, someone will find me.

"Welcome to Page Turner Books. May I help you?"

I turn, smiling at the familiar voice. "Hi, Rachel."

Her eyes widen briefly, then her business smile deepens into a genuine one. "Hey, Meredith. I saw your interview on the news the other day. Congratulations!"

"Thanks. And thanks for helping my business take off. It's been overwhelming, but I'm also excited."

Rachel shrugs. "It was a crazy fluke, but you're welcome." Her eyes fall to the package in my hand. "Are you looking for Brett?"

"Yeah, I have news I wanted to share with him."

Her smile turns sympathetic. "He's not working today. You should try calling him."

And risk him sending it to voicemail and continuing to ignore me? That's a big nope. I want to see him so I can gauge his reactions and have no doubt about where we stand. But the longer I stand here looking into Rachel's pitying face, the more my courage wanes. "No, that's okay." Maybe if he sees I'm trying to patch things up, he'll reach out. I'm not super optimistic, but it's my last shot. "Would you give this to him the next time he's in?"

She takes the misshapen gift with the card taped to the top. "Sure. If you want to tell me your news, I can pass that along as well."

I'm dying to tell someone and, since my first choice isn't here, why not Rachel? It rockets out of me like fire. "I've been hired as the full-time events director for the Arboretum!"

Rachel squeals and pulls me into a hug. "Yay, Meredith. Congratulations!"

I squeeze her back before letting go. "Thanks. I'm pretty excited. I have to go tell my family, but hoped to catch Brett on my way home."

"Don't worry, I'll pass along the information the first chance I get." She holds up the small package. "And this too, of course."

Rachel's enthusiasm was just the reaction I needed. I'm disappointed it wasn't Brett who heard the news first, but I can't say I didn't try. Yes, I know I'm kind of chickening out, but can I be blamed after being shut down so definitively after Winter Lights? I made another move with the gift, and now will wait and see what Brett does with it. In the meantime, I'm off to the house to share the news with my parents. I'm so excited to be staying in Asheville. This year is already looking pretty bright.

38

Brett

RUSHING THROUGH THE front door of Page Turner Books, I'm surprised to find the inside displays neat and tidy. The fire alarm is silent and the wood floors are completely dry. I peek around shelves and down rows, methodically working my way through the store until I find Rachel nonchalantly placing books on shelves in the Fantasy section near the back. "Rach, you know SOS texts are only for genuine emergencies. I was in the middle of cooking."

She looks over at me and giggles. "Checks out."

I look down and realize I forgot to take off the apron I wear while making spaghetti sauce. It has a cartoon drawing of three peppers with the words *Hot & Spicy* above and *And the food is pretty good too!* below. "My mom gave this to me."

Rachel smirks. "Sure she did. It's totally improbable that you'd pick that out yourself."

I consider this, nodding in acknowledgment that it's not out of the realm of possibility that I'd buy it for the humor, though my mom really did give it to me. "Touché. However, I noticed that the building wasn't flooded or on fire when I came in. What's going on?"

She blushes, looking away. "Okay, so maybe it wasn't a *true* emergency, but I didn't think this could wait until you came back in at the end of the week."

She leaves the cart in its spot and ushers me back out to the front of the store. Walking behind the checkout counter, she bends down and then drops a present onto the counter in front of me. "Meredith brought this in for you today."

I was just about to go into a rant about belated Christmas presents not being an emergency, but Meredith's name stops me cold. She was here? Today? I look around the store like she might still be here, though of course she isn't. "What is it?"

Rachel rolls her eyes and shrugs. "She didn't say."

"What *did* she say?"

Her eyes sparkle and I know she has information I want to hear. "Open the present first and then I'll tell you."

She knows me too well. I was planning to take the gift to my car and open it in private, but I suppose this is payback for teasing her about all the gifts from Tom. "Fine."

I start with the card, deciding to draw out the mystery of what's in the package. When I press down on the wrapping paper to unstick the tape attaching the card, whatever's inside, depresses. From all my years trying to figure out my gifts as a kid, I'd say it's probably clothing.

The front cover of the card is a red and white diagonal stripe pattern reminiscent of a candy cane. Inside, the only words are in Meredith's handwriting. The large looping letters suit her warm personality. I read silently. *Brett, I'm sorry for whatever I did that pushed you away. I wish we could be friends again. I miss you. Thank you for helping my Crafty business grow. Here's a small token of thanks. Sincerely, Meredith*

The "I" of her name is dotted with a heart, and I wonder if it's significant or how she always signs her name. My throat feels tight at the fact that Meredith thinks she caused my distance from her. I mean, she did, but not like she thinks. And even I've realized how dense I was to let her go without a fight. If she dropped this off today, then it means she hasn't gone to New York yet. I can still turn things around. That's a key part in making the plan I'm working on a success. Maybe I can contact her sisters to help with that part. Doesn't one work for a local newspaper? My eyes roam back over the third sentence. She misses me? I certainly miss her. I've thought about her every day, wondering what she's doing, if she had a pleasant holiday.

"What's it say?"

I look up into Rachel's curious and eager face. Remembering how I made her give me the notes Tom sent, I reluctantly hand it over.

Rachel reads and then looks back up at me. "She misses you, Brett!"

"Yeah, I read the note."

Turning my attention to the package, I run my finger under the tape, creating an opening. I tip the paper to the side and out slides a knit beanie the same color as my gloves. I pick it up to try on my head and papers fall out, fluttering to the ground. The hat fits nicely on my head, just like my favorite pair of gloves. How does she get the fit so perfect? Another way she's so fantastic. I bend down, pick up the two white rectangles, and flip them over. I'm surprised to be holding two tickets to the Metalhead show in town next month. The show's been sold out since before Thanksgiving. How did she get these?

"Brett, what is it?" I hold them out to Rachel, who takes them. "That's more than a small token of thanks."

I nod, suddenly at a loss for words. My first instinct is to call her up right this second and tell her how I feel. Say I'm sorry for pushing her away, that I was afraid of my feelings for her and realize now I'd rather risk being hurt if it means even one day of having her in my arms again. If she'd even be open to that. Though she did just give me an incredibly thoughtful gift, so there's a good chance the answer would be yes.

"Hey, what did Meredith tell you when she was in here?"

Rachel smiles widely and my heart lifts, hopeful I'm going to like whatever she has to say. "Meredith got a full-time job."

My heart sinks like a stone. She took the hotel job. Well, I'm just going to have to hope she's still in town for my big surprise. "That's good."

"You don't want to know what it is?"

"It's the job in New York, right?"

Rachel shakes her head, her eyes sparkling. "Nope."

My heart kicks against my chest. It's getting quite a workout and I'm not even moving. "Tell me."

She rubs her hands together, obviously enjoying drawing out the suspense. I groan. "Rachel, please." Can't she see I'm in agony?

"She's the full-time events director at the Arboretum!"

What?! That's perfect for her. How did I not know that was even a possibility? I want to drive right over to her parents' house, wrap her up in a big hug, and spin her around. But that might be too strong after weeks of silence. Now I'm more determined than ever to make my idea a reality.

"Thanks for everything, Rachel. You're a good friend."

She winks at me. "I know."

I dash out the door to my car, thinking of all the things I need to do. My feet barely touch the ground knowing that Meredith's staying in town. I'd love to know if I factored into that decision, but have no right to ask. How could I have been a factor when I wasn't willing to be honest with her about my feelings? *Man, Brett. You're an idiot.* I hope "Operation Make a Fool of Myself for Meredith" works.

39

Meredith

I CAN'T BELIEVE I let Zach talk me into coming to trivia night. There's still a mountain of MerryDesign orders waiting to be tackled, plus it's the middle of my first official week working at the Arboretum. I have been overwhelmingly busy, though, so maybe a little down time with friends will do me some good. I really haven't seen any of the Winter Lights crew since the season ended.

I've been doing everything I can to get up to speed on the summer camp situation, which has mostly been reading through reports from the last three years to get a handle on what we might need this year. The camps have filled up early every year, so I'd like to add one or two more to meet the obvious demand for our programs, but that will require more staff, more initial funds, and curriculum.

When I'm not holed up in my new office, I'm shut up in my room at my parents' house knitting until my fingers are too tired to hold the needles anymore. With a break or two to refuel, of course. Which reminds me. I need to add *find a place of my own to live* to my agenda. Now that I'm staying in town, I'd like to find a place closer to the Arboretum. I've appreciated my parents' hospitality, especially since it gives me more time with Olivia, whom Ali brings over most days.

My life is very full right now. The knitted butterflies I added to my shop have been selling well and the Arboretum job is a dream come true. Olivia and I had our first one-on-one so her parents could eat a meal alone together, and we managed quite well. I've even figured out where I'm going to go on my adventure—Moab, Utah. I haven't spent any time out west and the photos of Arches and Canyonlands look incredible. Plane tickets were purchased for April and I even booked a helicopter ride.

There's still one thing missing in my life which pricks my heart whenever I'm around my parents and Ali and Rich—love. I would like to find someone to go on grand adventures with. Someone who looks at me like I'm a dream come true and can't stop thinking about me when we're apart. I know that sounds like a lot, but I think you should go big with love.

Paige finally convinced me to download one of the dating apps, but so far, no one has piqued my interest. Not to say there aren't cute guys in the area, but my heart is still stuck on Brett. I really thought there was some chemistry between us, but I haven't heard a thing from him since I asked him out. Not even after I gave him the concert tickets. I'd thought for sure he'd respond to that, but no dice.

Truth be told, part of me is still hoping he'll call. I really do need to give up on this idea of Brett and me. That door is obviously closed and locked tight. My head just has to convince my heart to abandon my last shred of hope. I did as much as I could do and now I have to accept that he wasn't interested in a relationship with me.

At Nothing But Wings, I settle into the usual booth where Zach, Ava, and Genesis are already waiting. They've ordered me a ginger ale and there are already appetizers at the table. We spend a few minutes catching up on the past few weeks. I receive a round of congratulations for my new position. I implore them all to come back next year, but only Zach will commit this early.

The Quiz Master gets everyone's attention, letting us know tonight's starting a little different. We're beginning with a Potpourri category that only has seven questions. The rest of the evening will be themed categories and eight questions like everyone's used to. Zach hands me his phone. Usually he inputs our answers, but everyone's allowed a break. I type in our team name, *Risky Quizness,* then watch the screen until it pops up, letting me know we're officially registered. Yes, I'm using a name Brett suggested. I know it's pathetic, but at least no one here knows where it came from.

The room is almost silent as the Quiz Master reads the first question. "Give the first name of the actor whose credits include *Star Trek*, *Stand by Me*, and *The Big Bang Theory*."

Easy peasy. I haven't seen either of the first two, but I loved *The Big Bang Theory*. I know Wil Wheaton is the correct answer because he played himself on the television show. I wonder if they're trying to trick us with the odd spelling. It's the only reason I can think of for wanting just the first name. Usually, answers require the last name. I type it in and hold it out toward the rest of the table for their approval before I submit it. Zach nods in confirmation.

"Question two. What do you call an adult female sheep?"

I roll my eyes. The first round is supposed to be one of the easier ones, but come on. Who doesn't know this? I answer, not bothering to check with the group.

Question three gives me pause. "This starting space on an iconic board game is also where you collect your salary with each turn around the board."

What are some famous board games? Chutes and Ladders? Candy Land? No, neither involve a salary. Life? But you don't return to where you start. You head toward retirement.

Ava leans in and whispers, "Monopoly."

I roll my eyes. Of course that's right. How did I draw a blank on Monopoly? I start typing it in, but Zach places a hand on mine.

"That's the game, but the question asks for the name of the correct square."

"Easy," says Genesis. "Go."

Duh, Meredith. I quickly erase the letters, type in *Go*, and send it off seconds before the Quiz Master starts reading question four.

"This word refers to a runner in baseball who's tagged by the ball while trying to steal home."

Uh…no idea. Sports are definitely the weakest spot of my trivia knowledge. Genesis's eyes light up and she leans forward to whisper her answer. "Out."

It sounds too easy, but I'm swayed by her confidence and send it in. The fifth question, a word which can be abbreviated using just the first letter and a right slash, doesn't stump Ava, an English major. She takes the phone from my hands and writes in her response.

A few teams start humming the song in order to find the answer to question six: the third note in a song sung by the von Trapp siblings. Another one that could trip people up with its spelling, though I sang in my middle school choir and had the scales drilled into me. I fire it off without hesitation.

The last question is as difficult for me as question three. "This is the first name of the fictional and titular character of a medical television drama that's been on the air for two decades."

Another response requiring just the first name. Weird. My mind cycles through options: *General Hospital*, *Doogie Howser*, *ER*, *House*, *Scrubs*. No, *Scrubs* was a comedy. *Chicago Med*, *Nurse Jackie*, *Private Practice*, *In Treatment*, *Grey's Anatomy*. I haven't watched most of them, so I turn to the table. "Is it Jackie for *Nurse Jackie*? Or maybe *Doogie*?"

Ava grins, shaking her head. "The question's referring to *Grey's Anatomy*. One of the doctors is Meredith Grey."

I quickly type the answer and send it off, then stare at the board while I wait to see which team is on top after the first round. Obviously, I hope it's ours.

"So, will you?"

I freeze at the familiar voice. Slowly, I turn my head, taking in a red holiday sweater with a green Grinch face right in the center. My eyes continue up to a bearded chin, pink lips that are twitching at one corner, probably suppressing a smirk, past the mustache and up to warm green eyes with small creases at the sides that betray a hint of nerves. My heart hammers in my chest. Is he really right here in front of me and wearing the sweater I gave him? I want to read everything into this, but I'm not one hundred percent sure what's happening. "Will I what?"

Brett waves his arm toward the television screen with the team ranks. The answers to the questions have been posted next to them.

1. *Wil*
2. *ewe*
3. *Go*
4. *out*
5. *with*
6. *mi*
7. *Meredith*

My mouth drops open. The cushion underneath me bobs up and down as my teammates slide out from the U-shaped booth and disappear.

Brett slides in next to me and gently takes my hand in his. "Meredith, I'm so sorry for acting like a jerk and pushing you away. I've really grown to like you these past few months. I tried to ignore my attraction to you because of some messed up thoughts regarding my past and I didn't want to jeopardize my job and lose the opportunity to help my mom.

"When I heard you might move to New York, I didn't think I could do a long distance relationship, but not seeing or talking to you these past few weeks has been agony. I deeply regret not being honest with you about how I felt after the closet incident. I don't want to live my life without you as part of it. I'll gladly get on a plane every weekend if that's what I have to do to be with you. You light up my life with joy and I can't go another day without it—without you. I never wanted to hurt you and I feel terrible that I did. Will you please forgive me?"

The warmth of my hand in his is comforting, but at the same time, his touch feels electric. My throat is tight and I feel tears welling up in my eyes. I blink to keep them at bay. It feels like a tidal wave of emotions is threatening to drown me, but in a good way. I had hoped beyond hope that I didn't misread things, and it's clear now I didn't. Not trusting myself to speak, I nod. The smile that unfurls on Brett's face in response lights me up from the inside and my body instinctively leans closer to him, like it's a flower and he's the sun.

"Can I take you to dinner sometime?"

The hopeful look in his eyes undoes me. My arms wrap around his neck, and I pull him to me until our lips press together. Heat zings through me and I sigh against his mouth. His arms gently pull me closer to him and I'm transported back to that night in the broom closet. Only this is better, of course, because I'm not left wondering what his lips feel like against mine. The scruff of his beard tickles my cheek and I giggle. He grins against my mouth, then pulls back, his smile just as devastating to my senses as it was moments before.

"I take it your answer is yes?"

I should probably be embarrassed that I just kissed a man in the middle of a restaurant, but I'm too happy to care. "Yes. I've missed you."

His smile dims slightly. "I've missed you, too. We have some catching up to do."

"We certainly do."

"I definitely want to hear about the new trivia team name," he grins, giving me a knowing wink that makes me blush, "but first I need to let the rest of the team know they can return to the table. Be right back."

"You better." I wink and bite my lower lip, hoping it looks flirty. He slaps a hand to his chest and groans, making my insides warm with delight.

He disappears, returning with the rest of the group. Zach tips his head toward Brett and gives me a thumbs up. The Quiz Master announces the start of the second round and I pick up the phone, ready to type in our next answer. Zach reaches over and snatches it from me, which turns out to be perfect, because Brett and I end up holding hands for most of the night. Now that he's back in my life, I don't want to let him go.

Epilogue

TEN MONTHS LATER

Brett

"ARE YOU SURE I can't convince you to play Santa this year?"

Meredith runs her hands up the front of my sweater, locking them together behind my neck. My hands wrap around her waist, the bells along the bottom of her skirt jingling as I pull her closer. "I'm sure you could provide a persuasive argument, but I much prefer the solitude of the cocoa shack. You know I'll fill in as needed, though. Gotta do everything I can to make the boss look good, right?"

She gives me a quick kiss. "Yes, please. And on the subject of looking good, while I'm fond of your green sweater, is there any hope of seeing you in something a little more festive at work this year?"

I point to the green Santa hat on top of my head. "What do you call this?"

Meredith rolls her eyes and smiles. "I suppose that's *some* progress. It'll have to do for now."

"Thank you."

She drops her arms and steps back. "I'm still determined to turn you into a Christmas freak like me." She turns, swaying her hips as she walks away, her bells jingling merrily. My eyes follow the movement. She turns to look back, giving me a knowing smirk. All I can do is shrug. I can't help how attracted I am to Meredith, not that she seems to mind. And she seems to enjoy the beard I've kept just for her. Though I've threatened to shave it all off if she tries to decorate it like a Christmas tree. I've seen the images of glittery, ornamented beards and that is a bridge too far.

Yes, I'm working Winter Lights again this year. Not because I need the money. It's because Meredith will spend most of her evenings here for the next six weeks and I want to be wherever she is. Simple as that.

The evening starts out pretty smoothly. I've still got my perfect pouring skills from last season, which is good because there's been a steady stream of customers since we opened.

I wonder if my brothers will show tonight. Josh said they'd try to come by after Victor's basketball game. I ended up going to quite a few games last year and was impressed by his athletic ability. He's got excellent ball handling skills and a pretty consistent three-point shot already. If he continues to improve, I bet he'll be able to play college ball.

I've learned a lot about my brothers this past year. JJ is obsessed with stars and planets and wants to go to Space Camp when he's old enough. Fisher is in a dinosaur phase, so we've read *Jurassic Park* and are working our way through *The Lost World* together. Josh says we can watch the movies together when we finish. It's been easier for me to continue calling him by name rather than force the "dad" thing. He seems to understand.

I've taken the boys snow tubing, fly-fishing, and river floating. We've even been on some of my favorite hikes. Josh initially came along to everything since they're minors and I'm a relative stranger. Or was. Now, he's offered to let me take them on my own, but I enjoy seeing him interact with his sons. It reminds me of how involved he was with me when I was their age. I've definitely thawed a lot in my feelings toward him. We may never be as close as we once were, but there's hope that we might become something like friends if things continue to progress.

Halfway through the night, there's a knock on the door. This is the moment I've been waiting for since October. I quickly remove my sweater and pull on the one I stashed in the shack earlier. I find the button and press it, double checking everything's in order, then press it again. Satisfied, I unlock the door and turn the knob, opening it a crack, then turning toward the window to find a woman with an odd look on her face. She must have just watched me change. I didn't even think about having an audience. At least I'm wearing a T-shirt underneath. I hold a finger up to my lips, which doesn't reassure the customer in the least. With all my planning, you'd think I'd have remembered that there might be customers staring into the service window. Well, too late now. The plan is already in motion.

Meredith steps inside the shack, shutting the door behind her. "How's it going in here?"

I reach into my left pocket, my fingers fumbling for the small velvet box. I use my right hand to steady my trembling arm. Sliding it out, I hide it in the palm of my hand, then turn to my right until I'm facing her, keeping my left hand slightly behind me.

Meredith's eyes drop to my sweater, and she sucks in a surprised breath. The back is plain green like my other sweater, but the front of this one is a swirl of colorful Christmas lights. Red, blue, and yellow bulbs decorate my chest and stomach.

"Whoa, Brett. Where'd you get that sweater?"

I take a breath to calm my pounding heart. It's time to shine. Figuratively and literally. "I ordered it from Crafty, just for you."

Meredith's eyes are shiny with tears, and she clasps her hands to her chest. "You got this sweater for me?"

I grin. "Yep, just for you." I take a deep breath, then dive into my speech. "Meredith, you're an extraordinary woman. You are smart, tough, hard-working, creative, and resilient. You don't let anything keep you down. You look for the good in everyone and are great at finding the bright side of every situation. You know how to make me smile when I've had a rough day. You are the best trivia player I've ever known. I love your joy for life and your Christmas spirit. I especially love all your crazy earrings. You are a unique and special person who deserves the best. I'm proud to know you and get to share this adventure called life with you. This past year has been one of the best of my life and it's because I got to spend it with you. I'd do anything for you."

Reaching down to the hem with my free hand, I find the hidden button and press it, turning on the actual string of lights sewn into the sweater. My eyes follow hers as she reads the question on my chest. Her hands cup her open mouth and her eyes slide up to mine.

I drop to one knee, opening up the box and holding it out between us. "So, will you?"

"Yes!" she yells, pulling me up to standing, then throwing her arms around my neck and kissing me hard. I kiss her back with all I've got, relief coursing through me. Did I think she'd turn me down? No, but you never know for certain until you ask and they answer.

Meredith slides a hand into my hair, tilting her head to deepen the kiss. My hands move up from her waist, my arms snaking around her back and drawing her flush against me. My thoughts are on nothing but how right and perfect this present moment.

A piercing whistle comes from my left. Meredith and I startle apart, turning our heads at the same time. There's a small crowd outside the shack window, smiling and clapping. My grin widens. I can't believe I'd forgotten about our audience.

I remove the ring from the box and slide it onto Meredith's finger. She holds it out in front of her and I must admit I like how the simple diamond solitaire I picked out looks on her finger.

Meredith grabs my sweater and pulls me to her for another kiss. I'm still aware of the people outside, but they can look away if our affection bothers them. I didn't invite them to my proposal.

Meredith releases her hold on me and steps back. "Maybe we should get back to work and celebrate later."

Someone knocks on the door. Right on time. "Actually," I say, reaching past Meredith to open the shack door, "I told Joanne what I was doing tonight, and she's letting us both leave early."

Tony steps inside. "Congrats, you two! I'm taking over, so get out of here."

The amazed look on Meredith's face turns to an amused smirk. "Pretty confident I was going to say yes, were you?"

I chuckle. "I mean, how can anyone who loves Christmas as much as you say no to a proposal at Winter Lights?"

She grins. "Way to stack the deck in your favor, Jacobs."

"Just trying to make it a perfect evening for my fiancée."

Her eyes light up. "Oooh, fiancée? I like the sound of that."

I pull up the hem of my sweater, intent on changing back to my regular one, when Meredith grabs my wrists. "No, leave it on. I like Festive Brett."

I obey, mesmerized by the adoring look on Meredith's face. "Yes, ma'am. Anything else?"

"Let's get out of here and celebrate our engagement." She looks down at her hand, her smile as brilliant as the diamond on her finger, before settling her gaze on me. "Fiancé."

I grin, knowing my love for her is written all over my face. Who knew it'd only take one special person to help me love Christmas again?

Thank you for reading *Merry & Brett*! If you enjoyed it, please consider leaving a review online.

❄❄❄❄❄❄❄

Want to stay in the know about future books? Sign up for my newsletter at MeganByrd.net/newsletter

Find additional *Merry & Brett* content including a bonus scene and recipes at MeganByrd.net/merryandbrett

ACKNOWLEDGEMENTS

Anna Booraem, thanks for all of the writerly support and cheering you've given me throughout each book endeavor. If I hadn't met you, I might not have ever started writing novels.

Heather Gerwing, again, thank you. I so appreciate your frankness. You help me stay on the right path and offer very useful wisdom and insight.

My Beta Readers through various stages—Heather, Cali, Anna, BJ, Sandy, Kelly, Anne Claire, Jan, Carrie, Hilary, Suzie, and Jane: Thank you! Your feedback was helpful and made this book better.

Maureen Ollivant (Mom), thank you for proofreading the manuscript and offering great feedback. You're officially hired for all future books. ☺

Thank you to my Sweet Reader Group for answering questions about the cover and providing general support throughout the process.

The North Carolina Arboretum, thank you for putting on a spectacular Winter Lights show each year and hosting many other wonderful programs and exhibits throughout the year. I appreciate your excellent walking and hiking trails and numerous benches with lovely views that help me ruminate on story ideas.

Biltmore Estate, your grand Christmas décor delights and inspires me every year.

Lioputra, thank you for the awesome character illustrations.

As always, thank you to my family for all of your love and support. Your encouragement and kind words keep me moving forward on this journey.

ABOUT THE AUTHOR

Megan Byrd lives in Asheville, North Carolina with her husband and two kids. She hates running, but loves hiking in the mountains toward a waterfall or scenic view and taking a variety of classes including kickboxing, HIIT, yoga, and Zumba. When she's not reading, writing, or chasing waterfalls, she enjoys visiting local bookstores, wandering through thrift shops in search of special finds, listening to live music, and catching up with friends.

Want to be first to know when the next book is available? Sign up on the website to receive a monthly e-newsletter and read about behind-the-scenes sneak peeks of her current work-in-progress, book recommendations, and other fun things. You can also visit MeganByrd.net/my_books to learn more about the inspiration behind her books.

Website: MeganByrd.net
Instagram: @megan.e.byrd
Facebook: Facebook.com/authormeganbyrd
Facebook Reader Group:
Facebook.com/groups/meganbyrdsweetreaders

www.ingramcontent.com/pod-product-compliance
Lightning Source LLC
Chambersburg PA
CBHW030134010826
48973CB00002B/557
9781964181011